Murder at the Marina

A Mollie McGhie Cozy Sailing Mystery #1

ELLEN JACOBSON

Murder at the Marina
Copyright © 2018 by Ellen Jacobson

This book is a work of fiction. Names, characters, places, and incidents either are products of the author's imagination or are used fictitiously. Any resemblance to actual persons, living or dead, events, or locales is entirely coincidental.

Print ISBN: 978-1-7321602-1-7
Digital ISBN: 978-1-7321602-0-0
Large Print ISBN: 978-1-7321602-2-4

Editor: Chris Brogden, EnglishGeek Editing

Cover Design: Mariah Sinclair | www.mariahsinclair.com

First Printing: June 2018

Published by: Ellen Jacobson
www.ellenjacobsonauthor.com

For my mother

CONTENTS

CHAPTER 1
SURPRISE!

WHAT WOULD YOU DO IF YOU found out your husband was having an affair? Would you:

(a) be understanding—he's just going through a midlife crisis;

(b) throw your glass of champagne in his face and storm out of the restaurant;

(c) tell him about the new love of your life —Sven, your Swedish masseur; or

(d) order an extra-large piece of chocolate cake?

You can cross (a) off the list—believe me, I wasn't in a very understanding mood. And

(b) is out too. Why would I waste a perfectly good glass of champagne? Of course it's not (c)—what kind of girl do you take me for? The correct answer is obviously (d), chocolate. Lots and lots of chocolate, washed down with lots and lots of champagne.

You know what made matters worse? He told me about her during our ten-year anniversary dinner. You're supposed to get diamonds after ten years, not your husband's confession about his torrid love affair with some hussy named Marjorie Jane. And, as if that weren't bad enough, it turned out that she was a redhead! I mean, Lucille Ball is great, but certain other redheads really made my blood boil.

There we were, dining at my new favorite seafood restaurant, Chez Poisson, when Scooter reached across the table, took my hand in his, and rubbed it softly. This was the moment I had been waiting for. Any minute now, he was going to reach into his jacket pocket and present me with a velvet jewelry box containing some lovely little thing encrusted with diamonds.

Instead, he pulled his cell phone out of his pocket. "You know how much I love you, don't you, Mollie?" I nodded, wondering why he was holding his phone. Maybe it was going to magically turn into a diamond bracelet. I kept my eyes on it, just in case.

He pressed a button, looked at the screen, and smiled. "Well, it turns out I've fallen in love with another pretty lady too. Her name is Marjorie Jane." He glanced at me and chuckled. "Not that anyone could replace you, of course, but Marjorie Jane is pretty special."

I was stunned. My husband, in love with another woman. And not only in love with another woman, but casually announcing it over dinner as if I'd be okay with it. I think I would have been less surprised if Scooter's phone had turned into a diamond bracelet than I was by his confession.

"Wait until you see these shots of her," Scooter said. He adjusted his tortoiseshell glasses, then swiped his finger across the screen on his phone, gazing at picture after picture of the new love of his life. "She has the sleekest lines. You won't believe how she moves through the water." He got a dreamy expression in his dark brown eyes. "You can really see her red coloring shimmering in this one."

Now I was starting to get angry. There he was, ogling photos of this red-haired hussy in her bathing suit, swimming in the water. I bet it wasn't a one-piece suit either, but one of those skimpy bikinis that left nothing to the imagination.

I leaned back in my chair, ran my fingers through my frizzy, mousy-brown hair, and stared at my empty crystal champagne flute. I really needed a refill. And where was the cake I had ordered earlier?

As I scanned the restaurant for the waiter, my eyes were drawn to a young couple sitting by a window overlooking the water. She toyed with her wedding ring while the waiter refilled her wine glass. I heard the young man tell his wife to close her eyes. He got up from the table and walked behind her. He pulled a small velvet box out of his jacket pocket, opened it, and removed a necklace. Brushing her long, black hair to the side, he gently placed it around her neck. She opened her eyes and squealed as she looked down and saw—yes, you guessed it—a diamond pendant sparkling on a delicate gold chain. I bet they hadn't been married for even a year and he was already giving her diamonds.

Our waiter bustled up to the table, interrupting my thoughts about sparkly diamonds and unfaithful husbands. "Voilà, madame," he said, putting a dessert plate down in front of me with a flourish.

"You call this big?" I pointed at a tiny slice of chocolate cake. Sure, it was beautiful, artfully arranged on a rectangular white plate with a drizzle of raspberry sauce and crushed hazelnuts sprinkled in the shape of a heart, but it was positively microscopic in size. "I specifically asked for the largest piece of chocolate cake you have. Can't you see that this is an emergency?"

I thrust the plate into the waiter's hands. "Take this back to the kitchen and add at least three more slices before you come back." As he started to walk away, I grabbed his arm. "How about a couple of scoops of chocolate ice cream while you're at it?"

I looked over at Scooter. He had been oblivious to the whole chocolate cake fiasco. I took the opportunity to switch my empty champagne glass with his full one. He didn't even notice.

"You're drooling all over your phone!" I said sharply.

Oops, that might have been a bit too loud. The young woman with the diamond necklace turned and stared at me. My mother would have been telling me to use my indoor voice right about then. She'd probably also have had something to say about ordering chocolate cake and what it could do to my waistline.

Just then my phone beeped. I pulled it out of my beaded evening bag. Yep, right on cue —a text from my mother.

What did Scooter get you for your anniversary this year? Something with diamonds?

I sighed. How was I going to explain Marjorie Jane to her? She had never been that crazy about Scooter to begin with. Probably best to get straight to the point. It was easier that way.

No diamonds, just a redheaded midlife crisis named Marjorie Jane.

I saw the waiter coming back to the table with a heaping plate of chocolate cake and enough ice cream piled on top to guarantee a healthy tip. My phone kept beeping. No doubt my mother wanting to know more about the other woman in Scooter's life. I tucked the phone back into my purse. Chocolate deserves one's undivided attention.

"Sir, can I get you anything else? Some more coffee, perhaps?" the waiter asked. Scooter barely glanced up from his phone. "No, thank you. I'm fine," he mumbled.

Who sits and stares at pictures of their mistress during an anniversary dinner with their wife? I could feel the muscles in my neck tense up. Too bad Sven wasn't around to work out the knots. Maybe that would have gotten Mr. Oblivious's attention—the sight of a cute, young, blond guy massaging my neck. Nah, probably not. He was so wrapped up in Marjorie Jane that he wouldn't have even noticed Sven.

I felt my eyes tear up, which I didn't like one bit. I pride myself on not breaking down every time something goes wrong. I took a deep breath. *You're in control.* I crumpled up my linen napkin and placed it next to my dessert plate, which sadly only had crumbs left on it, took aim, and kicked Scooter under the table. I was wearing very pointy shoes. That got his attention.

"So, did you think you could just find another woman and I'd be okay with it?"

He looked at me with surprise. "What are you talking about, my little sweet potato? What other woman?"

"Are you serious? You've been staring at pictures of her for the last half hour." I was proud of myself for using my indoor voice this time. "Sure, I know men have midlife crises, but they usually get a sports car or a toupee or something like that. But no, you had to go and get yourself a mistress. And a redhead at that!"

Scooter's brow furrowed. "But Marjorie Jane isn't my mistress. She's a sailboat. I'm buying her for you as an anniversary present."

I put my champagne flute down. "What? An anniversary present? A sailboat?" This wasn't making any sense. I wondered if he had had too much champagne to drink, but I think it was possible I had finished off the entire bottle myself. Normally, I would guess that's why my head had started to hurt, but let's be realistic—my husband was talking gibberish. Who buys their wife a sailboat as an anniversary present?

"Yes, a sailboat. See, she's gorgeous." He passed me his phone. "Look at those classic lines, those teak decks, the red hull, and the white-and-gold trim. Snazzy, huh?"

He leaned over the table and squeezed my hand. "I've arranged for us to meet the boat broker at the marina tomorrow so that you can see her. I know you're going to love her as much as I do."

I was so flabbergasted I didn't say anything. Trust me, that's highly unusual.

I've typically got a lot to say. All of it very interesting, I might add, and none of it about sailboats.

I didn't talk to Scooter as we left the restaurant.

I didn't talk to Scooter on the car ride home.

I didn't talk to Scooter when we got home.

I didn't talk to Scooter when we went to bed.

A normal guy would have figured out by this point that he was getting the silent treatment. Nope, not Mr. Clueless. He was so wrapped up in his daydreams about Marjorie Jane that he didn't even notice.

Marjorie Jane was seriously getting on my nerves. Something was going to have to be done about her.

CHAPTER 2
THE RED-HAIRED HUSSY

I STARTED TALKING TO SCOOTER again in the morning, but that was only because he asked me if I wanted a mocha. I need caffeine to function, preferably caffeine that's made by someone else.

I could have just nodded in response to his question, but I noticed that he wasn't putting nearly enough chocolate syrup into my cup. After the events of last night, I deserved an extra chocolaty start to the day. This required words.

"Scooter, why are you skimping on the chocolate?"

He turned and smiled. "Sorry, I was lost in thought about *Marjorie Jane*." He stirred in a few more spoonfuls.

I put my head in my hands. I couldn't believe it. *Marjorie Jane* was even getting in the way of my morning mocha.

Scooter tapped me on the shoulder, placed the steaming cup on the counter in front of me, and gave me a kiss on my forehead. I took a sip and sighed. It was delicious. That man sure could make a tasty mocha. It was almost hard to stay mad at him.

He sat on the barstool next to mine with a bowl of Froot Loops. Just like I can't start my day without caffeine, Scooter can't start his day without cereal. He prefers it to be full of brightly colored, sugary nuggets that crunch loudly when you eat them, disturbing those of us who prefer to quietly sip our mochas.

As he munched away, Scooter sorted through a pile of mail. He passed some catalogs and bills to me, then pulled out a magazine that had a picture of a couple of geeky-looking guys underneath a headline declaring them the winners of this year's telecommunications technology innovation award.

"Why do they keep sending me this?" He clenched the magazine in his hands. "The last thing I want to be reminded of is these two idiots. The only reason they're on the cover is because of my research." He tossed the magazine across the counter, pulled his bowl toward him, and pushed the rest of his Froot Loops back and forth with his spoon.

I reached over and squeezed his arm. He gave me a half-hearted smile. Ever since he had been forced to sell his stake in the high-tech telecommunications business that he had founded with the two geeks in question, he hadn't been himself. Sure, he had made enough on the sale that he didn't have to work again, but he was struggling to figure out what to do next with his life, especially as he was only in his forties. Although the gray that had begun to appear in his dark-brown hair made him look distinguished, it was probably due to stress.

I pulled out one of his sailing magazines from the stack. "Here, why don't you read this instead? That should cheer you up."

He leafed through the pages for a few minutes, then seized my hand. "Thanks for being so understanding. I'm sorry if I've been a real pain to live with lately."

"It's okay. You've been going through a rough patch."

He put the magazine down and slurped up the last of the milk in his bowl. "What do you say we head over to the marina after I take a quick shower?"

I shrugged. Might as well get it over with. Maybe I could talk some sense into him about the boat once I saw what I was up against. "Sure, as long as you make me another mocha for the road."

* * *

"Are you excited to meet *Marjorie Jane*?" Scooter asked as he pulled into the marina parking lot.

"Sure, as excited as that time the dentist told me I was doing an excellent job flossing my teeth." I gave him a big grin to prove my point. "See, good dental hygiene does pay off."

"Why do I think you're being a tad sarcastic?"

"Sarcastic? Me? Never. No, I'm dying to meet this red-haired hussy of yours."

I stepped out of the car and closed the door. It might have sounded like I slammed the door, but I swear that's just the acoustics you get when you're near the water. Sound carries farther over water; at least that's what I think my science teacher said back in high school.

While I reminisced about my struggles getting a passing grade in physics class, Scooter was busy grabbing a navy-blue tote bag out of the back. It had a picture of a sailboat with "Let Your Dreams Set Sail" printed underneath. No doubt he had bought it at one of those boat shows he was always going to.

"What's in the bag?"

"You'll see. It's a surprise."

"You know I don't like surprises."

"Sure you do. Remember how thrilled you

were last night when I surprised you with *Marjorie Jane*?" He bent down and gave me a quick peck on the cheek before hurrying down the path.

"You really are dense sometimes, aren't you?" I shouted after him as I tried to catch up.

Scooter sure can move fast when he's focused on something. And by focused, I mean obsessed. He has two modes of operating—fixated on something 24/7 or completely disinterested.

His interest in sailing had started a couple of years ago when he had gone on a weekend charter trip with some buddies. After that, he spent countless hours looking at sailing websites, leafing through glossy boat magazines, and reading books on rather dull subjects like diesel engine maintenance and repair.

I had hoped it was just another one of his temporary preoccupations, like the time he decided he was going to learn to make Ethiopian food. He bought all sorts of unusual ingredients, scorched several pots and pans, and couldn't speak for days after adding too much hot pepper to a chicken dish and burning his mouth. After one final failed attempt at making an Ethiopian spice blend, he lost interest and ordered pizza for dinner instead.

I should have realized that his fixation with sailing was a lot more serious. Buying a sailboat was probably a good clue. Maybe that's what a midlife crisis was—an obsession gone wrong.

When he arrived at the boardwalk, he turned and wiggled his finger at me. "Come on, my little sweet potato. This is no time to dawdle. We're due to meet the boat broker soon."

I certainly wasn't dawdling. Okay, maybe a little. I really wasn't in any hurry to see *Marjorie Jane*. But my short, stubby legs could never keep up with his long ones. He had been a star basketball player in college, and it was his speed running up and down the court that had earned him the nickname "Scooter." I glared at him. He caught my meaning.

"Sorry about that." He clutched my hand and gave it a squeeze. "It's just that I'm so excited to see my new girl."

I glared at him again. My patented knock-it-off-or-you'll-suffer-serious-retribution glare. The last time I'd given him a glare like that, I hid his Froot Loops and he had to eat oatmeal every day for breakfast for a week instead. Oh, how he'd suffered.

He gave my hand another squeeze and quickly said, "Of course, *you're* my best girl, Mollie. No one could take your place."

When Scooter calls me by my first name instead of a silly pet name, then you know he's serious. Or worried he might be served more oatmeal.

"All right. We better get a move on if we're going to meet this boat broker of yours," I said. I tried to see what was in the tote bag he was carrying.

"Hey, no peeking." He switched the bag to his other hand and walked down the boardwalk to a creaky dock that had seen better days. He pointed to a sign that said B Dock. "She's just down here. There are three other main docks: A Dock, C Dock, and D Dock."

"Do you think they hired external consultants to come up with those clever names? Probably the same team that came up with the name Palm Tree Marina on account of all the palm trees. And let me guess, they came up with the name Coconut Cove on account of all the coconuts floating in the water?"

Scooter suppressed a smile. "There's also a fuel dock and a dinghy dock. And yes, before you ask, they have clever names too—Fuel Dock and Dinghy Dock." He pointed at the boats bobbing in the water near the breakwall. "People who keep their boats in the mooring field use their dinghies to get back and forth to shore, and have a special dock to tie up at. And the fuel dock is—"

I held up my hand. "Let me guess. The fuel dock is where you get fuel."

"You're catching on quick. Do you want to know about the boatyard?"

"Not really."

"Of course you do. If you need to do

repairs or maintenance to your boat, you have it hauled out and taken there to work on it."

"Fascinating."

I gingerly stepped along the dock, avoiding planks that looked like they were missing nails. It reminded me of that kids' game where you avoided stepping on cracks so that you wouldn't break your mother's back. Except, in this case, I wasn't worried about my mom as much as I was worried about one of the planks breaking and tumbling me into the water. Sure, I like splashing around in the water, but only in pools and hot tubs. I find the chlorination in the water reassuring —it's a sign that humans are in charge and that you're less likely to find scary critters, like sharks and alligators, lurking about. When it comes to the ocean, you're on your own. You never know what sea monsters might be waiting for you. I'm not a very strong swimmer, so I'd much prefer to fight off someone trying to steal my lounge chair by the pool than fend off a great white or a gator.

We had only moved to Florida a few months ago, so worries about sharks and alligators were pretty new to me. When Scooter's uncle passed away and left him his cottage in Coconut Cove, a small tourist town on the Gulf Coast, we decided it would be a good opportunity to make a fresh start, away from reminders of Scooter's old business and former partners.

Across from the marina, stairs led down to a sandy beach. I watched some tourists wading in the water, a dog carrying a large piece of driftwood to his owner, and a couple of kids flying colorful kites. Maybe I could convince Scooter to go for a stroll after we were done looking at this boat of his.

After successfully navigating the rest of the dock, I saw him standing in front of a red wooden boat. He stared at it rapturously, his mouth hanging open.

I grabbed a tissue out of my purse. "Here," I said. "You're drooling again."

He wiped the corner of his mouth. "She's so beautiful!"

I'm not sure "beautiful" was the word I

would have used. Paint was flaking off the side. The teak decks looked like they had seen better days. And to top things off, the name *Marjorie Jane* was written in an ostentatious, flowery gold script on the front of the boat. "Tacky" is the word that came to mind, not "beautiful."

I was all set to explain exactly what the difference between beautiful and tacky was when Scooter gazed at me with those dark brown eyes of his.

We used to have a chocolate Labrador dog with the same exact eyes when I was a kid. One day, he came bounding up to me with my Barbie doll in his mouth, dropped it at my feet, wagged his tail, and looked at me with his soulful eyes. Sure, Barbie was missing a leg and covered in dirt, but how could I stay mad at a dog who oozed so much cuteness? It was the same with Scooter, except this was a boat and not a mangled doll.

"How much did you pay for this thing?" I asked. "She looks like she should have sunk to the bottom a long time ago."

"I've only put down a deposit," Scooter said. "That's why we're meeting the boat broker. To sign the papers and finalize the deal."

"You mean you can get out of this?" I asked hopefully.

Scooter didn't answer my question. He had a faraway look in his eyes as he caressed the side of the boat. Either he was lost in daydreams about sailing or he was deliberately ignoring me. I wasn't sure which was worse. I hated it when he pretended he couldn't hear me, but daydreaming about a boat, of all things—especially this boat— really took the cake.

He rubbed his hands together. "Come on, let me show you the cockpit. Imagine relaxing there at night over one of those tropical cocktails you're fond of. Sounds romantic, doesn't it?"

It's true. I do like tropical cocktails. Especially when they're served in coconuts with tiny umbrellas. But I wasn't sure you needed a boat to enjoy coconut drinks. They had these beach bars that did the trick just fine.

Scooter slipped off his shoes, then jumped athletically up from the dock onto the teak deck, as though he were going for a slam dunk. He ducked under the red canvas shading the cockpit from the sun and sat behind the steering wheel, grinning from ear to ear. He looked like a lovesick teenager.

He patted the seat next to him. "Hop on up. But first, take off your flip-flops. You should never wear shoes on a boat."

I placed my sandals on the dock next to his shoes and tried to pull myself up onto the deck. I didn't get very far. Stupid short legs.

Scooter whistled some sort of sea shanty while he pretended to steer the boat. At least I thought it was a sea shanty. It might have been the latest girl-group song we'd heard on the radio on the drive over to the marina. Either way, it was annoying.

"Are you coming or what?" he asked as he spun the wheel from side to side.

"Exactly how am I supposed to get up there?" I said, putting my hands on my hips. "The boat is like twenty feet above the dock here and I'm only five feet tall."

He peered down. "Math never was your strong suit, was it? It's only a few feet, not twenty." He pointed at a twisted metal cable that ran from the mast to the deck. "Just grab onto that and hoist yourself up." Then he went back to steering the boat and whistling away to himself.

After several attempts, I eventually managed to scramble on board, holding on for dear life. I teetered precariously on the edge, trying to figure out how I was going to get my legs over the lines that ran around the boat. "Hey, Scooter, mind giving a girl a hand here?" I asked.

He stepped out of the cockpit. "See, I knew you could do it. You're going to love being on a sailboat. It's great exercise, isn't it, climbing up and over things?" He held onto my hand. "Now, just put one leg over the lifelines here. That's good. Now the other one."

The boat rocked back and forth as a powerboat sped past *Marjorie Jane* and headed toward the inlet, which led out of the marina and into the deeper waters of Sunshine Bay. I clung to Scooter so that I wouldn't lose my balance and land back on the dock. The last thing I wanted was to have to climb back up again.

"Welcome aboard *Marjorie Jane*," he said as he clasped my waist and gave me a kiss. "This is the greatest day ever. My very own sailboat that I get to share with my best girl."

When he let go of me, I nearly lost my balance again. I clutched the lines I had just climbed over. "What did you call these again?"

"Lifelines. They keep you from falling off the boat and into the water. They can save your life, so to speak."

I thought about all the potential sea monsters circling below, just waiting to gobble me up. I tugged on the lifelines. "These feel kind of loose. If I fell against them, they'd just give way. Shouldn't they be tighter than this?"

"Nah, they seem fine to me. Don't worry. You're not going to fall in the water. Sailing is perfectly safe." Scooter sat back down behind the wheel.

I climbed into the cockpit, stepping on tattered white cushions with a red starfish pattern. "These are in pretty bad shape."

"That's just cosmetic stuff. You have to look past that and see the beauty that lies underneath. Besides, that's why we're getting *Marjorie Jane* at such a bargain price."

"And what exactly is a bargain when it comes to sailboats?" I asked as I sat at the other end of the cockpit.

"She's a steal," he said evasively. "Captain Dan says we're lucky that we snapped her up before anyone else did."

I had a feeling I wasn't going to get a straight answer. I reached out and touched the wooden boards at the entryway to the boat. Red paint flaked off on my hands.

"That's the companionway," Scooter said. "You push back the hatch and pull out those washboards to get into the boat. I know you can't wait to see down below. Captain Dan will be here any minute to unlock her."

I picked up a broken padlock from the

cushion next to me. "You mean this lock? I think someone may have used bolt cutters on this."

Scooter narrowed his eyes. "Bolt cutters. Of course you'd know it was bolt cutters."

"Do we have to go into that again? It was just that one time," I said quickly. "Besides, there's a bigger issue here. Who broke into the boat and why? There's much nicer boats to break into around here than this piece of junk." I looked around the dock at the fancy powerboats and well-maintained sailboats nearby.

Scooter elbowed me out of the way. "Let me see that," he said, grabbing the padlock. He turned it over in his hands. "Looks like you're right. This was cut. That's definitely your area of expertise, isn't it?"

"Focus, Scooter, focus. The past is the past. More importantly, do you think anyone's still down there?" I asked.

"Move over," he said. He slowly pushed back the hatch and peeked down into the cabin.

"Do you see anyone?" I asked.

He put a finger to his lips. "Shh. I'm going to check it out. You stay here and keep quiet." He pulled the washboards out, setting them down gently on the cockpit floor. He carefully climbed down the ladder.

"I can't see anything with your big head in the way. Can you move over to the side?" I asked, trying to peer down below.

"What part of keep quiet didn't you understand?" he whispered. "Just stay there. I'm going to try to find the light switch."

I heard a lot of banging and a few swear words followed by a loud exclamation. "Ouch, that hurt!"

"Scooter, are you okay?" I asked.

"I'm fine. I just banged my foot on something."

"What was it?"

"How would I know?" He sounded grumpy. "It's dark down here. I can't see a thing."

I reached into my purse, pulled out a flashlight, and pointed it down the companionway. There were cushions and clothes scattered everywhere, cans of food piled haphazardly on a table in the center of the cabin, cupboard doors hanging open, and books strewn about.

"There's the light switch," Scooter said as he turned an overhead fixture on. The place looked even worse when illuminated.

Scooter sat on one of the couches, bent down, and rubbed his left foot. I quickly climbed down the ladder and rushed over to him. "Is your foot okay?"

"It'll be fine. I stubbed my toe on that winch handle over there." He pointed at a large metal object next to the ladder.

"Did you say *witch* handle? Are you saying this boat is haunted?" I picked up the long metal object. "What do witches do with these? Wave them over their heads and cast magic spells to ensure good fishing?"

"No, not witch, *winch*. You insert the handle into the winch to grind the sails in. You know that metal drum you tripped over getting into the cockpit? That's a winch." He must have seen the confused look on my face. "Never mind. I'll show you how it works later. Here, give it to me." I passed the handle to him, being careful not to step on an overturned toolbox.

Scooter examined it closely. "It appears to be brand new. But the size is all wrong for our boat. This handle is way too big for the winches on *Marjorie Jane*."

"How is it you know the sizes of the winch handles on this boat but you don't know what shoe size I wear?"

"What are you talking about? I bought you fuzzy bunny slippers a few years ago for your birthday."

I rolled my eyes. "Yeah, I remember. That's why I started leaving sticky notes on your desk for you with gift suggestions."

"Oh, is that what those were?" he asked with a smirk on his face.

"Yes, and if you'll recall, there wasn't a note that said dilapidated sailboat on it."

"Trust me, *Marjorie Jane* will look great once she's all tidied up. Why don't you go check out the rest of the boat while I clear up this mess?" He pointed toward a tiny hallway running along one side of the boat. "That's the kitchen. Or, as we sailors like to say, the galley. Just imagine yourself whipping up some tasty treats in there for us."

I watched in surprise as Scooter began putting books back on the shelves and cans into cupboards. At home, he usually left stuff all over the place and I picked up after him. This stupid boat inspired tidiness in Scooter, whereas I had failed miserably in my efforts to domesticate him. Just another reason to despise *Marjorie Jane.*

I sighed and walked into the galley area. I could see why they called it a galley. A space as small as this certainly didn't deserve to be called a kitchen. There was barely enough room to turn around. The stove and oven were tiny, the counter was practically nonexistent, and there wasn't a fridge to be seen.

"How are you supposed to survive on this thing without a fridge?" I asked Scooter.

"There's a fridge." He pointed at where I was leaning on the countertop. "Right there, underneath your hand."

I glanced down, and sure enough there was a tiny, hinged door on the top of the counter.

I pulled it open and stared into something that appeared to be the size of a small cooler you'd take on picnics. As I was puzzling over this, I heard a man call out, "Ahoy, is anyone there? Permission to come aboard?"

Scooter poked his head up the companionway. "Hey there, Captain Dan. Come on down." He chuckled. "Although I'm not sure I can give you permission to come aboard. *Marjorie Jane* isn't our boat yet."

"Don't you worry. This pretty lady will be all yours once we sign these papers and you hand me a check," Captain Dan said in a slow Texas drawl. I admired his agility as he made his way down into the cabin. He made climbing down a ladder seem easy. He was wearing a denim shirt with mother-of-pearl buttons tucked into well-pressed jeans. My eyes were drawn to his shiny red cowboy boots and an even shinier belt buckle in the shape of an anchor. I looked up, expecting to see a cowboy hat. Instead, the boat broker had a navy-blue captain's hat perched on top of his head. He had neatly trimmed salt-and-pepper hair and a bushy beard and moustache. Something about him was familiar, but I couldn't figure out what it was.

Captain Dan shook Scooter's hand heartily while he surveyed the cabin. "My, oh my, what happened here, li'l pardner?"

"Oh, it's nothing," Scooter said.

"Nothing?" I said in disbelief. "It isn't nothing. It looks like someone cut through the padlock, broke in, and was searching for something."

Captain Dan turned, stared at me, and gave a low whistle. "Now, let me see here. This must be the missus. Whew-whee, you sure are one lucky fella, Scooter. She's got more curves than a barrel of snakes. And what color are those lovely eyes? It's hard to tell in this light, but they sure are sparkling."

I was pretty sure the sparkle in my eyes was due to my surprise about how corny this guy was. "They're hazel."

Scooter wrapped his arm around my waist possessively. "This is my wife, Mollie. But you better not talk about snakes around her. She had a run-in with one a while back."

"Okay, no more talk about snakes," Captain Dan said. "Well now, missy, have you seen the rest of the boat?"

"Not yet. There are more important things to worry about, like who broke into the boat and why."

"Oh, that? That's nothing, probably just some of the high school kids on a dare. I wouldn't worry your pretty little head about it, Mrs. McGhie. Now, why don't you have a look back here at the aft cabin." The captain slapped Scooter on the shoulder. "We menfolk are gonna sort out the paperwork."

Scooter grinned. He seemed to be having fun watching my reaction to Captain Dan's patronizing comment about my pretty little head. Not that I didn't like being told that my head was pretty. Given the perpetual frizzy state of my mousy-brown hair, it didn't happen very often. But somehow I didn't think Captain Dan was complimenting my efforts at trying to tame my unruly locks with hair straighteners.

"Go on," Scooter said. "The aft cabin will be our bedroom. You're going to love it. It's really spacious."

"Aft?"

"Just walk through the galley to the back of the boat. That's what 'aft' means—toward the back or the stern."

I thought about giving the boat broker a piece of my mind but decided I might as well see if the burglars had rifled through the aft cabin too. I wasn't buying his explanation that a bunch of high school kids had broken in on a dare. How many teenagers carry around bolt cutters?

Scooter called after me, "Make sure you duck your head."

"Too late," I said as my head smacked into a low ceiling. After making my way through a tiny door suitable for Hobbits, I found myself in a cabin with a full-size bed against one wall and a small seating area against the other. What I didn't see were any walk-in closets or dressers. Yet another thing to add to the list of complaints about *Marjorie Jane*.

The cabin was neat and tidy. Nothing was out of place. Had the intruders found what they were looking for in the main cabin, or had they been disturbed before they could search this part of the boat?

I made my way back through the galley, remembering to duck my head this time. I could have sworn I felt someone swat me on the butt as I inched into the main cabin. Captain Dan winked at me.

Unaware of the captain's flirtations, Mr. Oblivious glanced at me and said, "There, doesn't it look better?" The cushions were back in place and all the items that had been strewn about the cabin were piled on one of the couches.

"I guess so. But it is a bit dark in here," I said. I pointed at the small windows set high up on the cabin walls. "Maybe we could replace those with some large picture windows to let in more light. And I bet a light-colored wallpaper would do wonders for those walls. All this dark wood makes the place feel so old-fashioned, kind of like the paneled den my dad had in the basement."

Scooter's eyes got wide. "Wallpaper... picture windows...," he sputtered.

Captain Dan chuckled. "Never mind about

that just now, missy. Why don't you have a look at the V-berth? Scooter, go on, show her the V-berth."

Scooter opened up a door at the front of the boat and showed me a room that was shaped like the letter *V*. Yep, V-berth— another highly original name. The room was taken up by a large raised platform topped with dark-green cushions. I bent down to get a better look at the pattern, when I realized that it wasn't a pattern at all—it was mildew. Gross. There were two floor-to-ceiling cupboards flanking each side of the berth. I didn't dare open them for fear of what bacterial cultures I might find growing inside.

As I was brushing a cobweb away from my face, I heard Captain Dan whispering to Scooter, "Let the ladies have their way when it comes to decorating. Your life will be so much more peaceful."

"But picture windows, wallpaper..." He was still sputtering.

"Y'all will have plenty of time to figure that all out. Maybe we should go ahead and sign these papers now."

"Captain Dan, what exactly do these papers say?" I asked as I closed the door to the V-berth.

"You know, standard stuff. Just a few signatures and a couple of initials, then this gorgeous little lady will belong to y'all," Captain Dan replied. He sat and put a folder on the table.

"Scooter, don't you think we should talk about this a bit more?"

Captain Dan opened up the folder and pulled out a stack of papers. "Well, little lady, I wouldn't take too long. There's a couple who are flying down from New York City tomorrow to see the boat and the phone's been ringing off the hook. Lots of other people are interested in *Marjorie Jane*. If you don't snap her up now, I can't guarantee she'll still be parked here on the lot. Um, I mean *docked* at the marina."

Scooter looked through the papers and then up at me with those cute little puppy-dog eyes. Okay, maybe he did need a new hobby to lift him out of his funk, but I wasn't sure a boat was the best solution. Especially this dilapidated one.

Captain Dan handed Scooter a pen. "And, it's a heck of a price. You won't find a better price on a boat like this anywhere. Captain Dan has the best deals in town, guaranteed!"

Scooter hesitated. "I don't think we can let this slip out of our fingers. You know we have the money from the sale of the business and from my uncle's estate. Besides, I think it would be a nice way to honor my uncle's memory. He always did enjoy sailing."

It was true; we did have some money in the bank, and his uncle always did talk fondly about his days sailing in the Caribbean. I suppose if you were going to have a midlife crisis, a sailboat was better than a bad toupee or a sports car.

I sighed. "I guess it's okay."

Scooter grinned from ear to ear. "It's going to be great. Just imagine us out there on the water with dolphins frolicking alongside *Marjorie Jane*. Just the two of us."

The way he was talking about *Marjorie Jane*, it was more like the three of us. But who's counting?

"Fine. While you two do the paperwork, I'm going to go outside for some fresh air. It's so stuffy in here." I looked around the cabin again. "I really think some picture windows that we can open up to get a breeze in here would do a world of good."

Scooter turned red and sputtered again. I wondered what it was about windows that got him so worked up. Captain Dan distracted him by pointing to a spot that needed to be initialed.

While Scooter was leafing through the paperwork, Captain Dan leaned back and looked me up and down. I was getting a little tired of how he leered at me. And Mr. Oblivious continued to be, well, oblivious. I knew his rather nerdy powers of concentration were what made him so successful in his line of work, but sometimes I wished he were able to pay attention to more than one thing at a time. Maybe it was a good thing we were getting this paperwork over and done with so we wouldn't have to deal with Captain Dan much longer. And what made him so special that he could wear cowboy boots on the boat, but I wasn't allowed to wear my flip-flops?

"Come on by the patio later, around four," Captain Dan said. "The marina hosts a barbecue every Friday. They'll provide the hamburgers and hot dogs. All you have to do is bring a side dish or a dessert to share. It'll be a good chance to meet some of the other cowboys and cowgirls who have boats here."

"We'll bring dessert," I said quickly. I always bring dessert to potlucks. Usually brownies. That way I know there's going to be something decent to eat. One time somebody convinced me to bring a salad. Well, that turned out to be a colossal mistake. There were salads of every kind, but no brownies. Not even any chocolate chip cookies. No desserts at all. The worst potluck ever.

I grabbed my purse off the table. "Since I don't have time to go back to the cottage and make brownies, I'm going to see what I can find in town and meet you back here at the marina."

"Sure thing," Scooter said while he continued signing papers and handing them back to Captain Dan. "Why don't you pick up a bottle of wine while you're out so we can celebrate?"

I looked around the cabin and sighed. I wasn't sure one bottle of wine was enough to help me come to terms with the arrival of *Marjorie Jane* in our lives.

* * *

I didn't know how to get back off the boat without breaking a leg or, at the very least, spraining an ankle. *Okay, just do everything in reverse.* Somehow, I managed to get both of my legs over the lifelines and was hanging on for dear life when a cat jumped up onto the boat, dashed past me, leaped back onto the dock, and darted off. I was so startled that I let go of the lifelines and ended up landing smack on my butt on the dock. Splinters in your butt are very awkward.

"Are you all right, sugar?"

I looked up and saw a woman, probably in

her midthirties, staring down at me with concern. She was wearing a pink baseball hat with a long blonde ponytail pulled through the back and sporting a pink-and-white-striped T-shirt and pink shorts. Even her sneakers were pink. If I had to go out on a limb, I'd say pink was her favorite color.

I'm not a big fan of pink. Don't get me wrong—I like girly things, like facials and diamonds. But pink? Ugh.

She held out her hand—bright pink nail polish, of course—and helped me to my feet. I stood and heard a rip as my jeans caught on one of the rusty nails sticking out of the dock. Great. Just what I needed. Splinters in my butt, a rip in my jeans, and a stupid sailboat as an anniversary present. Could the day get any better?

"They really need to do something about fixing these docks. Someone could get seriously hurt one of these days," she said. She had a sweet-sounding drawl that was far more pleasant on the ears than Captain Dan's.

"Yeah, don't I know it," I said, brushing

dirt off my rear end. "My name's Mollie McGhie, by the way."

"And I'm Penny Chadwick." She pointed at *Marjorie Jane*, who gently bobbed up and down in the water as if she didn't have a care in the world. And why should she? She had just suckered someone into buying her. "What were you doing on *Marjorie Jane*?" she asked.

"My husband decided to buy her for me as an anniversary present."

She furrowed her brow. "He bought *this* boat for you?"

"Exactly!" I said. "Who buys their wife a boat for their anniversary when everyone knows diamonds are a girl's best friend?"

"Well, diamonds are nice," she agreed. "But what I meant was, why did he buy *this* particular boat, especially when there are so many nicer ones available on the market?"

"Honestly, I have no idea. I guess when Captain Dan told him what a bargain it was and that there were lots of other people interested in her, he figured it was too good of a deal to pass up. Plus, he's been wanting a boat for a while and when our anniversary came up, it probably seemed like the perfect excuse to take the plunge."

"Did Captain Dan really say other people were interested in the boat?" She bit her bottom lip. "Did you sign any papers yet?"

I hesitated for a moment and then said, "My husband is signing them now."

A loud cheer erupted from *Marjorie Jane*. I heard Scooter yell, "Whoo-hoo! I own a boat!"

I sighed. "I guess he's finished signing them now." Penny continued chewing on her lower lip and looked at *Marjorie Jane*. My stomach started to churn. "Why, what's wrong?"

"I don't know if I should say," she said.

"Please, you have me worried. What's the deal with this boat?" I asked. "My husband can be impulsive at times. I really would like to know what he's gotten himself into this time."

"Well, you have to wonder why the previous owners are in such a big hurry to get rid of her. They've priced the boat to sell quickly."

"Where are they now? Maybe I can talk to them and find out what's going on."

"Easier said than done. After they sailed the boat over here from Texas a few days ago, they skipped town right away. From what I understand, they gave Captain Dan power of attorney to sell the boat. I guess that's what he's doing now with your husband—completing a bill of sale and transferring the title over to his name on their behalf."

"But why did they leave town? Why didn't they complete the sale themselves?"

Penny shrugged. "Who knows?" Then she smiled slyly. "Wait until Ned and Nancy hear about this!"

"Who are Ned and Nancy?"

"The Schneiders? You haven't met them yet?" I shook my head. "Oh, well, they own the marina. They were already pissed at Captain Dan about the previous owners. They're going to be livid when they find out that he helped them by selling their boat."

"Why would they be so mad?"

"When they brought *Marjorie Jane* into the marina, they rammed into one of the docks, causing a lot of damage. Captain Dan told them not to worry, that they were good for the money. They believed him and didn't get a deposit or credit card details. Then the owners left in a hurry, leaving a big unpaid bill behind, which they blame Captain Dan for."

I rubbed my temples. I could feel a headache coming on.

"Hey, it'll be okay," she said. "I'm sure your husband knows what he's doing. Has he restored a boat before?"

I laughed. "Scooter? Restore a boat? Not that I know of."

"I'm sure he's an experienced sailor, at least. He must know a lot about boats."

"He used to sail on Lake Erie when he was a kid, but that's quite a while ago now. Does that count?"

She tilted her head to one side. "I suppose he might be a little rusty. And what about you? Do you have much experience on boats?"

I shook my head. "No. *Marjorie Jane* is the first sailboat I've ever been on."

"Goodness gracious," she said. She paced back and forth on the dock. "Listen, sugar, there's no way Captain Dan will let you out of this deal. I've known him for a while and with him, all sales are final." She paused for a moment. "But considering you and your husband's lack of sailing experience, not to mention lack of experience restoring older boats, I might be able to do you a favor and take her off your hands. I was thinking of getting another boat anyway. I always thought fixing a boat up would be fun. *Marjorie Jane* might be too much for the two of you to cope with."

"Really?" I said enthusiastically. "I'd love to get rid of this piece of junk."

She smiled. "Well, talk it over with your husband and let me know what you think. I run the sailing school here at the marina. You can find me on my boat, *Pretty in Pink*, on D Dock or just ask for me at the marina office."

"You have no idea how much I appreciate

your help. I'll give it a while before I talk with him about it. I think he's a little too excited right now to see reason." I reached into my bag and grabbed my phone. "Before you leave, let me take a picture of you with what hopefully will be your new boat, and not ours." Penny stepped over to the front of the boat and smiled while I snapped a photo.

"Hope to see you later, Mollie," she said over her shoulder as she walked down the dock.

I turned, looked at *Marjorie Jane* for what I hoped was the last time, and went in search of brownies. And wine. Scooter thought the wine would be for celebrating getting *Marjorie Jane.* I hoped it would be for celebrating getting rid of her.

CHAPTER 3
MY LITTLE SWEET POTATO

AS I MADE MY WAY BACK down the dock, I tried to figure out the best way to convince Scooter that we should sell *Marjorie Jane* to Penny. Once he had his heart set on something, it was hard to get him to change his mind. I thought about pointing out all the things that were wrong with the boat and what a huge project it would be to restore her. Nope, that probably wouldn't work. Scooter is one of those guys who loves the idea of fixing things up. Unfortunately, he's not one of those guys who's good at fixing things up. Just ask me about the time he tried to install a garage door opener at our old house. On second thought, don't. I ended up having to park on the street for almost a year. It's possible I might still be a little bitter about that.

I reached the end of the dock and stepped onto the brick patio area in the center of the marina. It really was a lovely spot. People were sitting at tables underneath large umbrellas. Some were chatting, others were reading, and a family with small children was enjoying ice-cream cones.

At the back of the patio, nestled among some palm trees, were a few buildings painted in the bright, cheerful colors common in this part of Florida. I was pondering which was my favorite color when my phone beeped, alerting me to yet another text from my mom. She must have sent a dozen last night wanting to know who *Marjorie Jane* was and asking why Scooter was too cheap to get me diamonds for our anniversary.

I really didn't want to deal with responding to her just then. My mom doesn't get the whole concept of texting and the fact that it's supposed to be a quick, shorthand way of communicating. One time I texted LOL to her. She was perplexed for a week. I figured it was easier to send her a picture of *Marjorie Jane*. No words. No chance of getting drawn into a long round of back-and-forth texts. I attached the picture, clicked Send, and chucked my phone back into my purse.

Enough thinking about Scooter, *Marjorie Jane*, and my mom. I really needed to get focused on my mission at hand—brownies. Normally, I bake my own award-winning, gooey, quadruple-chocolate brownies, but I didn't have enough time to make them before the barbecue. I decided to pop into the marina office and see if they knew of a good bakery in town.

The office was located in a small two-story wooden building. The white trim and shutters were freshly painted and contrasted nicely with the bright yellow clapboards. As I stopped to admire the colorful flower beds in front of the office, the screen door flew open and a ball of fur streaked past me, followed closely by a woman brandishing a broom.

"If I see you in here again, you'll be sorry, you mangy cat!" she yelled, waving the broom back and forth for emphasis. I jumped back quickly to avoid getting clobbered. Unfortunately, I stepped straight into the flower bed, crushing some purple impatiens under my flip-flop.

"Look what you did," she said, shaking her fist. She stared at the flower bed in dismay. "I just planted those, and now they're ruined!"

She glared at me over the top of her reading glasses without saying a word. I figured she was in her late fifties or early sixties, based on the wrinkles around her eyes and her laugh lines. Although in her case, I suspect they were more like frown lines. Unpleasant reminders of childhood popped into my head. My mom was the master of long, uncomfortable, silent stare-downs. Ultimately, I would confess to whatever it was that she thought I was guilty of, like polishing off the cookies she had been saving for her bridge group. Not that I ever did anything like that as a child, mind you. As the stare-down continued, I began to think that my mom was just an amateur compared to this woman.

I wasn't sure what made me more uncomfortable—her piercing blue eyes peeking out from underneath her immaculately coiffed hair, or how tightly she was gripping the broom handle. I averted my gaze and noticed she was wearing white capri pants and a navy-blue polo shirt with the Palm Tree Marina logo embroidered on it. A name tag that said "Nancy, Office Manager," was pinned underneath.

I'd read somewhere that if you use a person's first name it defuses the tension. "This sure is a nice place you have here, Nancy," I said. She continued to glare at me while increasing her death grip on the broom. I wondered who was going to crack first, the broom handle or me. Probably me.

I decided to try a new tack. "Your cat's awfully cute. What's its name?" People love it when you ask about their pets.

"That is *not* my cat," she said. "Cats don't

have any business being here at the marina. Next time I see the owner of that vile creature, I'm going to give her a piece of my mind." Her eyes narrowed as she saw the mangled impatiens.

"Um, sorry about the flowers, Nancy. I was just trying to get out of the way and stumbled. I'm a bit of a klutz."

She relaxed her grip on the broom slightly. "Humph. Well, accidents happen. Especially if you're klutzy." She inspected me up and down, pausing when she saw the rip in my jeans.

I put my hand over the tear, trying to cover it up from her disapproving look. "Like I said, I'm klutzy. I ripped my jeans getting off our boat."

"Your boat? What's your boat's name? I don't think I've seen you around here before," Nancy said, tightening her grip on the broom again. I didn't think the broom was going to live to see another day. "Did you dock here without getting permission first?"

"No, the boat was already here," I

stammered. "We just bought her from Captain Dan. She's the red boat on B Dock."

"You don't mean that floating monstrosity, *Marjorie Jane*, do you?" I nodded, both in agreement to her question and with her assessment of *Marjorie Jane* as a monstrosity.

Nancy started to sweep the area around the flower bed furiously. "That man, I swear, he's always up to something. I'm going to wring his neck when I see him," she muttered.

"What do you mean, he's always up to something?" I darted out of the way as Nancy swept the dirt back into the flower bed. She ignored me and kept sweeping.

I tried again. "Listen, I just met a woman named Penny who told me that *Marjorie Jane* isn't in the best shape. I'm worried that my husband bought a lemon. Do you think it's possible that Captain Dan pulled a fast one on us?"

Nancy snorted. "Whatever deal you made with Captain Dan is between you and him. I don't want any part of it."

"Well, can you at least tell me a little bit

about him? Scooter—that's my husband—doesn't really think things through before he buys something. He even bought a case of Elmer's glue once because it was on sale. I asked him what he thought we were going to do with that many bottles of glue. He was at a loss for an answer but was still convinced it was a great deal. I'm worried that this is another one of his rash decisions. People have taken advantage of him before. I'd hate to think Captain Dan did the same thing."

Nancy stopped sweeping and looked at me with concern. "Oh, you poor thing. I know all about foolish husbands." She paused before adding, "To be honest, I don't really know too much about Captain Dan. He moved down to Coconut Cove about a year ago and opened a boat brokerage business at the marina. We lease him space for his office, and he keeps some of the boats he's selling here at the marina. It's purely a business arrangement."

She leaned the broom on the wall next to the office door. "Now, why don't you come inside with me, and we'll get you registered as *Marjorie Jane*'s new owners."

I wasn't convinced that Nancy didn't know more about Captain Dan, but I was relieved that she had finally let go of the broom. I followed her into the office, wiping my feet on the mat by the door first.

Nancy sat behind a counter, adjusted her reading glasses, and tapped away on the computer keyboard. "It will be just a minute while I pull up the records, dear."

I thought I saw a faint smile when she called me "dear." Maybe she wasn't so scary after all. Turned out it was a short-lived feeling.

"You didn't track dirt into here, did you?" she barked, peeking over the counter at the gleaming pine floor.

I gulped. "No, I wiped my feet on the mat."

"Good. We like to run a tidy ship. Being neat is a good thing, wouldn't you agree?"

"Of course," I said, while I thought about the fact that I hadn't made the bed this morning and that the sink was full of dirty dishes.

I looked around the room while she

worked away on the computer. The wall behind Nancy was painted turquoise and had framed photographs of dolphins, tropical fish, and seashells on display. Nancy looked up from the computer. "Those are for sale if you're interested. My daughter took them. We also have some guidebooks and nautical charts by the door. Those might come in handy, considering you just bought a boat."

I walked over to the shelves stocked with cereal, cans of soup, crackers, and other basic groceries that boaters might need. As I contemplated the mystery of canned artichoke hearts, the screen door opened.

Nancy pursed her lips and glared at the entryway. "Is that you, Ned? Don't just stand there letting all the flies in. Get in here and close that door."

A man wearing a matching navy-blue Palm Tree Marina polo shirt tucked into neatly pressed khaki pants entered and quickly shut the door. "What happened to the flower bed?" he asked tentatively, running his fingers through his gray hair.

Nancy pointed at me. "That's what

happened."

He looked over at me and gave me a warm smile before turning back to Nancy, who was picking some papers off the printer. She stapled the pages together so firmly that I thought the stapler might break. She put the papers down and waved the hunk of metal at Ned angrily. "Her husband just bought that old boat, *Marjorie Jane.* Can you believe Captain Dan went and did that behind our back?"

Ned stepped back to avoid being hit by the stapler. Nancy certainly had a way with office equipment and cleaning supplies. He rubbed his chin for a few moments. "But maybe that's a good thing. We won't have the hassle of trying to track down and deal with the previous owners any—"

Nancy slammed the stapler down on the counter, cutting him off. "Never you mind about that. Shouldn't you be setting up the tables for the barbecue?"

Ned took that as his cue to leave, nodded at me, and scurried out the door.

"I've got your paperwork for you." Nancy

motioned me over to the counter and explained the monthly rates and marina rules and regulations. She became quite animated when she got to section 8.1—pets must be on leashes at all times. I discreetly moved the stapler a safe distance away and filled in my details while Nancy quickly fired questions at me. "You don't have a pet, do you? You do have a credit card, don't you? Do you have loud parties at night?" I must have answered yes and no correctly, because she eventually handed me a copy of the papers and a credit card receipt.

As I opened the door, I noticed Ned setting up a folding table next to the grill, which reminded me that I needed to get brownies. I looked back at Nancy, who was busily tapping her perfectly manicured pink nails, each adorned with a white starfish, on the computer keyboard.

"Do you happen to know a good bakery around here?" I asked.

"Try Penelope's Sugar Shack. It's just off Main Street. Big purple awning. You can't miss it." She stared at the screen door, which

I had left partially ajar. "Hurry up now and close the door on your way out. The last thing we need is more flies in here," she said as she whacked one unfortunate victim on the counter. I'm surprised flies even dared to come into the office when Nancy was on duty. I don't think I would unless I had to.

As I walked across the patio, I noticed the cat that Nancy had chased out of the office sitting on top of one of the tables. Ned was scratching behind its ears to the accompaniment of a loud purr. He caught my eye and motioned me over.

"Listen, don't mind my wife. Her bark is worse than her bite. It's just that she's very, well, how should I put it..."

"Organized?" I offered.

"Yes, that's a good description for it—organized."

I actually thought scary was a better description, but organized seemed more polite. The cat nudged Ned's hand, reminding him that his primary duty should be ear-scratching, not chatting with people.

"Sorry about that, Mrs. Moto," Ned said.

"Only a few more scratches, then I have to get back to work."

"Mrs. Moto is an interesting-looking cat." I stroked her white fur while she purred approvingly. "I love the black rings around her eyes. And her black-and-orange patches remind me of a calico cat I used to have when I was growing up. Except my cat had a fluffy white tail, while this one doesn't have much of a tail at all."

"That's because she's a Japanese bobtail. I think it's kind of cute, like a rabbit's tail." Mrs. Moto meowed in agreement. "She's such a sweet cat. Aren't you, Mrs. Moto?" Ned gave the cat one last scratch on her head, picked her up, and set her on the patio. "Time for you to run along now before Nancy catches you out here."

Ned turned to me. "Do me a favor, will you? Don't let Nancy know that you saw me out here petting Mrs. Moto. I think she gets jealous when I pay attention to her."

"No problem. Your secret is safe with me."

I watched the calico scamper down the dock while Ned returned to setting up tables on the patio. My phone beeped. Another text from my mom.

I thought you said Marjorie Jane was a redhead. She has blonde hair in the picture you sent.

I checked the picture. Sure enough, Penny was in the corner at the front of the boat. She must have thought that Penny was *Marjorie Jane.* I sent her a quick text before heading over to Penelope's Sugar Shack.

That's Penny. Gotta go. Need brownies.

* * *

By the time I got back to the marina, the barbecue had already started. I put my box of brownies down on one of the tables. I saw lots of different types of salads, but no desserts. People sure were going to be glad I stopped by the bakery.

I saw Scooter walking down the dock toward the patio. I waved at him but he didn't notice. He kept stopping and admiring each one of the sailboats along the way. It was bad enough that he'd paid more attention to *Marjorie Jane* than to me, but now he was paying more attention to all sorts of other sailboats as well. He was so lost in his daydreams that he bumped into me at the end of the dock.

"There you are. I was wondering what happened to you. Great news—I finished signing all the paperwork, and *Marjorie Jane* is officially ours!" He grinned. It was a cute grin, and I really hated to crush his spirit, but he needed to know about Penny's offer.

"I know. I heard you cheering earlier when I was speaking with this lady named Penny. She seems to think Captain Dan did a number on us. *Marjorie Jane* needs a lot of work. She's a major fixer-upper. It might be a little too much for us, don't you think?"

"Penny, you said? She doesn't happen to be the sailing school instructor, does she?"

"Yes, that's her. Why?"

"Captain Dan warned me about her. He said she's been dying to get her hands on *Marjorie Jane* and will say or do anything to warn prospective buyers off."

"But she sounded quite sincere and she

even offered to buy the boat off us."

"Well, there you go then. I bet she would offer a really low price and we'd lose money on the deal. No, I trust Captain Dan. Everything is going to be fine, you'll see." Scooter glanced at the patio. "There he is now. Let's go say hi. I'm sure he'll put your mind at ease."

Captain Dan waved us over. "Glad you could make it!" He turned to the couple standing next to him. "Let me introduce you. This here is Scooter and Mollie McGhie. They're the proud new owners of *Marjorie Jane*. And this here is Jack Holt. Just look at those freckles on him. He looks like he swallowed a quarter and broke out in pennies." Captain Dan playfully punched Jack in the arm as though they were best buddies.

Jack pulled up the sleeve of his brightly colored Hawaiian shirt and rubbed his arm before shaking hands with us. "Why would you buy *Marjorie Jane*?" he asked in disbelief. He took the words right out of my mouth. Why would anyone buy that boat? Or any boat, for that matter.

Scooter beamed. "I bet you're jealous, Jack, that I snapped her up. Captain Dan's been telling me that his phone has been ringing off the hook with people wanting to buy her."

Jack raised his eyebrows at the bearded man. "Your phone's been ringing off the hook?"

Captain Dan nodded. "Sure has. Captain Dan is the number one boat broker in all of Coconut Cove." He inched over to the woman standing next to Jack, draped his arm around her shoulder, and winked. "Isn't that right, sweetheart?"

Jack stared at him. "That's my wife, Sandy." I wasn't sure if he was introducing her to us or reminding Captain Dan whose wife she was. Sandy brushed her curly, silver hair behind her ears and smiled at us.

The captain gave Sandy's shoulder a squeeze and looked over at us. "She's as cute as a calico kitten, isn't she?" Sandy blushed, unaware that her husband's stare had turned into a glare. She looked at Captain Dan wistfully when he took his arm off her shoulder.

He reached into a cooler, pulled out a couple of beers, and offered one to Scooter. "Anyone else want one?"

A young man tapped Captain Dan on the shoulder. He had a scruffy beard and long, greasy, brown hair tied back in a ponytail. When I saw the tattered shorts he was wearing, I self-consciously put my hand over the tear in my jeans, wishing I had been able to change before the barbecue. But while I was embarrassed by my ripped clothing, he seemed unfazed. I wondered if wearing a bright orange T-shirt that said "Trust Me, I'm a Pirate" and a leather cord with a skull-and-crossbones pendant around your neck was the latest in sailor chic. I really hoped not, because I didn't think it was a look that Scooter could pull off.

"I'll take one of those," he said, holding out a rather grimy-looking hand.

"I can always count on you to show up when there's free beer." Captain Dan sneered as he handed him a bottle. "This is

Ben Moretti. He lives on a sailboat out on one of the mooring balls. It's cheaper out there than getting a slip on the docks. You're always trying to save a buck, aren't you, Ben?"

Ben took a large swig of beer. "You know good and well why I'm broke." He nodded at us, pushed past the captain, and walked toward the barbecue.

Our boat broker shook his head. "Well, somebody's a little touchy, aren't they? Oh, I see Nancy and Ned over there. I need to have a word with them. I'll catch y'all later."

Sandy gazed after Captain Dan longingly. Jack grabbed her by the elbow. "It looks like the hamburgers and hot dogs are done. Why don't we go over and get some food, Sandy?"

Sandy pulled her arm away from Jack and took mine instead. "Sure thing. Mollie and I will meet you guys over at the barbecue."

* * *

After loading my plate up with a cheeseburger and all the fixings, I checked out the buffet table, where everyone had placed their contributions. I bypassed the healthy-looking salads, opting instead for a large helping of baked beans and some corn on the cob. I snagged a brownie while I was at it too.

Captain Dan sidled up to me. "You sure are a sweet little thing, just like those brownies. Go on and pass me one of those, darlin'."

I reluctantly put one on his plate. "Are you originally from Texas, Captain Dan?"

"Sure am. Texan, through and through."

"You look so familiar. Did you ever spend time in Cleveland? Scooter and I lived there before we moved down here. Maybe we ran into each other up there?"

"Nope, never been to Cleveland."

"What brought you to Coconut Cove?"

"Um...I just wanted a change of scenery." He winked at me. "I heard the ladies are real purty out here."

I was officially creeped out. I changed the subject. "Have you always been a boat broker? It seems like an interesting job." It didn't really seem that interesting, but one thing I've learned in my line of work is that people love to talk about themselves and what they do.

"I've always been in sales," Captain Dan said. He hesitated, then pointed across the patio. "Look, the gang's got a table over there." While he hurried off, I put another brownie on my plate.

* * *

"There's my little sweet potato." Scooter pulled out a chair next to him for me.

Sandy cocked her head. "Sweet potato?"

"I think Scooter has a hard time remembering my name," I said. "He's always calling me these strange pet names. Lately, they've all been related to vegetables, which is odd because Scooter isn't really a big fan of vegetables."

Scooter pointed at his plate. "That's not fair. I've got some baked beans right here. Those are vegetables, aren't they?"

"I guess. But I really meant vegetables like broccoli and cauliflower. Like the ones on that list your doctor gave to you."

Scooter shuddered at hearing the names of two of the vegetables he'd least like to make an appearance on his dinner plate. He scooped up some of the baked beans. "Yum, these are delicious. I wonder who made these."

Sandy beamed. "I did. I'm glad you like them."

I took a bite and had to agree. "They're fantastic. What's your secret, Sandy?"

"It's an old family recipe. The trick is to add a touch of cocoa powder and some maple syrup. I bring them to all the potlucks we go to. They're always a big hit."

"I can see why. Everything's better with chocolate in it." I batted Scooter's fork out of the way when he tried to get the last of the baked beans on my plate. "Hands off, buster. These are all mine."

As I finished off the rest of my beans, I heard my phone buzzing. My boss, Brian Morrison, had sent me an email. I quickly scanned it between bites of my cheeseburger.

"Scooter, you'll never believe this! Brian says they're down to two candidates for the promotion at work. It's between me and Lola."

Scooter furrowed his brow. "Work? Promotion? What are you talking about?"

I clenched my phone and glared at him. "How can you say that? I've told you a million times that I'm up for a promotion."

Sandy leaned over. "I know what you mean about having to constantly repeat yourself. Jack doesn't listen to a word I say."

Scooter's brow was still furrowed. If he kept this up, he was going to get a headache. "I always listen to what you say, Mollie. But since you don't have a job, how can you be up for a promotion at work?"

I looked at Sandy. "See, he called me by my name, rather than a vegetable. He knows he's in trouble." Then I turned to Scooter. "You know good and well that I have a job. I do important work for FAROUT."

Scooter leaned back in his chair. "Oh, that. I thought you meant a real job."

"You know what I was thinking I'd start

making you for breakfast, Scooter?" I asked. "Oatmeal with broccoli and cauliflower on it."

Scooter blanched. "How about if we just stick to Froot Loops? I don't want you to go to any trouble making a fancy breakfast for me." He quickly added, "Of course the work you do for FAROUT is a real job."

Jack pushed his plate aside. "Well, at least your wife has a job. I can't remember the last time Sandy worked for a living."

Sandy glared at Jack. The way she held her plastic fork made me think she was considering stabbing him in the hand. She scooped up some baked beans instead. Wise choice. When your husband is annoying, my philosophy is to eat chocolate. Or in this case, baked beans with cocoa in them.

Captain Dan held up his bottle of beer. "You know what we need? A little toast. Here's to Scooter and Mollie on the purchase of their new boat."

Scooter looked cautiously at me and raised his bottle. Sandy and I raised our wine glasses while Jack stared off into the distance.

Our boat broker nudged Jack. "What's wrong with you? You look as mean as a mama wasp. Come on, let's congratulate these fine folks." Jack grudgingly raised his bottle.

After a few minutes of silent eating and drinking, Captain Dan leaned back and rubbed his belly. "That sure was some good grub, and the company wasn't half-bad either." Sandy gave a sudden yelp and fidgeted in her chair. I could have sworn that the captain had put his hand on her knee under the table. He pushed back his chair, stood, and looked at some kids building sandcastles on the beach.

"Scooter, why don't you take your missus out for a sunset stroll on the beach. Y'all can get a good view of the marina from there. While you're off doing that, I'm going to pop by *Marjorie Jane* and leave a little boat-warming present for you on board."

Scooter got up from the table. "That's awful nice of you." He reached into his pocket. "I found another padlock on the boat. Here's a spare key for it."

Captain Dan took the key, then shook Scooter's hand heartily. He nodded at the rest of us. "Have a good night, y'all."

As he ambled across the patio, I saw Penny come up and grab his arm. Captain Dan stopped and tried to remove her hand. She tightened her grip on his arm and spoke to him in an agitated manner. Whatever she was saying appeared to be making him angry. His eyes narrowed and he pushed her away from him. The others at the table were busy talking about injector valves on diesel engines, which was not a conversation I wanted to be a part of. I decided it was time to do a little bit of investigating.

"Here, why don't I throw all of this in the trash," I offered, gathering up the paper plates, utensils, and cups.

"Thanks," Scooter said absentmindedly, and turned back to his conversation with Jack and Sandy.

I headed toward the trash can and hid behind some potted palm trees so I could listen to Captain Dan and Penny's conversation.

"You promised me that we'd be partners in the boat brokerage," Penny said.

"I never did any such thing," Captain Dan said.

"Yes, you did. And you owe me, especially after I lost all that money I put into your last business."

"It was an investment. Sometimes you win and sometimes you lose. If you can't stand the heat, you should get out of the kitchen, as my mama always said." He folded his arms across his chest. "You knew when you put that money up that it was a risk."

"You told me it was a sure thing. Otherwise, I would have never given you the money."

"Well, I don't know what to tell you, darlin'. It's not my problem, is it?"

"I'm going to make it your problem. You better watch your back, Bob. It isn't just me who's livid. Ned and Nancy are pretty hot under the collar. And wait until those new marks of yours find out what you sold them."

He shook Penny by the shoulders. "You better not say anything, you hear me?" He pushed her back, turned, and stormed off. Penny chewed on her nails while she watched him walk away.

I was left with two questions—why did Penny call Captain Dan "Bob," and who were these new marks she was referring to?

CHAPTER 4
UNEXPLAINED LIGHTS

WHEN I GOT BACK TO THE table, Scooter, Jack, and Sandy were engrossed in conversation. "You wouldn't believe it—there was oil everywhere, even on Sandy's T-shirt and hair!" Jack chuckled. "Yep, those were the good old days, weren't they, honey?"

He leaned over to Sandy, smiled softly, and rubbed her hand. Sandy looked at him in surprise, then pulled her hand away. Jack's smile faded, and his eyes got steely.

"But those days were a long time ago," Jack said bitterly. Sandy blushed while Scooter did his best to pretend that things weren't incredibly uncomfortable.

"So, Scooter, what about that stroll on the beach?" I asked.

He looked at me with relief. "Yes. That would be great."

"See you guys tomorrow," Scooter said as we walked toward the boardwalk.

I glanced back and saw Jack staring angrily off into space while Sandy rubbed her hands together anxiously.

"What was that about?" I asked.

"I'm not sure. One minute we were talking about changing oil filters and the next minute they were, well, you saw it."

"Do you think there's something going on between Sandy and Captain Dan?"

"What?" Scooter asked incredulously.

"Didn't you see how Captain Dan kept flirting with Sandy? I even think he had his hand on her knee at one point during dinner."

"I think you're reading things wrong. Before you came back to the table, Jack was telling me that he and Sandy were high school sweethearts. They've been married for over thirty years."

"Just because you've been married a long time doesn't mean you're happy."

Scooter puzzled over this while we walked down the wooden steps from the boardwalk that led to the beach. "I can't imagine not being as happily married to you after thirty years as I am now. These past ten years have been wonderful." He added with a smirk, "Even if you do hog the covers at night."

"That's not true! *You* steal them during the night and wake me up. All I'm doing is getting back my rightful share."

"Anyway, we won't need covers once we sail *Marjorie Jane* to the tropics. It'll be too warm at night."

"Let's not get ahead of ourselves. I'm still not convinced that we should keep this boat. Do you really think we're cut out to be boat owners?"

"Of course we are. It'll be fun—something we can do together. Don't let Penny mess with your head."

"I don't know. There's something fishy

going on between Penny and Captain Dan. I happened to overhear them talking, and based on that conversation, I think our boat broker is a pretty shady character."

"You *happened* to overhear? Isn't that another way of saying you eavesdropped?" Scooter asked. "Kind of like the time you told me you *happened* to open a padlock without a key while you were holding bolt cutters in your hand?"

I shook my head. "How else was I supposed to get into the storage shed behind that grumpy old man's house? You knew as well as I did that he stole my bike and locked it up in there. The police didn't take me seriously, so I had to take matters into my own hands. And I was right, wasn't I? My bike was there. Honestly, are you ever going to let that go?"

Scooter laughed. "Probably not. You're too cute when you get all worked up."

"Humph. Anyway, Penny was complaining angrily to Captain Dan about how he had conned her out of some money and—get this —she called him Bob. I don't think Dan is his real name!"

"Sure it is. He gave me a business card." Scooter fished in his wallet and handed it to me. "See? Right there. Captain Dan Thomas. There's even a little anchor logo next to his name that proves he's a certified captain."

"Uh, yeah. You do know anyone can get business cards printed up, don't you? And how do you know he's a certified captain anyway? How does this prove anything? Besides, he wore those cowboy boots of his on the boat. I thought you told me you always had to take your shoes off. Wouldn't a legitimate boat broker know that?"

Scooter chewed on his lower lip. "Um, I'm not sure what that was about. It's a bit strange, but I'm sure he had a good reason. Maybe they're orthopedic cowboy boots?"

I decided not to press Scooter on Captain Dan or *Marjorie Jane*. I needed to figure out another approach to get him to sell her.

I slipped off my flip-flops and walked down the beach, relishing the feel of the warm sand between my toes. The sun was beginning to set, its waning light glistening on the water between the boats moored in the cove.

After a few minutes, Scooter caught up with me and handed me a sand dollar. "I thought you might like this for your collection."

I tucked it into my purse. I'd started collecting seashells when we moved to Florida. I'd found a number of pretty specimens, but this was my first sand dollar.

"I think your shells are going to look great on the boat. You should start thinking about how you want to decorate. A nautical theme might be nice. But no picture windows or wallpaper, right?"

As far as I was concerned, my seashell collection was staying right where it was—in a basket by our bed at our cottage. I was about to make that clear when I noticed red and green lights flashing on the water and moving toward the far end of the beach.

Scooter was walking along the beach, his eyes downcast, scanning for more shells. I ran over to him and grasped his arm. "Do you see that?" By the time he looked up, the lights had vanished.

"See what?"

"Those lights. They were there for a few seconds, and now they're gone. I wonder if it was a—"

Scooter put his finger on my lips. "No, it wasn't what you think it was."

"It was. I swear it was. After all, I've got a lot of experience with this kind of thing because of my work with FAROUT."

Scooter rolled his eyes at the mention of FAROUT.

"Stop with the eye-rolling. I wish you'd take my work more seriously."

"But it's not work. It's some organization you volunteer for. You don't even get paid for all the hours you put into it."

"Just because I don't get paid doesn't mean I don't do important work." I stomped my foot on the ground for emphasis. Unfortunately, the emphasis part of it didn't work. I just ended up kicking sand everywhere.

"I know, I know," Scooter said soothingly after he wiped sand off his shorts. "Your work is important. I should take it more seriously. I really do hope you get that promotion. You deserve it far more than Lola." He took my hand. "Come on, let's find a place to sit for a while."

As we walked down the beach, I kept glancing over my shoulder to see if the lights reappeared. If they were what I thought they were, then the Palm Tree Marina and Coconut Cove could make the national news.

* * *

Later that night, as we walked across the patio toward the dock, I stopped to check the buffet table. Sure enough, all the brownies I'd brought were gone, but there were plenty of salads left. We waved good-night to a couple of stragglers who were having a nightcap before heading back to their boats. I saw Mrs. Moto chasing a lizard near one of the palm trees. After she trapped it under a paw, she looked at me and meowed. "Good girl," I said. "You sure are cute, aren't you, with those black markings around your eyes?"

We turned down the dock toward *Marjorie Jane*'s berth. I tripped over an empty beer bottle and grabbed Scooter's arm to steady myself. The bottle reminded me of how angry Ben had been at Captain Dan, although not angry enough to refuse an offer of a free beer. I wondered why Ben was so short of money. Had the Texan conned him like he had Penny?

By the time I reached the boat, Scooter was already in the cockpit. "Can you hand me a flashlight?" he asked as he pushed back the hatch. "It looks like Captain Dan didn't lock up the boat. I want to have a look around here and see if I can find the padlock."

I reached into my purse and found the flashlight tucked beside the sand dollar and other shells we had collected on the beach. I climbed onto the boat and handed it to him. "Do you think someone broke in again?"

Scooter shook his head. "No. You heard what Captain Dan said. That was probably just some kids. I don't think they'd come here twice. Captain Dan probably forgot to put the padlock back on." He pointed the flashlight around the interior of the boat while I climbed down the ladder into the main cabin.

"Be careful. There's something on the floor there next to your foot. Don't trip on it."

I squinted in the dark. "Isn't that one of those winch handles you were showing me earlier?"

Scooter poked his head down. "I think so. Hang on a minute; I can't see very well from up here."

While Scooter made his way down the ladder, I turned on the overhead light. Nothing happened. I moved over to the galley and tried the light in there. Nothing again.

"One more reason to sell *Marjorie Jane*. The lights don't work."

Scooter rolled his eyes. Or at least I think he rolled his eyes. It was hard to tell in the dark.

"Here, I'll trade you," I said as I handed him the winch handle and plucked the flashlight out of his hand. As I pointed the light around the main cabin, I noticed a pool of liquid on the floor near the V-berth. I walked over and pulled open the door. That's when I saw a foot hanging off the mildew-patterned cushions. And not just any foot, but a foot wearing a red cowboy boot.

"Uh, Scooter. We've got another problem."

"Don't worry about the lights. I'm sure it will be an easy fix," he said while he examined the winch handle.

"This is a far bigger problem. I found Captain Dan in the V-berth—and I think he's dead."

CHAPTER 5
EMERGENCY CHOCOLATE

"DID YOU JUST SAY CAPTAIN DAN is dead? Are you sure?" Scooter asked as he stepped toward me, clutching the winch handle in his hand.

"Of course I'm sure," I said.

"But how do you know?"

"Just trust me on this. You really don't want me to describe what I saw." Scooter took a few more cautious steps. I pointed the flashlight down on the floor near the V-berth. "Watch out—you're going to get blood on your shoes."

"Blood?" he asked in a shaky voice.

I shined the flashlight directly at Scooter. He just stood there with his mouth open, staring in horror at the floor. "I think that might be blood on the winch handle too," I said.

He gasped and dropped the handle on the table. He was never very good with blood. Every time Scooter cut his finger, he would close his eyes and scream for me to bandage it up quickly so he didn't have to see the blood. Don't even get me started on the time he cut open his forehead and needed stitches.

"Why don't you go sit down on the couch? I'll call the police." I dug my cell phone out of my purse and dialed 911. While I was talking to the dispatcher, I pointed the light at Scooter. He was looking rather pale. I ended the call and sat next to him. "They'll be here in just a few minutes. In the meantime, we're supposed to sit tight."

I pulled a Hershey's bar out of my purse and broke off a piece. "Here, have some. It'll make you feel better." I always keep a supply of chocolate handy for emergencies. Scooter nodded, ate the chocolate, then put his head between his hands. I squeezed his arm and passed him a few more pieces of chocolate.

"It'll be okay, Scooter. Why don't I get you something to drink?" I cautiously made my way back to the galley to get a bottle of water. Waving the flashlight from side to side, I hoped I wouldn't run across any more unpleasant surprises. I stopped in my tracks when the narrow beam of light illuminated a shiny object on the floor. Praying it wasn't something else covered in blood, I bent down and shined the flashlight directly on it. To my relief, it was just a pink fingernail. I picked it up to examine it more closely.

"Hello, is anyone down there? This is the police," a loud voice boomed.

"Yes, we're down here with the body." I looked at Scooter, worried he might faint at the mention of a body. He stared into space blankly and held out his hand for more chocolate.

"All right, ma'am. We're coming on board. Step aside."

It's not easy to step aside in a boat. I

squeezed as far into the galley as I could, while a burly man climbed down the ladder, followed by a petite woman carrying a large black plastic case. The man said briskly, "Sir, ma'am, I'm Chief Dalton and this is Officer Moore. Officer Moore is going to have a look around while I ask you some questions." He reached up and flicked the overhead light on.

"I thought the lights weren't working," Scooter said. I think he had been hoping they still didn't work. He closed his eyes so he could avoid looking at the blood on the floor and on the winch handle.

Officer Moore stepped into the galley and set the case on the counter. "We noticed your shore power cord had been disconnected, so we plugged it back in."

Chief Dalton asked us what we knew about Captain Dan and why he was on our boat, our whereabouts prior to discovering the body, and when and why we'd purchased *Marjorie Jane.* I told him about the break-in earlier and Captain Dan's theory that it had been high school kids. He scribbled down notes while Officer Moore took photographs.

Once he was done questioning us, he told us to wait on the patio while they examined the boat and removed the body.

* * *

Scooter slumped into a chair and I passed him the rest of the chocolate. While he scraped every last morsel from the wrapper, I looked around the patio, wondering if someone who had been at the barbecue earlier in the night had killed Captain Dan.

A small crowd had gathered, watching the police go back and forth between the parking lot and B Dock. Sandy and Jack stood at the edge of the group. Sandy appeared agitated, pulling on Jack's arm and whispering something in his ear. Everyone gasped as two officers wheeled a gurney with a body bag on it past them.

Sandy hurried over to us, Jack in tow. "Did you see that?" she asked, pulling up a chair next to mine. "I wonder if Mr. Kennedy had a heart attack. Did you know he's in his late eighties and still living aboard his boat? He's been having heart problems for years."

"No, I don't think it was Mr. Kennedy," I said, glancing at Scooter to see how he was holding up. He was searching through my purse, presumably looking for more chocolate. I leaned over to Sandy and whispered, "Captain Dan was murdered on our boat."

Sandy shrieked, "Captain Dan was murdered? Are you sure?" Everyone on the patio turned and stared at her.

Scooter dumped the contents of my purse on the table and pawed through them. "Where's the rest of the chocolate?" he muttered.

Sandy tugged Jack's arm. "Did you hear that? Captain Dan is dead."

Jack looked at her quietly for a few moments. "It's not really a great loss, is it?" He walked over to the boardwalk and gazed blankly out at the water.

The color drained from Sandy's face as she wiped away tears. She probably could use some chocolate too. Clearly, I wasn't prepared for a chocolate emergency of this magnitude.

Ned and Nancy pushed through the crowd and walked over to us. They looked like they had just woken up. Nancy was wearing a fleece robe cinched tightly over her nightgown. Ned had a matching robe over striped pajamas.

Nancy eyed the police officers milling around the patio. "Is it true that Captain Dan was found murdered on your boat? At this time of night?" she asked, peering over her reading glasses. I had a feeling she thought murders should be scheduled ahead of time at a more convenient hour. The way she was staring at me, I wondered if she was going to make a citizen's arrest for disturbing the peace, or rather disturbing *her* peace.

"It's true. I found him in the V-berth."

Nancy frowned and made tsk-tsk sounds. Ned looked woozy. He grabbed onto the back of a chair to steady himself.

Chief Dalton marched toward us, followed by Officer Moore, who was still carrying the black case.

"Mr. and Mrs. Schneider," Chief Dalton said. He pulled a notebook out of his pocket. It wasn't a question, but Ned and Nancy nodded while the chief scribbled something down. "A Daniel Robert Smith was found dead aboard a boat named *Marjorie Jane*." More nodding. "I understand Mr. Smith was a boat broker at the marina." Ned and Nancy continued to nod. I was beginning to like Chief Dalton's effect on Nancy.

The burly man flipped over a page in his notebook. "Is it true that the two of you had an argument with Mr. Smith earlier in the evening?"

Nancy stopped nodding. "Now, just you wait a minute here, mister," she said, jabbing the chief in his stomach with her long nails. The stout man looked down at her hand. She jabbed him again. "The people you should be talking to are them." She stopped jabbing his stomach and pointed at us. I pulled back in my chair, worried she might poke me in the eye with her fingernail. "They bought *Marjorie Jane* from Captain Dan, realized after the fact that they got conned, and then 'discovered' his body on their boat." She used her fingers to make air quotes around the word "discovered," then jabbed Chief Dalton in the stomach again for emphasis.

Ned seized Nancy by the shoulder and pulled her back. "Hang on there a minute, honey. There's no need to get worked up. The police chief is just doing his job." He looked over at the beleaguered man. "Maybe we could continue this inside our office?"

Chief Dalton snapped his notebook shut. "That sounds fine, sir. While we're at it, we'll need you to make a list of everyone who was at the marina tonight."

Ned nodded while Nancy glared at me.

The chief pointed at the marina office. "After the two of you." Before following them, he looked at us. "I'm afraid you won't be able to get back onto your boat until sometime tomorrow. Why don't you head home for the night? We'll follow up with you in the morning with any additional questions we may have." Scooter appeared relieved. He didn't want to get back on a boat covered in blood anytime soon.

Then it hit me. This was our way out. There was no way that Scooter was going to want to keep *Marjorie Jane* after this. He'd have to agree to sell her to Penny now, although selling a boat that someone had been murdered on might not be so easy. I thought about this while I put everything back in my purse that Scooter had dumped out.

Sandy snagged a pack of tissues off the table before I could put them away. "Do you mind?"

"No, they're all yours." She wiped her eyes and then blew her nose. "I just can't believe he's dead."

Jack wandered back to the table. "Come on, Sandy. The police said it's okay for us to head back to our boat." He walked down the dock without waiting for her.

Sandy got up and gave me a hug. "Thanks for being so understanding, Mollie."

I hugged her back. "I'll come by tomorrow and check to see how you're doing." I silently cursed Jack for ignoring Sandy. His wife was falling to pieces and he didn't seem to care. Then again, he didn't really seem to care that Captain Dan had been murdered either.

* * *

The next morning, Chief Dalton called and asked us to come to the police station. As we drove down Main Street, I pointed at Penelope's Sugar Shack. "That's where I bought the brownies for the potluck yesterday. They were good, weren't they? Captain Dan had a couple of them. That's the kind of last supper I'd like to have."

Scooter gripped the steering wheel tightly while he pulled up in front of the police station. It was painted bright blue and had flower baskets hanging from the windowsills, like the rest of the buildings on Main Street. It almost felt cheerful until I remembered why we were there.

Officer Moore greeted us and ushered us into the chief's office. After exchanging a few pleasantries, we tried to make ourselves comfortable in the hard wooden chairs in front of his desk. He reached into a cardboard box and pulled out a large plastic bag. He placed it on the desk with a thud. Inside the bag, I saw the winch handle that had killed Captain Dan. It was still covered in blood.

Scooter pushed his chair back. I reached into my purse, grabbed a bag of Peanut M&M'S, and passed them to him.

Chief Dalton looked at Scooter popping M&M'S rapidly into his mouth and raised his right eyebrow. "What can you tell me about this winch handle?" he asked, raising his eyebrow even higher.

I hadn't really noticed with all the commotion and the dim lighting yesterday, but he had the bushiest eyebrows I had ever seen in my life. They were fascinating in a strange sort of way, conjuring up visions of two dark, fuzzy caterpillars playing tug-of-war on his forehead.

Scooter crumpled up the empty M&M'S bag and tossed it in the trash can. "Is that the winch handle that, um, you know..."

"Killed Captain Dan?"

Scooter shifted in his seat and nodded.

"It is," Chief Dalton said. "What can you tell me about it?"

"It isn't ours. I mean, it doesn't belong to *Marjorie Jane*."

"Go on."

"Well, *Marjorie Jane* came with two winch handles. I saw them both when I did the original inventory with Captain Dan a few days ago. This isn't one of them. It's designed to fit a much larger winch."

"So you're saying that you had never seen this before last night."

"Yes, that's correct. I mean no, that's not correct." Scooter took a deep breath. "What I mean to say is that we did see this handle earlier in the evening. Mollie almost tripped over it. But it wasn't covered in..." Scooter clenched the sides of the chair.

"Blood?" Chief Dalton offered.

Scooter nodded.

"And you, Mrs. McGhie. Had you ever seen this winch handle before last night?"

I snorted. "Are you kidding me? I hadn't even seen *Marjorie Jane* before yesterday, when Scooter signed the papers to buy her, let alone any of her winch handles."

Chief Dalton raised his other eyebrow. "You mean to say you bought a boat without seeing it first?"

Scooter smiled. "It was a surprise. I bought *Marjorie Jane* as an anniversary present for Mollie. I took her over to see her for the first time yesterday afternoon, then signed the papers to buy her."

"Wow, that's some anniversary present. You must really like sailing, Mrs. McGhie."

I snorted again. "I've never been sailing before in my life."

The burly man looked at me in surprise, then at Scooter in disbelief. He picked up the winch handle and put it back in the cardboard box. Scooter breathed a sigh of relief now that it was out of sight.

"Tell me again, where were the two of you between six and eight last night?"

"We were walking along the beach," Scooter said nervously.

"That's a long walk."

Scooter gulped. "Well, we did sit for a

while and talk."

"What did you talk about?"

"Oh, you know, this and that." Scooter took his glasses off and rubbed his eyes. "I've been going through a tough time lately with work stuff. We were talking about plans for the future, that kind of thing."

The chief chewed on his pen for a moment. "Did anyone see you?"

Scooter looked questioningly at me. "I'm not sure. I didn't notice anyone. Did you, Mollie?"

I shook my head. "I don't think so, but it was dark out once the sun went down. It would have been hard to see anyone." I tried to recall the details of our walk, then remembered that I had seen something important. "But there were these bright red and green flashing lights out on the water. I think they might have been a—"

Scooter interrupted. "Chief Dalton is asking if we saw any people, not if you saw any flashing lights."

The chief wrote something down on a piece of paper and tucked it into a file folder.

"I'll need to go over the documents of sale."

"Wait a minute," I said excitedly. "Maybe the sale didn't go through because Captain Dan died. Maybe we don't actually own *Marjorie Jane*."

The chief thumbed through a pile of papers. "From what I can see here, it all looks legitimate. I'm afraid you're the owners of the boat."

"Does Mollie need to stay for this? I was the one who signed the paperwork," Scooter said.

"She can go, if she wants."

I grabbed my purse. "Great. I told Sandy I would check in on her this morning. You go through those papers, Scooter. Maybe you can find a loophole to get us out of this sale, while you're at it. I'll meet you at the marina later."

As I walked toward the door, I turned to Chief Dalton and asked, "Who's on your suspect list?"

He seemed taken aback by my question. I could tell by the twitching of his eyebrows. They were enough to frighten small children, let alone murder suspects. "I'm afraid I can't share that with you. It's confidential."

"You know, I'm an investigative reporter. I've got a knack for getting people to open up and admit things they don't want to talk about. I bet I could help you out by chatting with some of the folks at the marina. There did seem to be a number of them that held a grudge against Captain Dan."

Chief Dalton raised both of his eyebrows and gave me a faint smile. "That's okay, ma'am. I think we've got it covered."

"Fine," I said. "Scooter, want to walk me out?"

He nodded and walked with me to the lobby. "What was that back there about being an investigative reporter?"

"Okay, I might have exaggerated a bit. I'm not technically one yet, but I'm sure I'm going to get the job."

"Are you talking about this thing with FAROUT?"

"Of course," I said with a frown. "How many times do I have to tell you about this?

It's between Lola and me. You remember Lola, don't you? That obnoxious redhead who wore those very tiny skirts at the FAROUT convention in Texas last year?"

"Oh, her," Scooter said with a faraway look. "Who could forget her?"

Yeah, of course he couldn't forget her. She had had Scooter and every other guy at the convention wrapped around her little finger.

"Scooter, snap out of it! Back to business. I'm going to go to the marina and start questioning people. Once you're done here, you're going to stop by Penelope's Sugar Shack and pick up a couple more of those brownies and meet me back at the marina."

"Sure thing. Brownies and then the marina." He leaned down and gave me a kiss on the forehead. "Don't worry about Lola. I'm sure you're a shoo-in for the job." I was pleased that he was referring to my work as a job now, and not a volunteer position. "But do me a favor and don't get in Chief Dalton's way. And for goodness' sake, don't tell him about FAROUT and your theory about those red and green lights." I pulled away from

Scooter, and he quickly added, "It's just that I don't think he'll understand—it's not that I don't believe you."

"Fine. Whatever," I said as I stomped across the lobby and out the door.

* * *

One of the advantages of living in a small town is that you can walk everywhere. As I made my way toward the marina, I breathed in the salty air and breathed out my irritation with Scooter. I knew he tried to believe in the work I did, but it was hard for people to accept the truth sometimes, especially when no one talked about it. That was one of FAROUT's missions—to raise awareness and make people more comfortable sharing their stories.

When I got to the marina, I popped in the office to find out where Jack and Sandy's boat was located. Fortunately, Ned was staffing the desk. He told me that I could find them on C Dock, then asked me how I was holding up. You would think that a little of

Ned's compassion would have rubbed off on Nancy after so many years of marriage.

We talked for a few minutes about what it was like to find a body, then I headed to Jack and Sandy's boat. As I walked down the dock, I ran into Penny. She was wearing another all-pink outfit. Pink tank top, pink shorts, and another pink hat.

"Can you believe what happened to Captain Dan?" I asked her.

"It's terrible to think he's gone, isn't it?" Penny started chewing her nails. Her manicure looked terrible. Half of her nails were long, shiny, and pink. The other half were short and ragged. She looked at me. "Is it true that you found him on *Marjorie Jane*?"

"Yes. In the V-berth."

Penny shuddered and continued mangling her nails. I thought about giving her a hug, but she didn't seem like the hugging type. I pointed at her hand. "My mom does that when she gets nervous." Penny quickly put her hands in her pockets.

"It's a bad habit. Besides, short nails are better for sailing. Otherwise, you end up breaking them." She stared down at the dock absentmindedly and mumbled something that sounded like "poor Bob."

"What was that you said?" I asked.

Penny looked up at me sharply. "Nothing. Just saying that I need to get going. I've got a sailing class starting in a few minutes." She hurried down the dock, leaving me to wonder if she was referring to Captain Dan as Bob, like she had when I'd overheard them arguing at the barbecue.

I remembered the pink fingernail that I had found on the boat when I'd discovered Captain Dan's body. When the police had come on board they'd startled me, and I'd completely forgotten to tell them about it. I'd have to figure out what I did with it and give it to Chief Dalton. It could be an important clue. Both Penny and Nancy had been sporting pink manicures. Could one of them have been on our boat?

I pondered this as I made my way to *Island Time*, Jack and Sandy's boat. I saw her halfway down the dock. Jack and Sandy were in front of her, arguing.

"How can you say that, Jack?" Sandy said. "You're the one who should be careful. After all, I heard it was a large winch handle that was the murder weapon."

Jack clenched his fists. "I had nothing to do with it, Sandy. But I can't say that I'm not glad he's gone. He's caused enough trouble for us financially and otherwise."

He stormed off, ignoring me as I tried to say hello.

Sandy waved me over. "Sorry you had to see that. I think this murder has stressed out all of us. Come on aboard and I'll fix us some coffee."

"Will Jack be joining us?" I asked as I followed her down into the boat.

"No. He has to take care of some business matters." Sandy put a kettle on the stove and pulled out a French press from the cupboard.

"What kind of business is he in? I thought the two of you were retired?"

"Oh, we are, but you know how it is. Retirement savings only go so far, and we've had some financial difficulties. Jack has been making extra money buying and selling used marine equipment, like outboard motors, replacement parts, that kind of thing."

"Does he also sell winch handles?"

Sandy shrugged. "I guess so." She pulled a container of milk out of the fridge and scooped some coffee into the press. "I try to stay out of his business, except for helping with the bookkeeping. He gets mad whenever I ask him anything about it. After so many years of marriage, I've learned to bite my tongue. You know what I mean, don't you?"

"I think Scooter would be surprised if I ever started biting my tongue."

Sandy smiled. "Go on, have a seat. It won't be long."

I sat down on one of the couches and was admiring the embroidered throw cushions when a calico cat jumped onto my lap, turned around a couple of times, and then settled down on my legs.

"Sorry about that," Sandy said. "I hope you don't mind cats. That's Mrs. Moto."

I scratched Mrs. Moto behind the ears. "I know you, don't I?" I explained to Sandy,

"She jumped onto our boat yesterday, and then I saw her again later at the marina office. Nancy was chasing her away with a broom."

"Oh, Nancy hates cats." Sandy held up a cup of steaming coffee. "How do you take yours?"

"Milk and sugar, please." Mrs. Moto perked up at the word "milk." "Do you like milk too?" The calico responded with a loud yowl, which I took to mean "Yes, please."

"She's not allowed to have milk. Vet's orders." Sandy passed me a cup of coffee and placed hers on the table. She sat next to me and started to sniffle. "I don't know what I'm going to do with her when we sell the boat. They won't let us have cats at the condo we're moving into."

"You're selling your boat?"

"Yes, Captain Dan was going to list her for us. Now we've got to find another boat broker and a home for Mrs. Moto." Sandy's sniffles turned into a loud crying noise. "I've put notices up everywhere, but no one wants her. I hate the idea of having to take her to a shelter."

The Japanese bobtail rubbed up against my hand, demanding that I scratch under her chin. I hated the idea of her going to a shelter as well.

I took a sip of my coffee while she dried her eyes. "Why exactly are you moving?"

"We can't afford to keep the boat and our condo. We'd been renting out the condo, but the tenants just left. We thought about selling it and staying on the boat, but to be honest, we're getting too old for all the work involved in boat ownership. So we decided to move into the condo and sell the boat. Things have been tight, so any money we can get for the boat would be a big help."

Sandy groaned and rubbed her temples with her fingers. "Feels like I've got another one of my headaches coming on."

"Oh, no! Can I get you anything?"

"Would you mind? There's a bottle on the counter in the head." I must have looked confused. "The head is what we call the bathroom. Just down the passageway before the aft cabin."

I nudged Mrs. Moto. She moved over to Sandy's lap and purred while I went in search of the head. I peeked in and saw Sandy's pill bottle. As I picked it up, I noticed a white pillowcase in the sink covered in red spots.

I came back out and handed Sandy the bottle. Her hands shook as she swallowed two pills with her coffee. While she sat back and rubbed her neck, I saw bruises on the back of her arms. "Sandy, what happened to your arms?"

She lowered them. "Those marks? Oh, I don't know. I'm always getting bruises and cuts and I don't remember how." She pointed down at her legs, which were covered in small cuts and deep-purple bruises. "Like these ones here. No idea how they happened."

"I saw the pillowcase in the bathroom—I mean, head. Was that blood on there?"

"Yes, I must have gotten a nosebleed during the night. It happens from time to time. I'm just glad I was able to sleep last night. Sometimes, it's hard to fall asleep and stay asleep. I'm constantly having nightmares. Did you know that last night I dreamed someone was operating on me in a dark metal room? Must be the financial stress. And worrying about finding Mrs. Moto a new home." She frowned and stroked the cat's glossy fur.

When I sat back down on the couch, the calico ran over, plopped next to me, and rolled over on her back.

"She must really like you," Sandy said wistfully. "She rarely does that for anyone. Go on, rub her belly. She loves that."

Mrs. Moto really did love having her belly rubbed. Her purring grew so loud that I could barely hear what Sandy was saying. "If you can't find anyone to take her, maybe I can talk Scooter into letting us adopt her," I offered impulsively.

"That would be fantastic," Sandy said. She hesitated and then added, "Maybe this is too much to ask, but Jack and I are running up to the condo later today. It's north of here, about four hours away. We'll be away overnight, possibly two nights. Maybe you could look in on her and feed her while we're gone?"

"Sure, I'd love to."

"You're a lifesaver," Sandy said. "I had originally asked Penny if she'd take care of her, but she told me last night that she wouldn't be able to."

"What time did you see her at?" I asked.

"Oh, I don't know. I went for a walk before going to bed and saw her sitting out on the patio. She seemed really distracted." Sandy lowered her voice. "Between you and me, I think she and Captain Dan had a thing going on. I heard a rumor that she even moved up here from Texas to be with him."

"Really? I didn't think she was all that sweet on him. I overheard them last night arguing about the boat brokerage. It sounded like she had invested money in his last business, and he'd promised to make her a partner in the boat brokerage." I quickly added, "Not that I was eavesdropping or anything."

"Hmm. That's interesting. I saw them fighting last week too. I couldn't hear what they were saying and just assumed it was a lovers' quarrel, but maybe it was more than that," Sandy said. "Do you think she could have had anything to do with Captain Dan's murder? I mean, I hate to think that anyone we know is a murderer, but you can never tell about people, can you?"

While I reflected on this, Mrs. Moto decided that I wasn't paying enough attention to her. She jumped onto the floor and chased after a toy mouse.

"When we spoke with Chief Dalton this morning, he said Captain Dan had been murdered between six and eight o'clock." Mrs. Moto dropped the toy mouse at my feet and was delighted when I threw it on the other couch for her to chase. "What time did you see Penny at?"

"It was probably around six thirty, maybe a little earlier. We left the barbecue around six and headed back to the boat. I'm not sure about the time, but it was probably fifteen minutes later that I went out for a walk. I needed a break from Jack and a few minutes to clear my head."

"Where exactly did you run into Penny?"

"On the patio. She was sitting there, biting her nails and looking at something on her computer."

"What was she looking at?"

"I'm not sure. When she saw me, she turned her computer off and put it away quickly in her laptop bag. I probably talked to her for about five minutes, and then I headed up to the trail that leads around the cove. There's a nice lookout there with a park bench."

"When did you go back to your boat?"

"Oh, not too much later. I was probably back by eight." She paused. "When I came back to the marina after my walk, I saw Penny walking down from B Dock—you know, the dock where you keep *Marjorie Jane*." She shook her head. "It's all probably a coincidence. I can't imagine Penny was involved in anything like that."

Mrs. Moto meowed loudly, jumped onto my lap, and deposited her toy mouse. I told her what a good cat she was. She seemed pleased with herself.

I thought about Penny and Captain Dan's argument. Was it possible Sandy was right, and the two of them were involved? If that were the case, why was he flirting with Sandy? And why did he look so familiar?

"I can't figure out why Captain Dan seems —I mean, seemed—so familiar," I said. Sandy winced at the reminder that Captain Dan was dead. "I keep thinking to myself that I've seen him someplace before. Has he always been a boat broker?"

"I'm not sure. I suppose so. I don't think you just become a boat broker overnight. It's not like just anyone can sell boats." Sandy rubbed her temples again. "It would appear that my pills aren't taking care of this headache. I think I'm going to lie down for a bit if that's okay."

"Of course," I said. "Is there anything else I can get you?"

"No, I just need to rest in a dark room." She hesitated. "So, you're sure you're okay to look after Mrs. Moto?"

"Not a problem," I reassured her.

"Okay, Nancy has a key to our boat at the

office, and I'll leave a note with some instructions with her later today. We'll be leaving later this afternoon. I'm really not looking forward to the long car ride with this headache."

I couldn't imagine the car ride with Jack would be very pleasant, headache or not, given their fight, but decided to keep that thought to myself. Their relationship certainly was a puzzler. Last night, Jack had alternated between hot and cold with Sandy. Maybe he was just jealous of Captain Dan's flirtations, but maybe it was more than that.

CHAPTER 6
FLYSWATTER

I WAS HALFWAY DOWN THE dock when I realized I hadn't checked my phone since the previous night. My phone's always stuck somewhere down at the bottom of my purse, and half the time I don't hear it go off, something that annoys my mom to no end. She hates it when I don't reply right away and then sends a million more texts asking where I am as some sort of punishment.

Yep, there were a million texts from my mom. Most of them said things like, *Where are you? Why are you ignoring your mother?* and *Why don't you ever check your phone? I could be dead for all you know.* I'm not sure how she could be texting me if she were dead, but knowing my mom, she'd find a way. I scrolled back to her original message.

Who's Penny? What happened to Marjorie Jane? Did he ditch her already? Has Scooter moved on to another bimbo?

As usual, she had gotten it all wrong. I thought about explaining that Scooter was stuck on a sailboat, not on another woman, but that would require a lengthy conversation, one I wasn't really up to dealing with just now. After her latest divorce, she tended to think the worst of men, including Scooter.

Nothing's going on, I texted back, hoping that would be the end of it.

Her response was quick. Almost like she had her phone glued to her hand. *Don't be so sure. Where there's smoke, there's fire.* Just as I started to respond, she followed up with another one. *Why did it take you so long to reply to my original text? You know I worry.*

I typed a response as quickly as I could. *Things have been crazy. Someone was murdered.*

I'll call later. For some reason, she didn't respond right away. Maybe the battery on her phone died. As I was waiting for her inevitable response, I saw Jack walking toward me pulling a cart. I quickly popped my phone into my purse and rushed over to speak with him.

"Hey, Jack," I said. He looked like he wanted to avoid me, but I stepped in front of him and blocked his path. "I'm so glad I ran into you. When I was visiting with Sandy earlier, she wasn't feeling well. I left so she can try to get some sleep."

Jack rolled his eyes. "Another one of her headaches, isn't it?" I was surprised by the bitterness in his voice. "She always seems to get one whenever there's work to be done. I told her that I need to get these parts inventoried and priced right away. She promised she'd help enter everything into the computer. Now what am I supposed to do?"

I thought he might start by offering to give Sandy a foot rub. Scooter always does that for me when I have a headache. Jack didn't appear very receptive to my suggestion, so I decided to change tack. "You know, I'm awfully worried about Sandy. Not only does she have a really bad headache, but she also has all sorts of cuts and bruises on her. She told me she had a nosebleed last night as well."

"If she wasn't so clumsy, then she wouldn't have all those cuts and bruises, would she?" he asked angrily. "You don't see me complaining every time I get a little boo-boo."

"But it sounds like more than that. She also said she has a hard time falling asleep and staying asleep."

"Well, she's always been that way. Terrible insomnia and waking up in the middle of the night screaming. Even sleepwalking sometimes."

"Sleepwalking?"

"Yeah, I can't tell you how many times I've woken up late at night and discovered she's disappeared. I go out and find her walking along the docks in the dark. I'm worried that one of these times she's going to fall in the water." His expression softened. "It wasn't always like this. We've been married for over thirty years. At first, things were great; she slept like a baby." He smiled gently at the memories. "But over the past few years, it's gotten worse."

"What do you think caused things to change?"

"I don't know. It was probably right around the time we moved onto the boat. Must have been around four years ago. She said it was the lights that kept her from sleeping well. She began sleepwalking a lot more."

"What lights are you talking about?" I asked. "Bright white lights shining in your cabin?"

Jack furrowed his brow. "You mean like moonlight?"

"Not exactly."

"Well, the moon can shine brightly, but it's more the lights here at the marina that bother her. There's also the fishing boats that are coming and going at all hours. Sandy did get some drapes made for the cabin that block out a lot of the light, but she's still sleepwalking."

"Maybe your trip will be a chance for her to relax," I said.

"What trip?"

"Sandy said that you were going to head up to the condo and that you'd be away for a day or two. She asked me to look after your cat."

"We're not going anywhere. I don't know where she comes up with these things. Besides, it's *her* cat, not mine." He looked down at his cart. "I should get going. I've got a lot of work to do, and it sounds like I'll be doing it all on my own."

I peered at the cart. I didn't recognize anything except for one item. "Is that a winch handle?"

"It is. I bought a bunch of them from a salvage dealer."

"Did you know that the murder weapon was a winch handle?" I asked, regarding Jack carefully.

Jack fidgeted with the cart. "I might have heard that. But I'm sure it wasn't one of mine."

"How can you be so sure?"

"I keep a careful inventory of everything I buy and sell. I know for a fact that all of my winch handles are accounted for."

"Sounds like something the police will be interested in."

"Excuse me, sir. We need to have a word with you."

I turned and saw Chief Dalton standing behind me. "Speak of the devil," I said.

He looked at me and scowled. "Your husband is on the patio, Mrs. McGhie. Perhaps you want to join him?"

"Definitely. He should have some brownies for me."

* * *

After grabbing a brownie from Scooter, I walked down to the beach and called Brian Morrison at FAROUT headquarters. I filled him in on my interviews with Sandy and Jack.

"I'm sure of it, Brian. She's got all the

signs. Her husband said she sleepwalks at night. There's been many times he's found her walking along the docks in her nightgown. He's been afraid that one of these nights she's going to fall in the water and drown. I also found a pillowcase with blood on it in the bathroom. I asked her about it, and she said that she had a nosebleed the night before."

"Hang on a minute, Mollie. Let me make sure I've checked off all the boxes on the official checklist. Okay, that's two indicators —sleepwalking and nosebleeds. What else do you have?"

"She has unexplained marks on her body. Cuts and bruises on her legs and arms. When I asked her about it, she said she can't remember how she got them. And, get this, she said they weren't there the previous night. She claims she must have bumped into something, but I don't think that's what it was."

I heard Brian scratching down notes. "Let's see. That's one more indicator—unexplained marks."

"Her husband mentioned that Sandy was complaining about bright lights shining into their boat at night. He tried to pass it off as moonlight and fishing boats, but he could be in denial or trying to cover things up."

"Good, lights," Brian said. "That's another indicator."

"And it's not just Sandy who's been seeing lights. When Scooter and I were out walking on the beach last night, I saw flashing red and green lights on the water."

"Oh, now that's interesting. Did you get any video?"

"No, they were gone too quickly. I'll have to get back out there one night and see if they reappear."

"Okay, but please tell me you'll be careful. I'd hate to think of anything happening to you."

"Don't you worry about me. I took your safety course last year, remember?"

"I do. You were my star pupil. Now, what about her dreams? Did she mention anything unusual?"

"She sure did. I was saving the best for last.

She says she has frequent nightmares. Last night she even dreamed that she was having a medical procedure in a dark metal room."

"Wow, this is amazing, Mollie. I'd have to agree with you. This is a clear-cut case of alien abduction. You write this up in a report, send it to the board of directors, and you're a shoo-in to be the Federation for Alien Research, Outreach, and UFO Tracking's investigative reporter! There's nothing that Lola can do to top this."

After hanging up with Brian, I celebrated by eating my brownie. Not only was I going to beat out that vile redhead, but I was also going to use all my investigative skills to figure out who killed Captain Dan.

* * *

I was in such a good mood after my call, I practically skipped up the steps from the beach to the boardwalk. Scooter was flipping through some magazines at one of the patio tables. I sneaked up behind him, put my hands over his eyes, and said, "Guess who?"

"Is that my little kohlrabi?" he asked as he pulled me onto his lap.

"What happened to 'sweet potato'? I don't know that I want to be your little kohlrabi. They're a really weird-looking vegetable."

"Your wish is my command, my little sweet potato."

"What are you looking at there?"

"Oh, it's a fascinating article on holding tanks. Doing something about our holding tank is on our project list. I was thinking that instead of a marine toilet, we might want to go with a composting toilet and get rid of the holding tank completely. What do you think?"

"I don't need to think about toilets. That's what plumbers are for." I opened up the box from Penelope's Sugar Shack. "What happened to the rest of the brownies?"

"Guilty," Scooter said as he snagged another magazine from the stack.

"Darn. I was hoping to nab another celebratory brownie."

"What are you celebrating?"

I slipped off Scooter's lap. "Long story. I'll

fill you in later. Suffice it to say, Lola is history."

* * *

Maybe one brownie was enough. Did I really need more celebratory chocolaty treats? Of course I did. I had a lot to celebrate. Besides, if I bought a chocolate bar at the marina store, it would give me a chance to question Nancy and Ned about Captain Dan's murder.

A bell rang as I opened the screen door. Nancy stepped out of the back room, holding a couple of large cans. "Hurry up, close that door. You're letting flies in." I shut it behind me, but not fast enough for Nancy. "Now look what you've done! There's a fly next to my computer. Grab that flyswatter and get it."

"Um, I don't see one."

Nancy pointed at the counter. "There. Right there. Are you blind?" All I saw were some large bars of chocolate next to a display of fishing lures.

Nancy marched up to the counter, slammed the cans down, reached behind a vase of flowers, and pulled out a flyswatter. I stepped back. I had a feeling she could turn a flyswatter into a deadly weapon—not just against flies, but also against people who didn't close screen doors quickly enough.

"There. Got it," Nancy said with satisfaction. She tucked the swatter back behind the vase and straightened up some brochures that had gone askew when she whacked the fly. "Good thing you're here," she said gruffly. "You forgot to sign one of the forms yesterday."

"I signed everything you asked me to. Maybe you forgot to give it to me."

Nancy pursed her lips. "I run a tight ship here. If you didn't sign something, it's because you forgot to, not because I didn't give it to you to sign. Are we clear?"

She didn't wait for my answer. After placing the cans on a shelf, she walked behind the counter, adjusted her glasses, and pulled out a stack of papers from a file cabinet. She thumbed through them while I looked at the chocolate bars.

"Those are homemade by a gal who lives in one of the old fishing cottages on Harbor Street," Nancy said without looking up. "She makes all kinds. The dark chocolate butterscotch crunch is popular with the tourists."

Who was I to argue with tourists? I placed a bar next to the cash register.

"Here you go. Put your initials here and sign at the bottom." Nancy tapped her fingers impatiently on the counter while I scanned the form. The click-clack of her nails was distracting me from the finer points of what to do in the event of a fuel or oil spill.

"Nice nails, Nancy," I said. "The navy-blue color matches your shirt perfectly. And I really like the tiny white anchors on each tip. Where do you get them done?"

Nancy stretched out her hands and admired the artwork. "I do them myself. It's my Friday night ritual. I sit down in front of the television, watch my favorite shows, and give myself a manicure."

"You painted on those anchors yourself? I would have thought you'd need a nail salon to get that done."

Nancy warmed up to the subject. "I'll let you in on a little secret. They're press-on nails. They're so simple to use. And if one falls off, you just press another one on." She looked down at my short, unpolished nails with disdain. "You might want to think about doing the same."

I took out my wallet to distract her from my nails. "How much do I owe you for the chocolate?"

After giving me my change, Nancy pushed the chocolate bar toward me. "Aren't you going to try some of it now? You might like it so much that you'll want to buy another one."

You don't have to ask me twice to eat chocolate. I tore open the wrapper and popped a square in my mouth. "Oh, that's delicious. I might need another bar."

Nancy watched as I broke another piece off. She reminded me of one of those cats that would stare at your tuna sandwich, slowly inching forward until it could steal a hunk off your plate. I was worried Nancy was going to grab the chocolate bar and stab my hand in the process with her nails. "Here, do you want—" She snatched the square out of my fingers before I could finish my sentence.

The situation reminded me that I might be kitty-sitting Mrs. Moto sometime in the future when Sandy and Jack rescheduled their trip. "Do you have any cat treats?"

The question brought a scowl to Nancy's face. "Of course I don't have any cat treats," she snapped. "What does this look like, some sort of pet store?"

I handed her another square of chocolate. Somehow, she managed to keep scowling even while eating chocolate. I didn't think that was possible.

"Nancy, I have a few questions."

"Electricity and water are included in the monthly slip fee," she said. "If you need quarters for the washing machine and dryer, come see me."

"Good to know, but what I really wanted to ask was what you thought about Captain

Dan's murder. You know everyone at the marina. Who do you think could have done it?"

"That sounds like a question you should be asking Chief Dalton, not me." I waved a square of chocolate in front of her as an enticement. She seized it and shrugged. "Could have been anybody. He didn't have a lot of friends, and he sure made a lot of enemies."

"You and Ned had some issues with him, didn't you? I'm sure the chief has asked you where you were between six and eight."

Nancy took the chocolate bar from me and broke off not one, but two squares. "Like I said, I was doing my nails last night. Ned and I were both in our apartment all night."

I pulled the chocolate bar toward me. "Captain Dan sure was a real smooth talker, wasn't he? I mean, look at Scooter. He managed to talk him into buying *Marjorie Jane*. I'm sure he pulled the wool over lots of people's eyes."

"Well, that's true. He sure suckered Jack in once." I nodded encouragingly and pushed the bar back to her. She took another square. "He sold him a whole bunch of anchor chain. Convinced him it was stainless steel, the best money could buy. Turns out it was a bunch of junk. Most of it was rusted out. It wasn't worth anything. Boy, Jack sure was mad. Captain Dan refused to give him his money back. He said that he sold the chain as is, and that Jack knew what he was getting into."

"Do you think that's all Jack was mad about? It looked like Captain Dan was awfully flirtatious with Sandy at the barbecue last night."

"He was like that with all the women. I bet Sandy played that up to make Jack jealous. They've been having difficulties for a few years."

I thought about this while I savored some more chocolate. "You could be right. Sandy mentioned that she thought Captain Dan and Penny were an item. Did you know anything about that?"

"When Penny first moved up here from Texas, they seemed to get along well, but then it was like things went sour between them. Can't quite picture them romantically involved."

"Maybe things got real sour. I heard them arguing last night, and Sandy said she saw them have a big fight last week."

"Well, they did have a pretty big argument a couple of days ago. I could see them waving their arms. But I couldn't hear anything."

So much for that line of questioning. Just then Ben opened the door. He headed to the coolers in the back, grabbed a six-pack of beer and a bag of potato chips, and put them on the counter.

Nancy shook her head. "I can't give you any more credit, Ben. You've got to pay in cash from now on."

Ben pulled out his wallet and thrust a few bills at Nancy. "Don't worry, I've got the money for both this and for what I already owe you."

While he was collecting his change from Nancy, I noticed that his wallet was crammed full of bills. Several even looked like hundreds. He snapped his wallet shut and stuck it back in the pocket of his cutoff jean shorts. He nodded at both of us and walked outside to the patio.

"Nice to see Ben has some money for a change," Nancy said, shutting the cash drawer firmly.

I went to corral the last square of chocolate, but it was gone. Nancy wiped chocolate off her fingers with a napkin, crumpled up the bright-pink wrapper, and threw both in the trash. "Want another one?"

After giving Nancy money for another dark chocolate butterscotch crunch bar, I was tucking it into my purse when the wrapper caught my eye. I turned to Nancy. "Weren't your nails pink yesterday before you redid your manicure?"

Nancy peered at me over her glasses. "Were they? I don't remember. Close the door. You're going to let flies in."

* * *

Ben waved me over when I came out of the office. He held up a can of beer. "Want one?"

"Uh, no thanks. It's a little early for me."

He chuckled. "It's always five o'clock somewhere."

"Have you seen Scooter?" I asked.

"He went up to Melvin's Marine Emporium to get a catalog," he said after taking a sip of beer.

I noticed Ben was wearing another pirate-themed T-shirt. This one let me know that drinking rum before noon made you a pirate. I had the feeling this was Ben's personal motto. He drained his can, then patted the chair next to him. "Come on, have a seat. I could use the company."

"I guess the events of last night have hit everyone hard," I said, assuming that was the reason he was cracking open another beer. "I still can't believe Captain Dan was murdered on our boat." I pulled out a chocolate bar from my purse. "Want some?"

"No thanks," he said, much to my relief. "Not sure chocolate goes all that well with beer."

I almost unwrapped the bar, but decided I should save it for later in case there were any other chocolate emergencies. "You know, I've talked to a few people, and it doesn't sound like too many folks are broken up by Captain Dan's death," I said, reluctantly tucking the chocolate back in my purse. "I was surprised. I thought the marina would be a tight-knit community. What about you? Were you and Captain Dan on friendly terms?"

Ben's eyes widened. "What exactly are you implying? I didn't have anything to do with his death. Not that I could have anyway."

"Why's that?" I asked, noticing Ben reaching for a third beer. I thought about the brownie and chocolate I'd eaten earlier. I guess we all have our own vices.

"I keep my boat out in the mooring field. You need a dinghy to get back and forth from your boat to the marina. When I headed back to my boat after the barbecue, my outboard engine was acting up. It ended up dying on me. I was lucky to have made it back to my boat, especially as I didn't have any oars on board." He added sheepishly, "I dropped them in the water last week. I wasn't able to get the motor fixed until this morning, when Jack came out to help me."

"I didn't see you leave the barbecue. What time did you head back to your boat?"

"I don't know. I guess around six-thirty. I don't really pay much attention to things like that."

"Wouldn't it be easier to get a slip rather than have to go back and forth on your dinghy?"

"It would, but the rates are practically double. I've been out of work for a while and things are getting tight."

I thought about all the money I had seen in Ben's wallet. It didn't seem like things were too tight. "What kind of work do you do, when you're not out pirating?"

Ben smiled. "Pirating would be more fun, but it doesn't pay as well. I work on boats. I'd been doing some work for Captain Dan. He bought old boats, fixed them up, and sold them, but that didn't work out."

It sounded like all those home improvement shows I liked to watch. "Have you ever put picture windows in a boat? I was thinking that's just what we need to brighten up *Marjorie Jane*. It's really dark down below."

"Picture windows?" he asked with disbelief. Then he laughed. "Oh, I get it— you're pulling my leg." I decided not to mention the wallpaper. Ben's eyes lit up. "Hey, are you guys looking to have anything done on your boat? It sure does need a lot of work, doesn't it?"

What was I doing thinking about making improvements to *Marjorie Jane* like picture windows and wallpaper? Someone had been murdered on the boat. We needed to get rid of her, not fix her up. Obviously I wasn't thinking clearly.

Just as I was about to tell Ben that I wanted to sell the boat, Ned walked over to the table and pointed at the empty beer cans. "Where'd you get the money for the beer? Next month's mooring fees are going to be due soon."

Ben raised his can in a mock toast to Ned. "No, it won't be a problem. I already settled up with Nancy for last month, and I've got stuff in the pipeline. I picked up a few gigs at the Tipsy Pirate. Plus, Scooter and Mollie might hire me to do some work on their boat." He tried to high-five me, but fortunately Mrs. Moto jumped onto my lap and saved me from inadvertently committing us to having Ben work on a boat I hoped to sell.

"Well, hello there, you pretty little thing," I said.

"Don't let Nancy see that cat," Ned cautioned. As he walked toward the office, he said over his shoulder, "You better not be joking about coming up with that money, Ben."

Ben reached over and gave the calico a scratch on her head. She purred loudly in response. "She's a sweet cat, isn't she? Did you know Jack and Sandy are selling their boat and looking for a new home for her? She seems to like you. Maybe you should take her. She's a great boat cat."

Mrs. Moto looked at me and blinked slowly. I think she was trying to tell me something. What she didn't know was that it wasn't me she had to convince. It was Scooter. I turned back to Ben. "Yes, Sandy told me that earlier over coffee. I was surprised that they listed their boat with Captain Dan. Jack didn't act all that friendly toward him."

"That's true. Jack didn't want to use Captain Dan, but when he heard that he'd managed to offload *Marjorie Jane* onto you and Scooter, he had second thoughts. He figured if Captain Dan could sell that boat, he could sell anything." Ben started putting his empty cans into a plastic bag.

"He did seem like a smooth-talking salesman. He sure fooled Scooter."

Ben turned bright red. "Um, that's not what I meant. I meant to say Jack was impressed that Captain Dan sold *Marjorie Jane* so quickly, not that he pulled one over on Scooter."

He got up and grabbed the plastic bag. "Uh...gotta go, Mollie. You'll talk to Scooter about working on your boat, won't you?"

"Wait, Ben. You forgot a full one."

"You can have it," he shouted as he ran

over to the dinghy dock.

Hmm. Ben giving away beer? Such a difference from yesterday, when he was happy to take a free beer from Captain Dan.

CHAPTER 7
NOSEBLEEDS

"THANK YOU, SIR," I HEARD someone say behind me. "We'll be in touch if we need any more information." I turned and saw Chief Dalton ushering a man out of the lounge next to the office. He caught sight of me, walked back inside, and shut the door. He wasn't going to get away from me that easily.

I seized my purse and Ben's beer and pushed the door open. Mrs. Moto ran in and jumped on the windowsill. The chief wasn't anywhere to be seen. He was stealthier than I would have guessed. There was a kitchenette at the back of the lounge. I decided to tuck

Ben's beer in the fridge and give it back to him later. I turned to close the door and saw the chief standing behind it rubbing his nose.

"Oh, there you are," I said. "What are you doing hiding back there?"

"I went to get my briefcase off the table when you smacked into me with the door." At least, I think that's what he said. It's hard to understand someone when they're pressing a napkin to their face.

"Is your nose bleeding?"

"Yes," he said. He arched one of his bushy eyebrows, then the other. Good. He still had full range of movement of the furry caterpillars adorning his forehead. He couldn't be too badly hurt.

"You should really sit down," I said. He raised his eyebrows again. "You might be more comfortable sitting while I give you my report."

He furrowed his brow as though he didn't understand what I was saying. Blood loss will do that to you.

"You know, my report on the investigation." I

sat in one of the comfy lounge chairs in front of the big-screen television. Chief Dalton continued to stand near the door. "Plus, I have evidence for you. Something I found on *Marjorie Jane* last night." Finally, he came over and sat in a chair.

"Evidence?" he asked as he pressed another napkin to his nose.

I reached into my purse and pulled out a plastic bag containing the pink fingernail. I had even labeled the bag with a description of where I had discovered the evidence at the crime scene. Chief Dalton was sure to be impressed by my professionalism. "Right before you arrived at our boat, I found this on the floor," I said proudly.

The burly man continued to press a napkin to his nose with one hand and took the bag in his other.

Mrs. Moto streaked across the room, jumped onto the chief's chair, pawed at him, and meowed loudly. He dropped the bag in surprise.

"Is that your cat?" he asked as he tried to push her off. Mrs. Moto pawed at him again, this time with her claws extended. Chief Dalton backed down. Smart move.

"No, she belongs to Jack and Sandy. I should probably start with them first."

"Start with them first?"

"Yes, I've got quite a lot to report."

The chief picked the evidence up off the floor, sighed, and sat back in his chair. "Go on."

"I interviewed Sandy this morning. Have you interviewed her yet?" He was too busy trying to keep Mrs. Moto away from the fingernail to respond. I continued. "Well, if you have, you're probably as concerned as I am. Not just about the murder, but about the abduction."

Chief Dalton looked at me with surprise. "Abduction? We haven't had any reports of an abduction."

"Oh, that's interesting. No other reports of bright lights, unexplained bruises, that sort of thing?"

"What exactly are you talking about, Mrs. McGhie?"

"The classic signs of abduction, such as

sleepwalking   and   strange   dreams.
Nosebleeds, like yours." He looked confused.
"Don't you guys get training in this?"

"Come again?"

"Alien abduction. What else could I be
talking about?"

Just when I didn't think the chief could
raise his eyebrows any higher, he managed
to. "Mrs. McGhie, we're investigating a
murder here, not an alien abduction. You
don't honestly believe in that sort of thing,
do you?"

He got up, threw the napkins in the trash,
and put the plastic bag with the fingernail in
his briefcase. Mrs. Moto padded over to him
and meowed loudly. He ignored her. "Now,
where exactly did you find this fingernail?"

"In the galley. Did you notice the color?
It's bright pink. Two women had bright pink
manicures   yesterday—Penny,   the   sailing
school instructor, and Nancy, the owner of
the marina. Both of them had reason to be
angry with Captain Dan. He cheated them
out of money. My theory is that one of them
came on our boat last night, whacked him

with the winch handle, and somehow lost one of their nails in the process."

"Why don't you leave the murder investigation to the professionals, and we'll leave the alien abduction investigation to the amateurs." He snapped his briefcase shut and left.

Mrs. Moto ran to the door and meowed loudly. She really didn't miss that infuriating man, did she? I opened the door. She walked across the patio toward the beach, stopping now and then to look back at me as though she wanted me to follow her.

* * *

While Sandy's cat chased seagulls on the beach, I sat on a piece of driftwood and thought about what the chief had said. I couldn't believe he had called me an amateur! It was bad enough that Scooter pooh-poohed what I did for a living—well, not exactly for a living, but you know what I mean—but now Chief Dalton was dismissing me too. You would think a professional law enforcement officer would take alien abduction more seriously.

That was the problem. Individuals who come forward with their accounts aren't taken seriously. As a result, people don't put two and two together when it comes to recognizing the signs of alien abduction. People like Sandy. Chances were she didn't even realize what had happened to her. I needed to figure out a way to help her process her experience and come to terms with it.

I got out a notebook from my purse. It was time to start a to-do list:

1) Type up the notes from my interview with Sandy and write a report on her abduction for FAROUT's board of directors
2) Type up the notes from my interviews with Jack, Nancy, and Ben
3) Buy more chocolate
4) Figure out how to get Scooter on board with adopting Mrs. Moto
5) Figure out how to convince Scooter that we should sell *Marjorie Jane*

6) Solve Captain Dan's murder

I underlined the last item and put a couple of exclamation points after it. I imagined the expression on Chief Dalton's face when I solved the murder before he did. It would be almost as sweet as seeing the one on Lola's face when I was promoted to the investigative reporter role over her.

As I was daydreaming about my promotion, Scooter called out, "There you are, my little bok choy." I wrinkled my nose. "Okay, I take it that's a no to bok choy."

He took a seat next to me. "I was just at Melvin's Marine Emporium looking at stuff we're going to need for *Marjorie Jane*. I know how much you like catalogs, so I brought one back for you."

I leafed through the glossy pages. "Um, Scooter, the catalogs I normally look at have things like sweaters and shoes in them. I don't know what anything is in here. Like this," I said, pointing at a strange rubber item.

Scooter leaned over and looked at the picture. "Oh, that's a joker valve. You need to replace them in marine toilets periodically. I've heard it's a really nasty job. One more reason to go with a composting toilet instead, don't you think?"

"Is there anything in here that's less gross and more interesting?"

Scooter turned to a page with pictures of inflatable dinghies. "We're going to need one of these."

"Wow, those are expensive."

"Yep, you know what they say BOAT stands for—Break Out Another Thousand, or in this case, several thousand."

"Don't you need an outboard motor for a dinghy too?"

Scooter laughed. "That's the spirit. See, you're really getting into boating."

"I was talking to Ben earlier and he said that his outboard died last night. I guess that's his alibi for Captain Dan's murder. He couldn't have come to shore during the time Captain Dan was killed because his engine wasn't working. Jack went out this morning to help him fix it."

Scooter shuddered at the mention of the

murder. He collected himself and smiled. "Yeah, that's the problem with boats. Everything breaks sooner or later." I wasn't sure why he was smiling. Who in the world likes it when things break? "Except the good news is that when stuff on our boat breaks, we'll be in exotic locations. We can fix things in the morning and then go for a swim in the afternoon."

"I don't know, Scooter. It all sounds really expensive. Just look at the prices on some of these things."

"See, it's a good thing we got such a deal on *Marjorie Jane*."

"But it's not much of a deal if we have to fix lots of things on her, is it? Everyone I talk to seems to think Captain Dan sold us a lemon."

"Nah, they're just jealous. We got a great deal that they missed out on."

"But are you sure you want to keep *Marjorie Jane* after someone was murdered on board?"

Scooter clasped his hands together tightly and took a deep breath. "To be honest, last night I started to have second thoughts, but what better way to honor Captain Dan's memory than by fixing her up?"

I could think of plenty of better ways to honor Captain Dan's memory, none of which involved fixing up a boat.

"What's that cat doing over there?" Scooter asked. Mrs. Moto was fishing her paw underneath a small overturned wooden boat on the beach. After a few tries, she managed to get the object out, then pounced on it. She tossed it in the air a few times, then came bounding over to us holding it in her mouth. She dropped it at my feet and meowed.

"Good kitty," I said. "What did you bring me?" I reached down and picked up a crumpled piece of paper.

I smoothed it out. "It looks like an IOU." I squinted at the torn paper. "Is that Ben's name on it?"

"Let me have a look at that," Scooter said. After examining it, he handed it back to me. "I can't really make anything out. It's probably nothing. I'm sure stuff washes up on the beach all the time." I folded it carefully and tucked it into my purse.

Scooter slapped his knees with his hands. "I can't believe I forgot to tell you the good news. I saw Chief Dalton on my way down to the beach. He said we're free to go back on board *Marjorie Jane*. They've cleaned everything up." He hesitated and looked a little woozy. "But there is one big issue. There are blood stains on the floor. I'm not sure I really want to see that."

"I think I have a solution to that. There's only one problem," I said, pointing at the mooring field. "We need to get out there."

* * *

We decided to walk back to the marina and see if anyone could give us a ride out to Ben's boat. I kept my eyes on the beach in search of seashells to add to my collection, while Mrs. Moto trailed behind me, keeping the seagulls in check.

I was picking through a pile of shells when Scooter stumbled into me, knocking me down. "Sorry about that," he said as he helped me up. "I was so caught up watching the racing that I didn't notice where I was going."

I held my hand over my eyes to minimize the glare of the sun bouncing off the water. I could see half a dozen small boats weaving through the bay, adjusting their sails as they changed direction.

"What are those?" I asked. "I didn't know they could make sailboats so small."

"They're Optimist dinghies. Kids use them to learn how to sail." He shouted encouragement to the girl who was in the lead. "I wish I had done something like that when I was their age," he said wistfully.

We watched as the tiny boats zipped back and forth, followed by a small pink speedboat. "Hey, I think that's Penny out there," I said, wondering what in Penny's life wasn't pink.

"Makes sense. She's the sailing instructor."

Mrs. Moto dropped something at my feet, and then twined herself around my legs.

"What did you bring me now, Mrs. Moto?

Oh, that's a pretty one." I rubbed sand off the small green seashell.

"How do you know that cat's name?" Scooter asked suspiciously.

"Oh, she belongs to Jack and Sandy." I gave Scooter a bright smile. "They're looking for someone to adopt her."

Scooter frowned as the calico played with his shoelaces. He pulled his foot away. "Why don't they want to keep her? She's really adorable." By adorable, I think he meant annoying.

"They need to sell their boat and their condo association doesn't allow pets." I watched as Mrs. Moto tried to untie his laces again. I suspect she thought Scooter pulling his feet away was part of the game. "You know, I feel bad for Sandy. They've got financial problems, and their marriage seems on shaky ground. And on top of all that she has to deal with what they did to her."

"They?"

I pointed at the sky. "You know, them. I'm writing a report on her abduction for

FAROUT."

"Sandy, an alien abductee? I doubt it." He laughed. "Heck, there's probably a bigger chance that she's the murderer."

"Murder? No, I don't think Sandy could have done that. She's in too much of a fragile state. The woman can barely function with her insomnia, headaches, nightmares, and sleepwalking." I picked Mrs. Moto up before Scooter lost patience with her. "My money is on Penny or Nancy. That pink fingernail I found in the galley could belong to one of them." Scooter looked at me quizzically. "Oh, yeah. I guess I forgot to tell you about that. Don't take it personally. Chief Dalton didn't know about it either until today. Both Penny and Nancy had pink manicures the day of the murder, which means one of them must have been on *Marjorie Jane* that night and killed Captain Dan."

Scooter flinched at the mention of murder but held it together. It was probably being in close proximity to Mrs. Moto. Cats have a calming effect on people. "But couldn't that fingernail have been there before?" he asked.

"Remember how you cleaned up the boat after the break-in?" Scooter nodded while keeping a wary eye on the Japanese bobtail. "You didn't see it then, did you?"

"No, I don't think so." He thought about it for a few minutes. "But still, I can't picture it, especially Nancy. She's an older lady. Could she really have had the strength to, you know—"

I interjected quickly before Scooter had to utter the word "murder." "You need to spend more time with Nancy. She's got a serious temper, and given the way I've seen her brandish brooms, staplers, and cans, I don't doubt that she could wield a winch handle if she were angry enough. She's definitely got motive. And so does Penny. Captain Dan cheated them, just like he cheated Jack."

"What did he do to Jack?"

"Sold him some worthless anchor chain."

"So maybe it was Jack," Scooter said. Then he added quickly, "I'm just kidding. Jack seems like a stand-up guy. I'm sure it wasn't him."

"Maybe I need to talk with him some more," I mused. "I did see him with a cart full of marine equipment earlier, including a large winch handle."

Mrs. Moto suddenly yowled, jumped out of my arms, and ran toward the water. I looked over to see what had her so excited. "Scooter, did that boat just capsize?" I asked in shock.

"Yep. That happens." He saw the concerned expression on my face. "They'll be okay." We watched as a boy righted the small boat and climbed back on board.

I breathed a big sigh of relief. "Falling out of a boat would be my worst nightmare."

"Don't worry. That will never happen to you."

* * *

We watched the end of the race, cheering along with the families who were gathered on the beach. The children brought their dinghies on shore, stowed their gear, and teased each other about who was a better sailor. Penny gathered the children and parents around her, debriefing them on the morning's activities, and giving them instructions for the following week's class.

"Come on, let's go over and talk to Penny," I said. "Maybe she can take us out to see Ben on that fancy pink boat of hers."

"That was an exciting race," Scooter said to her. "Those kids are fearless."

"They sure are," Penny agreed. "Teaching the children's course is one of my favorite parts of being a sailing instructor. They're so eager to learn." She turned to me. "What about you, Mollie? You're going to need to learn how to sail now that you're a boat owner. I do ladies' lessons every Thursday. I find women have more confidence learning sailing skills when their husbands aren't around." She glanced at Scooter. "No offense."

"None taken." Scooter put his arm around my shoulder. "I think it would be a great idea. Let's sign you up."

Penny was giving us the details when the

young girl who had won the race came bounding up wearing a polka dot swimsuit with an octopus on it. She wore her light-brown hair in two braids, and her green eyes sparkled. "Can you believe I won, Miss Penny?"

"Of course I can, Katy. You've been working really hard, and you had a great race."

"I just wish my grandparents could have been here to see it," Katy said. Her eyes got big. "Someone was killed at the marina last night. Grandma and Grandpa have been busy with police and reporters all morning."

My ears perked up at the mention of reporters. Was someone trying to steal my story about Sandy's abduction? Was it about the mysterious lights I saw?

Penny tugged at the girl's braids gently. "It's okay, Katy. They'll be able to watch you next week. Maybe you'll even win again."

Katy grinned, showing off two gaps in her front teeth. I wondered how much the Tooth Fairy was paying out these days. I use my credit and debit cards for practically everything and never have any cash on hand. Does the Tooth Fairy have the same problem?

She hugged Penny good-bye and ran up the stairs from the beach to the boardwalk. "Katy is Ned and Nancy's granddaughter," Penny said. "She's a regular little mermaid. She's only seven years old, but she's taken to sailing quickly."

"I didn't realize Ned and Nancy had grandkids," I said, watching as Katy stopped to scratch Mrs. Moto on the head.

"They raised their kids in Coconut Cove. Their sons moved away, but their daughter and her husband settled here and had two kids—Katy and her younger brother, Sam." Penny adjusted her hot-pink baseball hat. "If Katy can learn to sail, then you can too. Unless, of course, you want to sell that dilapidated sailboat of yours. I'm still interested in taking her off your hands."

"Thanks for the offer, but we're committed to fixing her up and sailing her off into the sunset," Scooter said.

"You're gonna need to do a lot of work to

her," Penny said. "That's a big job for just two people."

Why was she looking at me? Did she think I was going to work on that boat with Scooter? Time to get that idea out of her head, and more importantly, out of Scooter's head. "Ben mentioned that he was looking for work. He might be a good person to help Scooter."

"That's not a bad idea," Penny said thoughtfully. "When he isn't drinking beer, Ben's actually a good worker. He knows tons about boats."

"Well, the first thing we need to get him to do is remove the stains from the floor," I said.

"Stains?" Penny asked.

"You know, from the, um..."

"Oh, stains. Gotcha."

"We were actually hoping you might be able to give us a lift out to Ben's boat to tell him that he's hired."

"Sure, no problem." She pointed at her pink speedboat, which was anchored a few feet from the shore. "Hop on in."

* * *

I was still wringing out my skirt, which had gotten soaked getting into Penny's boat, along with the rest of me, when we pulled up to Ben's boat. I didn't think it was possible to find a boat that looked worse than *Marjorie Jane*, but Ben had achieved that dubious honor. What appeared to have been blue paint at one time was chipped and faded, the canvas was ripped, and the decks were long overdue for some varnish. I could just about make out the name, *Poseidon's Saber*, next to a carving of a scantily clad mermaid.

Penny knocked on the side of the boat. "Ben, are you there? It's me, Penny, along with Scooter and Mollie from *Marjorie Jane*."

I heard some banging, followed by a few salty phrases that any pirate would be proud to have in his vocabulary. Ben came up on deck, stretching his arms. "Sorry about that. I was having a bit of a nap down below." He grabbed a rope from Penny and tied off her boat to the side. "Come on aboard," he said, pointing at a rickety ladder.

I wasn't too sure that I wanted to climb up that. "Maybe I should just wait here," I suggested.

"Nonsense," Scooter said. "It'll be a good chance to check out another sailboat and get ideas for *Marjorie Jane*. Climb on up." He held the ladder steady while I cautiously made my ascent.

"How's it going, Mollie?" Ben said, offering me his hand and helping me up on deck. "Long time, no see. To what do I owe the pleasure of this visit?"

"I talked with Scooter and we want to hire you to do some work on the boat."

After agreeing to an hourly rate, Ben said, "This calls for a celebration." He shoved aside an old guitar and a pile of rags and motioned for us to sit down. "Who wants a soda?"

Obviously, Ben didn't realize that celebrations involved chocolate, not a can of warm generic cola.

Scooter took him up on his offer and popped open a can. "How long have you had this boat?"

"I bought her earlier this year from Captain Dan. You should have seen what she looked like before I got my hands on her. Boy, was she a wreck."

"She used to be owned by that old guy, didn't she?" Penny asked.

"Yep, a real old salt. He circumnavigated the globe on this boat. I'm hoping to do the same thing." He combed his fingers through his hair, then pulled it back into a ponytail. "But it'll be a while yet before I can get her off this mooring ball. She needs a new engine and a million other things." He slapped Scooter on the knee. "Working for you is sure going to help a lot. I'm gonna save up my money, point *Poseidon's Saber* toward the Caribbean, and never come back."

"You'd sail down there all by yourself?" I asked.

Ben sighed. "I guess so. It's really hard to find a woman who wants to live aboard a boat and share the sailing dream." He punched Scooter in the arm. "You're a lucky fellow. Not every guy has a wife who's willing to sell everything, move aboard a boat, and sail around the world."

My jaw dropped. Selling everything and sailing around the world was news to me. Scooter's midlife crisis was taking on new proportions.

Scooter patted my arm. "One step at a time, Ben. First, we need to get *Marjorie Jane* fixed up. When do you think you'd be able to start work?"

Ben's eyes lit up. "How about later this afternoon?"

"Sounds good. The first thing we have to do is some cleaning." I noticed Scooter didn't mention exactly what needed to be cleaned up. "The boat's in a bit of disarray given what happened last night."

"Oh, yeah, the murder. Do the police have any idea who did it?"

"Not yet," Scooter said. "I think they've been interviewing everyone today. Hopefully, they'll solve the case soon, and we can all move on with our lives."

"Did they interview you, Penny?" I asked.

"Bright and early this morning," she

replied.

"I bet they asked you the usual questions, like what you were doing at the time of Captain Dan's murder."

"They did."

I was hoping for a little more information. Fortunately, we'd received training on questioning techniques for reluctant interviewees from FAROUT. I tried again. "What exactly were you doing at the time of Captain Dan's murder?"

Penny looked flustered. "I was on my boat reading a book about old whaling captains and their crews. Did you know some of the captains took their wives with them on trips that lasted for years?"

I wasn't going to be sidetracked. "Were you all alone?"

"Yes, they were alone. No other women on the ship," Penny said. "Can you imagine raising children on a whaling ship?"

No, I couldn't. I couldn't imagine raising children at all, let alone on a boat. Now, a cat, on the other hand—that was something I could imagine. Just the right level of responsibility for me to deal with.

I mentally shook myself. Somehow, Penny had managed to distract me. I was thinking about cats instead of Captain Dan's murder. I was determined to get an answer to my question. "No, I meant were *you* alone?"

"Yes," she said, frowning.

"So no one can vouch for you, Penny?"

Penny began to look irritated. "Not everyone lives with a husband or partner like you do, Mollie."

"No, that's not what I meant," I said quickly, realizing that my blunt questions weren't having the desired effect. I've been told that subtlety is not my strong suit. "All I meant was that they asked us about our alibis and who could vouch for us. I was just curious if they asked you similar questions. I wasn't sure if you had someone special in your life."

Ben inched closer to Penny. "I guess we're in the same boat. I don't have anyone special. You don't have anyone special. Neither of us has anyone to back up our alibis."

Penny moved closer to me and farther from Ben. "Maybe we should do something to change that. Whaddya say we hit up happy hour tonight at the Tipsy Pirate?"

"Sorry, sugar, but I've got plans tonight," Penny said.

Ben slumped on the bench. "Sure, I understand," he said slowly.

Penny stood and clapped her hands together. "All right. Let's get this show on the road and head back to the marina. I've got a million things to do this afternoon before my date."

This time, I managed to stay dry, which made the boat ride more enjoyable. The gentle breeze and clear blue water didn't hurt either. During the trip back, I remembered that Sandy had said that she had seen Penny at the marina on the night of the murder. Why did Penny say she was on her boat alone? Something wasn't adding up.

CHAPTER 8
TO-DO LISTS

AFTER PENNY DROPPED US OFF at the marina dinghy dock, we walked into town to the Sailor's Corner Cafe for a late lunch. It was popular with locals and tourists alike, and we were lucky to get a table. We had been coming here regularly since our move to Coconut Cove. I always thought the nautical decorations were cute, but now that we owned a sailboat, I looked at the old steering wheels, oars, ship's bells, and anchors dotted around with more interest.

I noticed the young couple I had seen at our anniversary dinner holding hands in a booth. The sunlight from the window made the diamond necklace he had given her that night sparkle brightly. "Aww. Aren't they sweet?" I said. "Look at how in love they are. I really like her necklace, don't you?"

Scooter glanced over at them. "It's okay." He put his menu down. "That reminds me—you have to stop trying to fix people up."

"What are you talking about? Who was I trying to fix up?"

"Penny and Ben."

"You've got to be kidding me. They are the least likely couple I can think of. She doesn't exactly seem like the type to go for an unemployed pirate wannabe."

"Then what were you doing asking all those questions about their alibis and pointing out that they're both single?"

"That's all I was doing—checking on their alibis. I'm done trying to fix people up. Remember what happened with your sister?"

"She's still not speaking to me." He picked his menu back up. "What are you going to get?"

"I can't decide. I'm torn between the

Pirate's Platter or a BLT."

Scooter's eyes followed a waitress who was bearing two large sundaes on her tray. "You should probably go for the BLT so you save room for dessert."

"Good call. The BLT it is."

Scooter waved the waitress over to our table. "We're ready to order, Alejandra."

Alejandra Lopez was one of the reasons we kept coming back to the Sailor's Corner Cafe. I envied her silky, black hair, which she wore in a French braid while at work, and her youthful energy. I certainly wouldn't have been able to put the hours in that she did, always with a big smile on her face.

After we placed our order, she asked, "Is it true that Captain Dan was killed on your boat?"

"Unfortunately, he was," I said.

"¡*Oh, Dios mío!* Are you doing okay?"

"We're trying not to think about it," Scooter said.

"You poor things. How awful." She scooped up our menus and tucked her pad and pen in her apron pocket. "Captain Dan used to come in here quite a bit. He always got the same thing—the Fisherman's Combo." She bent down and said in a low voice, "Between you and me, for all of his boasting about how great of a salesman he was and how much money he made, he sure was a lousy tipper. He used to try to hit on me too. Like I'd be interested in somebody like him." She gave us a smile. "Anyway, enough about him. I'll be back with your meals in a jiff."

After we polished off our sandwiches and hot fudge sundaes—complete with extra sprinkles and whipped cream—I got out my notebook. "We should probably make a list of what needs to be done on *Marjorie Jane*." I really shouldn't have been encouraging Scooter's midlife crisis, but I figured that if he was going to have one, I might as well make sure it was organized.

"You do love making lists, don't you?" Scooter said. It was true. I do love to-do lists. It's the doing stuff on the to-do lists that I don't like so much.

"So where should we start?" I asked.

"First, we should probably do a full

inventory of everything that's on the boat. After they found that winch handle, it makes me wonder what else is on there that we don't know about." I was proud of Scooter. He didn't look like he was going to pass out at the mention of the winch handle. I think the hot fudge sundae had had a fortifying effect. "Although there's so much stuff crammed in the lockers, it could take a while," he warned.

I wrote down "inventory" on the list with "VBT" next to it. "VBT" stands for Very Boring Task. I like to categorize my to-do lists by how interesting the items are. That way I have a better sense of how to prioritize my time.

We continued our discussion about the list, and I added a number of other items with various codes such as "EBT" (Extremely Boring Task), "NTWL" (Need to Win the Lottery First), and "AAAC" (Avoid at All Costs).

While I was trying to figure out how to code the installation of a composting toilet, I heard the squeal of children behind me. I turned and saw Nancy walking toward our table with Katy and another child in tow. Katy saw me and waved. "Grandma, they saw me sailing today," she yelled. She tugged on Nancy's hand and pulled her toward us. "Tell my grandma what a great job I did sailing today."

"She did a wonderful job," Scooter said. "And who's this?" He pointed at the boy standing shyly behind Katy.

"This is Sam, my little brother," Katy said enthusiastically. "I'm going to teach him how to sail! But first, we're going to have lunch!"

Nancy smiled and patted Katy on the head. She seemed a lot less grumpy when surrounded by her grandchildren.

"Where's Ned? Isn't he joining you for lunch?" I asked.

Before Nancy could answer, Katy shouted, "The police took him in for questioning!"

"Is everything okay, Nancy?" Scooter asked with concern. "I thought they had spoken with you both already."

"Everything's fine. It's all routine. All right, children, let's grab a table and get some lunch," she said as she ushered them to the back of the restaurant.

"I wonder what that's all about," I said.

"I don't know, but it doesn't sound routine to me at all."

"Nancy told me that both of them were at their apartment watching television while she did her nails. But now I'm wondering if Ned was there the whole time. After we pay the check, let's go back and see what we can find out."

* * *

After lunch, we met Ben back at the marina. While he and Scooter went to start work on *Marjorie Jane*, I headed to the lounge to type up my report on Sandy's abduction. The air conditioning was going full blast, which was a nice relief from the hot, humid afternoon weather. Looking at the gray clouds forming overhead, I figured we were due for the usual afternoon showers. Sitting inside on one of the comfy chairs with my laptop seemed like a good idea.

I kicked off my flip-flops and stretched out my legs on the ottoman. After opening my laptop, I had the funny feeling that someone was staring at me. I looked around but didn't see anyone. I poked behind the drapes, just in case someone was hiding there. You never know. Puzzled, I walked past the bookshelves to peek out the window. Then I heard a loud meow from above. There was Mrs. Moto, perched on a pile of sailing manuals on the bookshelf. She blinked at me a few times, then jumped down and rubbed herself against my legs. I picked her up, had a quick cuddle, and deposited her on the coffee table. Just as I settled back into my chair and got my laptop situated, the calico plopped down next to me and wiggled her way between my right leg and the side of the armchair. She started kneading my leg and purring loudly. After a few minutes, she put her head down and settled in for a nap.

I positioned my hands on the keyboard just like Mrs. Purdy had taught us at school—my index fingers poised above the *f* and *j* keys— and waited for inspiration. I waited some more. And some more. I stroked Mrs. Moto's soft fur for a few minutes, then hovered my hands over the keyboard, ready to write the report that was going to propel my career forward. Nothing. Absolutely nothing. This must be what they called writer's block.

I took a break and checked email. Brian Morrison had sent me a note marked urgent.

You'd better hurry up and submit your report. I heard a rumor that Lola has uncovered a major government conspiracy that might top your alien abduction case. I think you're the best candidate for the investigative reporter job, so please send your report in today, if possible. I'll put in a good word for you with the board of directors.

The mere thought of Lola motivated me to get cracking. I clicked away at the keyboard furiously, documenting Sandy's abduction in detail. From time to time, Mrs. Moto would open her eyes and demand to be scratched. I'm pretty sure aliens never abducted cats. They were far too demanding as test subjects.

As I was trying to write a scintillating conclusion, Ned walked in carrying a bucket full of cleaning supplies.

"How did she get in here again?" he asked. The Japanese bobtail peeked over the side of the armchair to look at him. She gave him the feline equivalent of a shrug and nestled back down to continue her nap. "Don't let Nancy see her," he warned.

"Don't worry, I'd be the last person to rat out Mrs. Moto," I said. "We saw Nancy and your grandkids at the Sailor's Corner Cafe earlier. They said the police were questioning you some more."

"Oh, that was nothing. Just routine." He pulled a rag from his bucket. "They all got back about ten minutes ago. The grandkids are helping Nancy out in the store this afternoon while their mom's running errands. By helping, I mean eating all the chocolate."

"Not only are they adorable, but they have their priorities straight," I said with a smile. "We saw Katy racing earlier today. I can't get over how good of a sailor she is for her age."

"She begged her parents for months for sailing lessons," Ned said as he started dusting and polishing the furniture. "She's loving it. Between you and me, Penny says that Katy is her best student." Ned glowed with pride. "I bet she'll even make the Olympic sailing team when she's older."

"Did you ever race?" I asked.

"I sure did. Every weekend I would be out there competing. My favorite part was the annual Coconut Cove regatta. We usually beat everyone else." Ned pointed at his knees. "These days, I don't move around as easily. I had both of these replaced a couple of years ago. Between that and my arthritis, my racing days are over."

"It looks like you keep busy around here."

"I do. It's the kind of job where you're never really off duty. We live in an apartment upstairs and have to be on call in case anything happens. But we enjoy it. It keeps us close to the water and involved in the sailing community. It's a close-knit group of sailors here in the area, as you've probably gathered."

"It must have been a real shock to everyone when Captain Dan was murdered."

Ned hesitated. "Of course. Anytime anyone is murdered it's a real shock."

"The memorial service should be packed with everyone from the marina." Ned suddenly became very engrossed in some dust bunnies near the window. I tried again. "Wasn't Captain Dan popular around here?"

Ned weighed up the question before answering. "Well, let's just say he didn't really endear himself in the short time he lived here. There are more than a few people who were cheated by him in one way or another, ourselves included."

"I heard he vouched for the previous owners of *Marjorie Jane*, which left you guys in the lurch with unpaid bills. Was it more than that?"

"It might have been," Ned said evasively. "What are you working on there?" he asked, pointing to my computer.

"It's a report for work. I'm actually really excited about it. It might even get picked up by newspapers nationally. It's a big story!"

Ned sat down in the other armchair. "Really? What's it about?"

Before I could tell Ned what had happened to Sandy, the door burst open, and Katy and Sam ran in. "Look what we got!" Katy shouted, holding out her hands. Sam ran up next to her and held out his hands eagerly too.

"Well, would you look at that!" Ned said, peering at Katy's and Sam's yo-yos. "What did you do to talk grandma into getting those?"

"We promised we wouldn't tell anyone what she said to Jack. She said it was a secret and that we couldn't tell anyone about it, not even you."

"Oh, is that right?" Ned pressed his lips together. "I'll tell you what—why don't we go back to the store to see grandma? Maybe she'll tell me her secret and give me one of those yo-yos so I don't tell anyone either."

"Oh, grandpa, don't be silly. These are just for kids," Katy said.

"Yeah, grandpa, you're a grown-up, not a kid," Sam added.

"Grandpa is being silly, isn't he?" Katy asked me. The calico hopped over to the coffee table, trying to get a glimpse of the yo-yos. "Don't be silly, Mrs. Moto," Katy said. "These aren't for cats either."

Sam laughed. "Yeah, Mrs. Moto, you're a cat, not a kid."

Ned got up from his chair. "Come on, kids, let's go next door and see grandma." He picked up his bucket of cleaning supplies, and the three of them left the lounge. Katy and Sam looked excited. Ned looked concerned.

* * *

After Ned and the kids left, I typed away for another hour, finished up my report, gathered my courage, and hit Send. Considering all that work, I figured I deserved a treat.

As I went to grab my purse, Mrs. Moto reached over and stuck her paw inside. She pulled out the piece of paper she had brought to me earlier on the beach and dropped it on my lap. I think she was trying to tell me something. I had another look at the IOU and wondered how big Ben's money problems were. I tucked it back in my bag and said thank you to Mrs. Moto for reminding me about it by way of a few scratches on her belly.

Sandy's cat followed me out of the lounge, but when I entered the marina office, she wisely scurried away. I quickly shut the screen door behind me, but not quickly enough. Nancy glared at me and got out her flyswatter. Hoping to avoid being mistaken for a fly, I hurried over to the back, where Katy and Sam were playing with their yo-yos.

"Is there any chocolate left? Or have you two munchkins eaten it all?" I asked.

"We want more chocolate!" Katy screamed.

"Yeah, more chocolate!" Sam agreed.

"You've had plenty of chocolate," Nancy said. "Maybe it's time for some apples instead?" Katy and Sam stared at her like she had developed some sort of dementia and went back to playing with their yo-yos.

"Their mother is going to be thrilled when she picks them up with all that sugar running through their system. But that's what grandmothers are for," Nancy said as she smiled fondly at her grandchildren.

Ned poked his head out of the back room. "Nancy, can you give me a hand with this?" She helped him carry out some heavy-looking boxes and stacked them next to the counter.

"It looks like this job keeps you fit," I said.

"I make an effort to stay in shape," Nancy said as she opened up one of the boxes and began stocking the shelves. "I go for a walk every morning on the beach, and I lift some light weights as well. That's the only way I can keep up with those two."

"Are there any more of those dark chocolate butterscotch crunch bars left?" I asked.

"Are we out already? I wonder how that happened?" Nancy smiled at Katy and Sam. "Let me just finish this, and I'll go in the back and get some more."

While I waited, I studied a display of sailing books by the door. I picked up one on cruising in the Bahamas and flipped through it. The glossy photos of sandy beaches, colorful fish, and picturesque towns almost had me thinking that this sailing thing might be okay.

The screen door opened, interrupting my daydreams of tropical cocktails. That young couple—whom I had started to think of as Mr. and Mrs. Diamond—seemed to be following me around. First at our anniversary dinner, then at lunch, and now here.

"Hi there," Ned said, looking up from the computer. "You're the folks out on the catamaran, aren't you? How can I help you?"

"We're not normally ones to complain, but there was someone speeding through the mooring field last night. I was worried he was going to ram into our boat," Mr. Diamond said. His wife nodded while she toyed with her diamond necklace.

"Could you make out who it was?" Ned asked.

"No, I didn't recognize him. I did see him anchor his boat on the far side of the beach and meet up with a couple of guys. It's probably no big deal, but we thought you should know."

"Well, I appreciate you letting me know. Folks shouldn't be driving through there like that. About what time was it, do you reckon?"

"Sweetie, what time was that at?" he asked.

Mrs. Diamond thought about it for a few seconds. "A little after we got back to our boat from the barbecue. Maybe seven."

Mr. Diamond and Ned continued to chat about reckless drivers, both on land and water, while Mrs. Diamond grabbed some milk and eggs from the cooler. As she walked past me, she pointed at the book I was reading. "Are you thinking of going to the Bahamas?" she asked. "If you are, that's a wonderful cruising guide. We'd definitely recommend it. It's got lots of useful information about anchorages, things to do in the area, and good charts."

"I don't even know how to sail," I said. "I can't even begin to imagine going to the Bahamas except on a cruise ship."

Ned overheard us and chuckled. "Can you

believe she doesn't know how to sail, and her husband just bought her a boat for their anniversary?"

"Wow, that's some present," she said. "Sailing must be something you've always wanted to do."

"Let's just say that it's something my husband is interested in," I replied tersely, staring at her necklace. I closed the book firmly and put it back on the shelf. While Ned was ringing their sale up, Nancy placed a stack of chocolate bars on the counter.

Katy and Sam looked up from their yo-yos and screamed in unison, "Chocolate!"

Ned peeked out the window. "I see your mom walking this way. Let's go show her your new toys." As they rushed out the door, followed by Nancy, Ned said, "That was a close call. They sure can go through a lot of chocolate."

I handed a bar to Ned to ring up. "It's never too early to learn good taste."

"Well, I suppose. I don't really have a sweet tooth myself."

"Good, more chocolate for the rest of us." I

glanced around to make sure Nancy was still outside. "Did you find out what Jack and Nancy discussed?"

"Oh, that was nothing. Kids exaggerate." He sat down and peered intently at the computer. "I better get this inventory done before Nancy gets back. You know how she is."

* * *

I sat at one of the patio tables and checked my phone for emails. I managed to resist sampling the chocolate, despite the anxious feeling I had in the pit of my stomach over the report I had submitted. Was it good enough to beat out Lola? No email from Brian, but plenty of texts from my mom.

Murder!! What murder??

Where are you? Is it safe to be there?

Why haven't you responded? If you don't text me back, I'm going to call the local police to check on you.

Yikes. I hoped she hadn't contacted the police. I could only imagine the acrobatics

Chief Dalton's eyebrows would perform if he had to field a phone call from my mother. I looked at my watch and realized I was late getting back to the boat. I sent a quick text to let her know everything was okay.

Don't worry. I'm fine. I'm hot on the trail of the killer. Gotta go.

As I got up, I noticed a copy of the local newspaper on a nearby table. I picked it up and scanned the headlines. Sure enough, Captain Dan's murder was the lead story. His picture still looked familiar, but I couldn't place how I knew him. I tucked the paper into my bag and walked down the dock, trying to figure out how I would have known a boat broker, when I'd known nothing about boats until recently.

* * *

"Ahoy, is anyone there?" I called out when I got to *Marjorie Jane*. I figured if we owned a boat, I might as well start getting used to talking like a sailor.

"We're down here," Scooter replied. "Wait

until you see what we found."

I climbed down the ladder, wondering if they had found a tasteful diamond brooch.

Scooter was jumping up and down with excitement. Well, not exactly jumping. When you're a six-foot-tall man and the ceiling height is only six foot two, jumping up and down can be dangerous. It was more like extremely enthusiastic hopping.

"Hold out your hands and close your eyes," Scooter said, finally coming to a standstill. Close my eyes? Hold out my hands? Maybe it really was a diamond brooch.

Scooter placed a flat, metallic object in my hands. It seemed kind of large and heavy for a brooch. I didn't feel anything that could be diamonds on the outside. Wait a minute— maybe this was a gift box, and the brooch was inside. I opened my eyes. Hmm...if this was a gift box, it looked an awful lot like an old compass.

"Isn't it amazing?" Ben asked. "Just look at the filigree work. And check out the etching of a whale on the other side. You don't see too many of these, do you?"

No, I had to agree. You don't see too many old compasses with whales on them. Then again, you don't see too many diamond brooches either. At least, I don't.

Ben blathered away for what felt like ages on the finer points of antique compasses. Scooter nodded and did that weird hopping thing again.

"Whoa, fellas. Calm down and take a deep breath. Where did you find this?"

"In the V-berth. It was behind a hidden panel under one of the storage lockers, wrapped in bubble wrap," Ben said. "I found it after I cleaned up the blood stains from the floor."

I checked out the floor. Not a trace of blood left. I glanced at Scooter. He looked pale. "Don't worry, we can put a throw rug or something over that spot. It'll be like it never even happened," I said. He looked unconvinced.

Ben, oblivious to Scooter's discomfort, motioned to me. "Come on over here, Mollie. Stand where the blood stains were and you can see better. Now, look where the floor meets the bottom of the berth. You can just about make the secret panel out near that wood trim." I saw a faint outline. Ben reached down, pushed on the corner, and the panel opened up. "The compass was right in there!"

While I inspected the secret compartment, Scooter picked up a magazine from the table. "We found a copy of *Nautical Antiquities* magazine in there too." He turned to a page marked with a paper clip. "There's an article on an antique compass that's identical to the one we found. You'll never believe how much it's worth."

Scooter named an outrageous sum. He was right. I didn't believe him. I grabbed the magazine and had a look for myself to make sure he hadn't inadvertently added a few zeros where they didn't belong. He hadn't. "Wow, that's some serious money," I said. "There's got to be a connection between the compass and Captain Dan's murder."

Ben held up the compass. "Imagine, someone bashing you over the head with a winch handle for this."

By this point, Scooter looked like he was in dire need of chocolate. I pointed at my purse. He pawed through the contents, clearly relieved when he found a dark chocolate butterscotch crunch bar.

While Scooter snarfed down chocolate and got some color back in his face, Ben and I tossed around ideas about the murder.

"But if someone killed Captain Dan for the compass, why didn't they get it out of the compartment after he was dead?" I asked.

"Maybe they didn't know how to open the compartment," Ben replied. "You've got to press on it just right for the door to open. Maybe they didn't even know about the compartment."

"Maybe they didn't even know about the compass," I suggested. "It could have been an entirely different motive, like revenge. A lot of people were mad at Captain Dan because he cheated them, including yourself."

Ben stiffened. "Yeah, he owed me for some work I did for him that he never paid me for. But like I told you before, I was stuck on my boat the whole night 'cause the engine on my dinghy didn't work." He exhaled slowly, then handed me the compass. "What do you want to do with this? It was found on your boat, so finders keepers, right?"

I glanced over at Scooter. He appeared to be doing better, probably due to the fact that there was a supply of chocolate at hand. He looked at the antiques magazine and sighed. "It sure is worth a lot of money. But we should give it to Chief Dalton. It could be related to the, you know, the..."

"Investigation?" I prompted. Scooter nodded. "I think you're right. How about if I go drop this off at the police station, give the chief an update, and pick up a pizza for dinner? It's late, and I'm sure you two have worked up quite an appetite. Meet you back on the patio in an hour?"

* * *

I decided to walk into town to drop off the compass and pick up the pizza rather than drive. I needed to work off some of the chocolate-related calories I had accumulated so that I could replace them with pizza calories. Sandy had told me about a path that ran through a wooded area along the beach and ended up behind Penelope's Sugar Shack.

As I trudged along the path, wishing I had worn sneakers instead of flip-flops, I heard arguing on the beach. I couldn't see who it was through the brush, but one of the voices sounded familiar. I pushed my way through the prickly shrubs growing among the palm trees. As I slowly inched forward, I stubbed my big toe on one of the coconuts littering the ground. I yelped in pain, cursing my sandals.

"What was that?" the familiar voice asked.

I peeked through the leaves, trying to get a glimpse of the speaker. Unfortunately, the man with the familiar voice had his back to me.

"Probably just a raccoon or a wild boar," grumbled a man with a dark crew cut. "If you're going to get spooked by some critters, then you're really not cut out for this." I looked around nervously for raccoons and wild boar. Sandy hadn't mentioned anything about encountering dangerous wildlife when she'd recommended this trail.

An older man with silver hair and a beard was standing next to crew-cut guy. He was holding a coconut, which he tossed between his hands forcefully. "Where's our money?" he demanded.

The man with the familiar voice held his hands up. "Like I told you fellows, I don't have it."

The man with the beard continued to slam the coconut back and forth between his hands. "That wasn't our deal. We delivered the goods, and now we want our money."

"I'll get it to you," he stammered. "It's just that with what's happened here at the marina, it's going to take some time to unload everything."

Crew-cut guy grabbed him by his collar. "You've got one more day. You remember what happened to the last guy who double-crossed us, don't you?" He turned to his bearded friend. "Come on, let's get out of here." They strode down the beach, got into a speedboat, and took off.

The man with the familiar voice put his head in his hands and started to shake. Then he drew a deep breath and turned to pick up a backpack off the ground. When I saw his face, I gasped. What was he doing here? What was he doing with those scary-looking guys?

I slowly backed up toward the path, trying not to make any noise, but then I tripped over a coconut, stumbled, and cried out in pain.

"Who's there?" he shouted as he pushed his way through the brush.

* * *

"Mollie, are you okay?" I opened my eyes and rubbed my head. It felt sore.

"Is that you, Scooter? What am I doing here on the ground?" I tried to get up.

"Just stay right there. The ambulance is on its way. Let's get you checked out first before you make any sudden movements."

"What time is it? I forgot to get the pizza!"

"I can't believe you're worried about the pizza," Scooter chuckled as he stroked my forehead. His expression sobered. "I'm so glad you're okay. When Sandy told me she found you lying here, I was so worried. What would I do without you?"

"Sandy found me?"

"Yes, she went out for a walk and came across you. Looks like you got hit in the head with a coconut and it knocked you out."

My head was throbbing. I reached up and felt my forehead. Scooter took my hand and kissed the back of it. "I think you're going to have a pretty spectacular lump," he said.

"I guess there isn't any blood."

"Why do you say that?"

"You're not eating any chocolate."

Scooter smiled. "Here come the EMTs. They'll get you to the hospital, and I'll meet you there."

As they started to wheel me down the path, I suddenly recalled something. "Scooter, wait! I remember what happened. It wasn't a coconut—it was Jack."

CHAPTER 9
PRETTY IN PINK

"OTHER THAN A NASTY BUMP on her head, your wife will be fine," the doctor said as she scribbled some notes on my chart. "Just keep an eye on her for the next twenty-four hours to make sure she's okay."

"Are you sure I should be the one monitoring her?" Scooter asked. "I'm not that good with medical stuff."

"He really isn't," I agreed.

"Oh, you'll be fine. It's just a minor head wound. There wasn't even any bleeding." Scooter didn't look convinced.

The doctor handed me a prescription for

pain medicine. "You're probably going to have a nasty headache. If it gets any worse, come straight back in. Otherwise, make a follow-up appointment with your regular doctor for next week." She patted me on the arm and walked out the door briskly.

Scooter slumped into a plastic chair by the side of the bed and breathed a sigh of relief. "I don't know what I would have done if anything had happened to you."

"I'm fine. It's just a bump on my head." I rubbed my forehead. Was it my imagination or had the bump gotten even bigger in the past five minutes? I shivered as I thought about how Jack had grabbed me as I'd tried to run away. "Have they arrested Jack yet for assaulting me?"

Scooter frowned. "Maybe we should have the doctor examine you again. You were hit by a coconut falling from a tree. Apparently, it happens more often than you'd think."

"I know what I saw. I overheard Jack arguing with two men on the beach. They said if he didn't pay them what he owed them, he'd end up just like the last guy. You know who the last guy is, don't you? Captain Dan!"

Scooter pushed himself out of his chair, then paced around the room. "You think those guys killed Captain Dan?"

"They were scary guys," I said. "The way they threatened Jack, I wouldn't put it past them to be killers."

Scooter got out his cell phone, dialed the police station, and explained what I had overheard. "Someone will be here soon to take your statement."

I texted my mom to let her know that I was in the hospital. Oddly, she didn't text back right away. It must have been bridge night with the girls. My stomach grumbled, telling me that I hadn't had dinner. I wondered what they had done with our pizza when I didn't pick it up. While I was contemplating the fate of unclaimed pizzas, Chief Dalton turned up.

"What's this I hear about you being hit on the head by a coconut?" he asked.

"It wasn't a coconut," I said. "Jack Holt did this."

He raised one of his eyebrows. "Why don't we start from the beginning." He took out his notebook and a pen. "I understand Mrs. Holt found you unconscious in the woods with a coconut beside you. Is that correct?"

"Well, since I was unconscious at the time, I can't be sure, but that's what they tell me," I said testily. My stomach grumbled loudly. The chief's eyebrows twitched.

"What were you doing right before the coconut fell on you?"

I seized my purse and searched for something edible inside. All I found were several empty chocolate bar wrappers and a packet of breath mints, which wasn't really going to cut it. I desperately needed pizza. "Let's cut to the chase, Chief. I overheard Jack and two men talking on the beach. Jack owed them money for some presumably stolen goods, and they threatened him if he didn't pay up. Jack caught me eavesdropping, shoved me, and bashed me in the head." I chewed on a breath mint. "If you haven't done so already, you should get out there and arrest Jack and those other two guys."

The burly man tapped his notebook with his pen thoughtfully. "What did these guys look like?" After I provided a description of crew-cut guy and his bearded friend, he jotted down a few notes. "I think I know who you're talking about, Mrs. McGhie. Don't worry, we'll have a word with them." He closed his notebook and put it in his jacket pocket.

"Great, but what about Jack? He's the one who tried to kill me."

"I spoke with Mr. and Mrs. Holt in the waiting room earlier. Mr. Holt was on his boat all evening. His wife was there as well, until she went for her walk and found you. So I'm afraid that you couldn't have possibly seen him on the beach. Maybe it was someone else you saw—that is, if you saw anyone at all. People with head injuries often have fuzzy memories."

"I know what I saw."

Chief Dalton pursed his lips. "Well, maybe it's not a fuzzy memory as much as an, ahem, overactive imagination." I glared at him, but that made the throbbing in my head worse.

He looked at the floor and suppressed a smile. "It's just that you've mentioned alien abduction before. You're probably one of those creative types. My ex-wife is like that. She does watercolors. She paints fairies sitting on flowers. Weirdest-looking pictures. But what's even weirder is that she claims the fairies actually talk to her." He turned to Scooter, looking for support. "She even said that they lived in our garden—can you believe that?" Scooter wisely declined to comment.

The nurse came in with my discharge paperwork, which I hastily signed. "If you can't be of any help, Chief, I'll just have to take things into my own hands." I grabbed my purse. "Come on, Scooter, let's get our pizza."

It turns out they don't throw your pizza away, even if it takes you hours to collect it. Good thing I like cold pizza.

* * *

The next morning, I had leftover pizza with

some painkillers for breakfast, followed by a strong cup of coffee. Scooter had a bowl of Froot Loops. After I spent ten minutes convincing him that my head was fine, we headed off to Melvin's Marine Emporium.

Scooter had a long list of items he swore we needed for the boat. He had a much shorter second list of items he wanted for the boat. I was pretty sure that a lot of the items on list number one could easily be moved to list number two.

When we walked through the door, we were cheerfully greeted by a gangly teenager with a bad case of acne. "Ahoy there, sailors! Welcome to Melvin's Marine Emporium. My name's Chad. How can I help you today?"

After I confiscated the nice-to-have list, Scooter handed Chad the need-to-have-right-now list. "We just bought a sailboat, and we want to get her outfitted. Our boat broker said this was the best marine store in town."

"You've come to the right place. Melvin's Marine Emporium is your one-stop shop for all your boating needs." Chad paused to admonish a girl with perfect, glowing skin who looked to be about his age. "Tiffany, the winches don't go on that shelf—they go over there." She scowled at him. He turned back to us and said importantly, "I have to keep on top of the staff. I'm the shift supervisor, you know." I had the feeling that if Chad asked her to prom, she'd turn him down flat.

Chad scanned the list. "Why don't we start with anchor chain?" We followed him to the back of the store, where large sections of chain were on display. "Over here, we have our stainless steel chain, over here is galvanized, and this stuff over here—well, you wouldn't be interested in this; it's just cheap chain." While Scooter and the boy discussed the merits of stainless versus galvanized, I had a look at the price tags.

"It costs this much for a foot of chain?" I asked incredulously. "How much chain do we need?" Scooter rattled off a figure, and I did a quick calculation in my head. Okay, it wasn't that quick of a calculation. I cheated and used the calculator on my phone. Wow, for that price, I could have had a very nice diamond necklace. Somehow it didn't seem fair that *Marjorie Jane* was going to be the only one with a sparkly chain.

Boredom set in as the two guys debated anchoring techniques. I wandered around the store, thinking Melvin could probably jazz up his displays of bilge pumps and marine toilets. I came to a section with flags from various countries. Finally, something interesting. As I was trying to decide which nation had the prettiest flag, I spied Jack walking toward the manager's office.

I put down a Bahamian flag, darted around the corner, and hid behind a display of sunglasses. Jack stood in the door, clenching his car keys.

"I can give you a good deal," he said.

"I don't care how good of a deal it is," replied another man with a high-pitched, squeaky voice. "I can't afford to get caught moving that stuff for you."

"But you used to deal with Captain Dan all the time."

"That was different."

"Different how? Now that he's gone, I'm

taking over the business. And I'm telling you, I can keep you stocked with everything you need at rock-bottom prices."

"Maybe after things cool down with the murder investigation. Why don't you come back next week and we can talk about it more then?"

"But I need the money now!"

"What do I look like? Your personal ATM? Get lost."

Jack turned abruptly and stormed toward the exit, pushing Tiffany out of the way in the process.

I hurried back to the anchor chain section and pulled Scooter aside. "I just saw Jack," I whispered. "He was trying to sell stolen goods to the store manager. Captain Dan was part of it all before he got killed."

"Are you sure it was Jack?" Scooter asked. "Maybe we should get the doctor to check your head out again."

"It's not my head that needs to be checked out, it's Jack who needs to be checked out."

Chad waved Scooter over. "Did you see that all our electronics are on sale?" My husband's eyes lit up.

I sighed. "Go on, have a look. Why don't you meet me at the marina later? Just promise me not to go overboard buying stuff."

"Scout's honor," Scooter said. "As long as you promise to stay out of this murder investigation. You've got to take care of yourself."

I crossed my fingers behind my back. "Promise." Then I headed off to confront Sandy on why she lied about Jack's whereabouts last night.

* * *

As I walked through the marina parking lot, I heard a horn. I turned and saw Penny pulling into a spot in a pink convertible.

"Mollie, perfect timing," she said as she hopped out and locked up her car. "Why don't you come with me to my boat, and I'll loan you an introductory sailing book."

"Sure," I replied, pushing my sunglasses back on my head.

"What happened?" She pointed at the big bump on my forehead.

I hesitated. I wasn't sure how close she was to Jack and Sandy. What if she thought I was imagining things like everyone else did?

"Mollie, did you hear me?" she asked.

"Sorry, yes, I heard you. I got hit in the head last night when I was out walking on the trail by the beach."

"Are you okay?"

"I'm fine. The doctor said there was nothing wrong, other than this bruise and the lump on my forehead."

"I bet it was one of those coconuts, wasn't it? Someone else got hit by one of them last year."

I decided to come clean. I figured seeing how Penny reacted could be useful. "It wasn't a coconut. It was Jack."

She stared blankly at me. "Jack hit you in the head with a coconut?"

"He grabbed me, then pushed me, and must have hit me in the head with something. It all happened so fast. But it was definitely Jack, and it was definitely deliberate." I took a deep breath. "You see, I overheard him talking to two guys on the beach. They were threatening him. If he didn't pay them the money he owed them, then things weren't going to go so well for him."

"You're kidding," Penny said. "Aren't you?"

"Do you think I'd kid about this?" I asked, indicating my forehead. "No, it was Jack all right. You know him pretty well, don't you?"

"I wouldn't say I know him well, but since we all live on our boats at the marina, I certainly see him and Sandy often enough."

"What do you think he's involved in?"

Penny shook her head. "I can't picture him being involved in anything. Are you sure it was Jack who attacked you?"

"It was definitely him." I shook my head angrily. That was a mistake. My headache was coming back. "For some reason, Sandy is covering for him. She says he was with her at the time. Chief Dalton thinks I made the whole thing up, and I don't think Scooter believes me either."

"Your own husband doesn't believe you? That's awful. I used to have a boyfriend like that. He never believed me about anything. Lying, cheating jerk!" Penny said.

"No, I think you've got Scooter all wrong. He's not like that at all. Sure, he tends to get obsessed about things, like *Marjorie Jane*, and not always pay attention to what I'm working on. But he'd never cheat on me or lie to me." I sat down on the hood of the car next to Penny's.

"Well, you're lucky then," Penny said, lost in her own thoughts. "I was there for this guy through thick and thin and believed in him, even when no one else would. I even..."

"You even did what?"

"Nothing, never mind," Penny said firmly.

We both sat lost in our thoughts for a few moments. "So what ended up happening with your boyfriend? Are you still together?"

Penny gave a wry chuckle. "No, we're not together. For a while there I thought we were going to get back together, but it didn't work out. And it's definitely never going to happen now." She stood and said, "Well, what about that sailing book?"

While we walked to her boat, Penny told me about her sailing experience. Like Katy, she had begun sailing as a kid. When she was a teenager, she had saved up her money and bought her own sailboat. After college, she crewed on boats in the Caribbean, helping less experienced owners learn how to manage their boats and sail properly. It wasn't long before she realized that she could get paid for teaching people how to sail. She got her certification and had been a sailing instructor ever since—first in Texas and now here in Florida.

I started to ask Penny how she knew Captain Dan in Texas, but she interrupted me by pointing proudly at her boat.

"Here she is: *Pretty in Pink*, my baby," Penny said with pride.

"Wow, I didn't know you could get pink canvas for a boat," I said, marveling at the liberal use of pink all over the boat.

"You can get pink anything these days," Penny said with a smile. "I've even written to several manufacturers of sailing clothing to ask them to make ladies' versions of their clothes in pink. You know, one day, I might even start my own ladies' sailing clothing and accessories line," she confided. "Everything would be in shades of pink."

I was speechless, but luckily Penny went down below before I could come up with a reply.

While she was gone, I checked my phone. A text from my mother, no surprise.

The hospital?! What's wrong?!

There were a number of other texts along that line. I ignored them for now. Probably a bad idea, but I was feeling reckless.

Penny hopped down to the dock, holding a book in her hand. "Here you go. Why don't you read the first couple of chapters and then we can talk through it later? You should also plan to join our ladies' sailing lesson on Thursday. Meet here at the boat at eleven."

As I took the book from Penny, I looked at her chewed-off nails. "Penny, I meant to ask you about your nails. You had such a lovely manicure when I first met you. Long pink nails."

"Oh, yeah. I don't normally go in for that sort of thing. Nancy had me over to her place for a girls' wine-and-nails night. Do you know Alejandra from the Sailor's Corner Cafe?" I nodded, trying to imagine Nancy hosting any sort of party without snarling at her guests. "She brought over all of these press-on nails for us to look at. She's a trained nail artist, you know. She's only waitressing until she can save up enough money to open her own nail salon. Alejandra is such a sweet girl, so I agreed to be her guinea pig."

"Did Chief Dalton tell you what I found at the murder scene?" Penny furrowed her brow. "A pink fingernail."

She smiled. "Oh, that. Yes, he told me about that. It wasn't mine. I ended up taking my nails off right after I saw you that day." She choked up but continued. "The day after the murder."

"So you weren't on *Marjorie Jane* that night?"

"Of course not." She tapped the book. "First two chapters, right?" She waved at someone docking their boat. "I better go help them. See you Thursday."

* * *

When I got to the end of Penny's dock, I saw Jack walking across the patio toward the parking lot carrying a tote bag. It reminded me that Scooter had said he had a surprise for me in the navy-blue tote bag of his. I'd have to remember to ask him about it later, but now was my chance to speak with Sandy while Jack was away. I hurried down C Dock to their boat. Sandy was sitting in the cockpit holding a book, but instead of reading it, she was staring blankly off into space. I tapped on the side of the boat to get her attention.

"Mollie, how are you?" she said. "We waited at the hospital to see how you were, but you must have left without us spotting you. Come on aboard and I'll make some coffee. I even have some chocolate chip cookies from Penelope's Sugar Shack to go with it."

At the mention of cookies, I felt my anxiety levels abate. She seemed happy to see me, despite the fact that her husband had assaulted me the night before. I sat in the cockpit while Sandy brewed the coffee. I picked up the romance novel she was reading: *Revenge of the Jilted Lover*. Not really my cup of tea.

She passed up the cookies and two mugs of coffee. "That bump on your head looks just awful," she said, settling back against the cushions. "A tourist got hit by a coconut last year. They should put signs up warning people about the dangers of falling coconuts."

I put down my coffee cup. "But I wasn't hit by a coconut. I thought the police talked to you about this."

She waved her hand at me. "They asked us about it last night. You really must have been delirious when you came to, saying that Jack was responsible. A concussion can do that, you know. Those coconuts sure are dangerous."

"But it wasn't a coconut."

"Of course it was. When I found you on the trail, there was a coconut next to your head."

"Maybe it was the coconut that Jack used to hit me on the head with," I said, gripping my coffee cup tightly.

"Are you sure they should have let you out of the hospital so soon?" she asked in a soothing voice. "You might still be experiencing some—what do they call them —delusions?"

"It wasn't a delusion, Sandy. I saw Jack on the beach with two guys. I think he's involved in some sort of criminal activity. I overheard their conversation, and when Jack caught me, he assaulted me. That's what happened. It wasn't any delusion."

"No, that can't be. Jack was with me all night, and he was still on the boat when I went for my regular evening walk. When I found you, no one else was around."

"Maybe you're the one who's suffering from delusions!" I snapped. I took a deep breath. That had probably been a bit harsh. I squeezed Sandy's hand. "It's just that you told me about the issues you and Jack have been having. You also mentioned your other symptoms, like your cuts and bruises." Sandy slumped in her seat. "How can you be sure Jack was really here with you? After all, you said that sometimes you have episodes where you don't remember what happened."

"I said Jack's innocent! He was here all night with me. He couldn't have done it!" Sandy shouted as she rubbed her temples. "See what you did. My headache has come back. I'm not supposed to get into stressful situations." She glared at me. "I think it's about time you left, don't you?" She stormed down below while I sheepishly climbed off the boat.

How could I have treated her like that? As a member of FAROUT, I was supposed to support those who suffered from the trauma of being abducted. I'd badgered poor Sandy and made things worse. Lola would have done a better job of managing this situation, I thought to myself bitterly. I might as well tell Brian that he should take me out of the running for the investigative reporter job.

I went back to the patio, sat at one of the tables, took a deep breath, and typed up an email.

Just wanted to check in and see what you thought of my report. I know it's not very good. The more I think about it, the more I realize that I'm not cut out for this job. I just made a mess of a follow-up interview with the subject. You should probably go ahead and tell the board of directors to give the job to Lola. I'll understand.

I hit Send, then leaned back in my chair and watched the boats slowly swinging back and forth on their mooring balls, while wondering if I should keep pursuing the murder investigation or give up on that too.

CHAPTER 10
WEEVILS

CHOCOLATE. I NEEDED CHOCOLATE TO help me figure out what to do. A lot of chocolate. I started to worry that Nancy and Ned might run low on their supply of dark chocolate butterscotch crunch. They probably hadn't counted on me being their biggest customer, no doubt followed closely by Katy and Sam.

As I walked across the patio to the office, I saw Mr. and Mrs. Diamond sitting at a table looking at some nautical charts and guidebooks. Probably their next adventure, I imagined. They seemed so carefree and happy together. Maybe that would be Scooter and me one day. Sipping on tropical drinks without a care in the world and making plans to sail *Marjorie Jane* to an exotic island.

Hopefully, Mr. and Mrs. Diamond wouldn't end up like Jack and Sandy: a criminal mastermind and an alien abductee. Although, having seen Jack in action, it was probably more like a wannabe criminal mastermind.

I swung open the screen door and walked straight over to the display of chocolate bars on the counter.

"Aren't you forgetting something?" Nancy asked, picking up her flyswatter.

"Oops, sorry about that," I said, quickly closing the door. I grabbed a bar and passed it to her.

"How do you manage to stay so slim eating all this chocolate?" she asked.

"Scooter eats his fair share, especially lately. He really doesn't handle things like blood and murder very well. Giving him some chocolate helps to calm his nerves."

"Sounds reasonable," Nancy agreed. She looked at my forehead. I was beginning to feel like some sort of unicorn with this thing sticking out of my head, a curiosity that everyone wanted to inspect. "That's a real beauty," she said. "Have you been putting any cream on it to help bring down the inflammation and speed up the healing process?"

"No, the only thing the doctor gave me was some painkillers. Personally, I find that chocolate works better than the pills." I wondered why she hadn't asked me how I got the lump. Then I realized that in a community as small as the marina, there probably weren't any secrets she didn't already know. I sighed while Nancy rang the chocolate up. She probably thought I'd imagined Jack attacking me too. Of course, she'd take his side. I was just the new chick on the block, or the dock in this case.

After she handed me my chocolate and my change, she reached into a drawer behind her and pulled out a tube of ointment. "Why don't you try this?" she asked. "It's something I concocted. I make herbal remedies using the plants that my daughter grows in her garden. It'll help soothe your head and bring down some of that swelling."

I was torn. I wanted to rip open the chocolate bar, but Nancy was being so nice that I thought I should take a look at the ointment. Greed lost. Politeness won. "What's in it?"

Nancy rattled off a whole list of things I'd never heard of, presumably the Latin names of plants. "There's nothing in there that can harm you. Go on, take it and give it a try. Let me know how it works. I'm always looking for feedback on what people think of my remedies."

I shrugged. It couldn't hurt. "How much do I owe you?"

"Nothing. It's my gift. It's the least I can do after what happened to you."

"So...what did you hear about what happened to me?" I asked cautiously.

Nancy replied just as cautiously. "I heard some conflicting stories. Everyone seems to think you got hit by a coconut. It does happen from time to time, but..."

"But what?"

"But I also heard that Jack attacked you." She fiddled with the brochures on the counter. "Is that true? Did Jack attack you?"

"You're the first person to think that might be what happened," I said as I unwrapped the chocolate bar and broke off two squares. I handed one to Nancy and kept the other for myself. "Everyone else thinks I imagined it."

She looked at me in silence while she ate her chocolate. Then she leaned over and lowered her voice. "Just between you and me, Jack has a bit of a temper. Lately, he's had a lot on his mind, so—"

She was interrupted by the door swinging open as Katy and Sam ran into the store. "Grandma, grandma!" they screamed. "Can we have some candy?" Nancy smiled and handed each of them a lollipop. Katy unwrapped hers while she said hi to me. Sam dove straight into his lollipop, ignoring me completely. I could relate. There were days when I just wanted to eat candy without having to go through all the social niceties.

It was apparent that Nancy was too caught

up with the grandkids to tell me any more about Jack. I went outside and sat on the patio. Mrs. Moto spotted me and ran over. I bet she believed me about Jack. Or she didn't care. It didn't really matter. Either way, she jumped on my lap and started purring. Who doesn't love a purring cat when they're feeling a bit down? She seemed offended when I told her she couldn't have any chocolate, even after I explained to her that it was poisonous to cats. Fortunately, all was forgiven when I gave her the empty wrapper to play with.

* * *

While Mrs. Moto batted the crumpled paper back and forth, I looked through the book Penny had loaned me. It was full of chapters on topics like "dead reckoning" and "points of sail." To be honest, it all seemed rather dull. Toward the end of the book was a chapter entitled "Cooking on Board." This was more my kind of thing.

I spent the next hour happily reading

about how to store grains so you didn't get weevils in them (use lots of bay leaves), keeping things (like cheese) in your bilge so they stay cool, 101 uses for your pressure cooker (clearly something I'd have to invest in), and recipes that were easy to make when you were underway. There was even a recipe for brownies.

I put the book down on the table and thought about everything that was involved in cooking on a boat in a tiny galley. Mrs. Moto knocked the wrapper off the table, stared at it for a few moments, then stared at me for a few moments. When I made no effort to pick it up off the ground, she lay on the book and closed her eyes. Clearly, all that playing had tuckered her out.

While the calico slept, I put my feet up on the chair across from me and thought about Captain Dan's murder and Jack's attack on me. I might have dozed off too. Next thing I knew, I heard a loud crash and someone screaming, "Put her in reverse, quick!"

I opened my eyes and saw Ned run out of the office to help a frantic-looking couple who were trying to tie up their boat to the fuel dock. "New boat owners," he muttered as he rushed past. He glanced back at me. "You better not let Nancy see that cat!" I think there had been a chapter in my book about how to dock a boat. That might be a good one to read.

The noise had disturbed Mrs. Moto from her slumber. She stretched and nudged at my hand, indicating exactly where she needed to be scratched. Once all of her itchy spots were tended to, she sniffed at the book, then poked between the pages with her paws.

"Be careful, Mrs. Moto," I said, trying to pull the book away from her. She batted my hand away, persisted in her labors, and eventually extracted a folded piece of paper.

"What's that?" I asked. I picked up the chocolate bar wrapper from the ground and gave it to her in exchange for her discovery. I unfolded it and smoothed it out on the table. It was a sales invoice for a car made out to Penny from a place called Cowboy Bob's Automotive Ranch, dated a couple of years ago. Could that be where she'd bought her pink convertible? If so, she'd gotten a heck of a deal on it. I guess Cowboy Bob could do amazing deals because he had such a big inventory. I knew that because it said so right under his logo.

I looked at the address for Cowboy Bob's Automotive Ranch with surprise. It was located in the same city in Texas where FAROUT was headquartered. I wondered if Brian was familiar with the place. Imagine what a coincidence it would be if Brian and Penny knew each other. Maybe Penny knew about FAROUT and was even a member. I thought about how great it would be to have a fellow believer to speak with. If that were the case, she would be able to help me out with Sandy's case.

While I tucked the paper into my purse, Mrs. Moto jumped off the table and ran down to the beach. Not one minute later, Nancy came out of the office and yelled to Ned, "Did you get those folks docked okay?"

"Yep, they're all tied off. Just going to fill them up with diesel and water, and then I'll be back in to help."

* * *

While I was napping, Scooter had texted to say that he and Ben were working on the boat, installing one of the new toys he had purchased at Melvin's Marine Emporium. Calypso music was blaring from the speakers when I got there. It brought back memories of the island where Scooter and I had honeymooned. It was the kind of music that made you want to kick off your shoes and dance on the beach.

Scooter and Ben were on deck, surrounded by toolboxes. Their heads were stuck in what Scooter called an "anchor locker," where the anchor chain was stored. I thought of it more as *Marjorie Jane*'s jewelry box. After all, Scooter was planning on buying a lot of expensive, sparkly chain to store in there. I could make out some swearing from inside. I guess the guys weren't exactly in a festive, dancing kind of mood.

"How's it going?" I yelled over the music. Scooter startled and bumped his head against the side of the anchor locker. He sat up and grimaced as he rubbed his head. "Oh, you poor thing." I rushed over and looked at his forehead. "I think you're going to have a bump there. Hey, we'll be matching!"

Scooter looked dubious about the merits of matching bumps. At least his would be hidden underneath his dark hair. "Ouch, that hurts," he said as he got to his feet.

"Maybe we can have a contest to see who has the biggest bump and who keeps theirs the longest."

"No thanks," he said. "Do you have any ibuprofen? I'm in agony." I fished a bottle out of my purse. It was a good thing he couldn't see the tiny cut on his head and the streak of blood. If he could, he'd need far more than some over-the-counter pain relievers.

"Why don't you go down below and take a couple of these?" I handed him the bottle. "While you're at it, you might want to get a wet washcloth and wipe the blood off your forehead."

Scooter moaned. "Blood? There's blood?"

"Just a little bit. You'll be fine. I'll be down in a minute. I want to see what you and Ben have been up to first."

Ben put down a screwdriver and gestured for me to look inside the anchor locker. I set my purse on the deck and peered inside. "We're installing a windlass."

"A wind-what?"

"It's an electric windlass. It raises and lowers the anchor for you so you don't have to do it yourself. I'd love to have one of these on my boat," he said as he stroked the metal contraption. "But at least I'm young and fit." He flexed his biceps. "So I can pull up my own anchor and chain by myself." When he saw the look on my face, he added, "No offense, Mollie, but you're a tiny lady and I'm guessing you don't work out." Hmm. Was it that obvious? "Scooter could probably manage just fine, but you both are getting up in age, and sometimes it's easier for older folks to use an electric windlass."

I didn't like where this conversation was

going. Sure, Scooter was a bit older than me, and he had an unnatural fear of blood, but he was still fit and strong. I'm sure that he could lift the anchor up manually. I glanced down at my arms. Maybe it wouldn't hurt to start hitting the gym.

"I'm having Scooter help me as I work on things so that he learns how everything operates. You should join in too. It can't hurt to have everyone on the crew be able to fix stuff."

"When my car breaks, I take it to the garage. Why would I want to fix things when the boat breaks?"

"Well, a lot of people hire folks to fix stuff for them, which is great for me. Keeps me in beer money, but there'll be a day when you're sailing somewhere, and you're all alone. Then who are you going to get to fix stuff then?"

Good question. I wasn't sure I liked the obvious answer. "I should probably go check on Scooter."

"Hope his head's okay. I've just got a few things to finish up here, and then I'll head off for the evening."

* * *

After reassuring Scooter that his forehead was fine, we decided to sit in the cockpit and have sundowners. Scooter had to explain what they were, but once he did, it made sense—a drink that you had while the sun went down. This was the kind of boating tradition I could really get into.

It was a pleasant evening, which was a relief after the hot, sticky day. A cool breeze blew off the water, causing the palm trees to sway gently. We sipped on our gin and tonics and watched the dolphins play in the bay. Scooter sighed with contentment. "This is what it's all about. This is why I bought *Marjorie Jane* for you. Moments like this. Relaxing in the cockpit, sipping on a sundowner with my best girl."

It was almost enough to make me forget that having a sailboat had never been at the top of my wish list, let alone having a sailboat that someone had been murdered on. I took another sip of my gin and tonic and tried to focus on the gorgeous sunset instead.

Unfortunately, the peace and quiet were shattered by the sound of a dinghy going by. "Scooter, look—that's Jack!" I watched as he pointed his dinghy toward the far end of the beach, where I had overheard him the previous night. "He's going back to that same spot. I wonder if he's going to meet those guys again. Do you think he managed to find the money he owes them?"

"That reminds me," Scooter said. "I forgot to tell you that Chief Dalton called earlier. He checked out those two guys you saw at the beach. Their names are Fred Rollins and Wayne Grimm. They've both been in trouble with the law before, but they couldn't have been involved in Captain Dan's...you know..." His voice trailed off. He took a sip of his drink and continued. "They both have an alibi for that night. Lots of people can confirm that they were at the Tipsy Pirate the whole night."

I thought about this. "So that must mean he believed me when I said I saw them on the beach."

"Well, he did say he had an obligation to follow up all potential leads. He also reiterated the fact that Jack had an alibi for the night of your accident as well." He hesitated. "The chief wanted me to mention to you again that people do get hit on the head from time to time by coconuts."

The thought of his coconut theory and those bushy eyebrows made me fume. I drained the rest of my drink. "Why don't you fix me another one, Scooter?"

A few minutes later, Scooter handed me a fresh drink, along with a bowl of pretzels. "What are you thinking about, my little sweet potato?"

"I'm trying to work through all the suspects in Captain Dan's...you know." I scooped up some pretzels. "If the crew-cut guy and his bearded friend didn't...you know...then who did?" Scooter looked relieved that I'd managed to avoid saying "murder" and "kill" out loud. "Let's see, we have five potential suspects—Sandy, Jack, Ned, Nancy, and Penny."

"What about Ben?" Scooter asked as he pulled the pretzel bowl toward him.

"He's a possibility."

"I was just kidding. I can't imagine Ben being involved. Heck, I can't imagine any of them being involved."

"Well, I can. Some more than others. Take Jack, for example. We know he's mixed up in selling stolen marine equipment, which he got from Captain Dan. It sounds like the deal went sour, and maybe that's why he...you know." Scooter appeared unconvinced. "And don't forget, Captain Dan cheated him before on some anchor chain."

"I don't know. Is that really enough to make you want to...you know...?"

"Well, if it wasn't over money, maybe it was over love. You saw how Captain Dan was flirting with Sandy. Jealousy is a powerful motive."

"That's true. I wouldn't like it if anyone flirted with you," Scooter said, kissing my hand with a flourish. "What about Sandy?

Does she know about Jack's illegal operation?"

"That's a good question. I'll have to follow up with her." I took a sip of my drink. "That is, if I can get her to talk to me again." Scooter looked at me questioningly. "Don't ask. Let's just say, I'm probably not cut out to be an investigative reporter."

I stared off into space, reflecting on the trauma I'd caused Sandy with my thoughtless questioning. "Earth to Mollie," Scooter said. "Tell me about your other suspects."

"Well, there's Ned and Nancy."

Scooter scoffed. "They're a bit older, probably in their late fifties. I can't picture either of them hitting Captain Dan over the head with a winch handle with enough force to kill him. Especially Nancy. She's a tiny thing. I know you said she has a temper, but still." Scooter gasped when he realized what he had said. He took a large gulp of his drink.

"I thought that at first about Nancy, but then I saw her lifting heavy boxes at the store, and I know she exercises regularly. As for Ned, even though he's had knee replacements and has some arthritis, he's still in really good shape as well, what with working outside and helping out with boats."

"Okay, so maybe they were fit enough, but why?" he asked.

"They blamed Captain Dan when the previous owners of *Marjorie Jane* stuck them with an unpaid bill."

"Sure, but is that reason enough to murder someone? It's not like that would help them get their money back."

"True. But Nancy implied that there might be more to their grudge than just that. And don't forget about the pink fingernail I found by the galley. Nancy was wearing pink press-on nails the day of the murder. She could have been on our boat that night."

"What about Sandy? Was she wearing press-on nails too?"

"No, her nails are neatly manicured, but she wasn't wearing any nail polish that day. I think I would rule her out because she's so sickly, what with her headaches and poor sleeping. But if she were angry enough and had adrenaline running through her system, then maybe she could have done it."

"What does she have to be angry about?"

"Captain Dan cheated Jack out of a lot of money. And they're already having financial difficulties. What if the fact that they have to sell their boat and move back to their condo pushed her over the edge?"

"I suppose."

"But, like we talked about before, it's more likely that it was the other way around and Jack did it."

"What about Penny?"

"Penny also had a pink manicure the day of the murder. The fingernail could be hers as well as Nancy's. And don't forget, I overheard Penny arguing with Captain Dan about how he cheated her out of some money." There were two pretzels left in the bowl. I took one and offered Scooter the other. "They knew each other before in Texas. I can't figure out why Penny is lying about that. She claims she didn't meet him until she moved up here."

I went down below and grabbed the bag of

pretzels from the galley. Sometimes it's nice to put snacks in decorative serving bowls, but then you have to keep refilling them. Eating directly from the bag is so much more efficient. I shoved a few pretzels in my mouth and passed the bag to Scooter.

"Did you know that Penny's car is pink? I'm sure the inside of her boat is completely pink too." He smiled. He knew how I felt about pink.

"So why wasn't Ben on your list?" Scooter asked, passing the bag back to me.

"Oh, I don't know. He seems so goofy. I can't imagine him being serious enough to, you know..."

"He was pretty serious the night of the barbecue," Scooter reminded me. "Remember how he got into it with Captain Dan?"

"That's true," I said. "But he did say his outboard was broken that night, so how could he get back to the marina?"

"Why didn't he row?" Scooter asked.

"He said he dropped his oars in the water. See what I mean about goofy? I also can't quite figure out his financial situation. One minute he's complaining about being broke; the next minute I see him with a wad of cash. Where did he get the money from? Maybe he did find a way to get back to the marina that night, after all. Did he steal the money from Captain Dan, after he offed him?" I thought about the scrap of paper Mrs. Moto had brought to me on the beach. "Don't forget that IOU with what looked like Ben's name on it. Did he owe money to someone, and was it enough to drive him to murder?"

Scooter put his glass down. "How about if we talk about more cheerful subjects for a while? Do you have any more chocolate left?"

"Sorry, you're out of luck. But I've still got some breath mints." I looked around the cockpit. "What did I do with my purse, anyway? Have you seen it?"

"Nope, I haven't touched it."

"Let's see, I gave you some ibuprofen, then you went down below. Ben showed me the windlass that you're installing...that's it! I set my purse down by the anchor locker." I walked up to the bow.

As I was on my way back to the cockpit, I remembered the compass. "Scooter, you know what I didn't do yesterday? Give the compass to Chief Dalton."

"Well, that's understandable, what with getting hit on the head. We can drop it off tomorrow."

I searched through my bag, unzipping all the compartments. "It's not here!"

"Of course it is."

"No, seriously, it's gone."

"You probably left it back at the house," Scooter said distractedly as he watched one of the dolphins leap into the air. "You've got so much crammed into that thing that the compass could be anywhere and you wouldn't know it."

"I know my purse inside and out. I know exactly how many chocolate bars I have in it at all times, whether I have any change, and if I have a valuable compass inside. It was there and now it's gone, and the only person who could have taken it was Ben."

CHAPTER 11
DISNEYLAND

SCOOTER AND I HAD A BIT of a lively debate the next morning on the subject of Ben. He was convinced that I had taken the compass out of my purse the night we came back from the hospital and that it was lying around somewhere in the house. I was convinced that the compass had been in my purse when I left it by the anchor locker. The only reasonable explanation I had for its disappearance was that Ben had taken it. Scooter suggested that aliens might have abducted the compass.

I'm pretty sure he was being sarcastic.

Personally, I think sarcasm is an unfair debating technique, especially before I've had my second mocha. I retaliated by eating some of Scooter's precious Froot Loops for breakfast when he wasn't looking.

In the end, we agreed that since I didn't have any proof that Ben had stolen the compass, we'd still have Ben work on the boat, provided Scooter kept a close eye on him. We also agreed that Scooter owed me a foot rub. It's possible he might not remember that last part of the agreement because he was upstairs getting dressed when it was discussed.

Scooter suggested that I meet up with them later, as while two was company, three was a crowd, especially on a thirty-eight-foot boat with stuff strewn all around the place. I wasn't hard to persuade. The thought of two guys working in a confined space without air conditioning in this hot, muggy weather sounded like a recipe for a real stink-fest.

While the guys toiled away on the boat, I headed to the marina lounge. I sat in one of the comfy chairs, got out my laptop, and connected to the marina Wi-Fi. I heard a scratching sound at the door. I ignored it. It got louder. I continued to ignore it. Then the yowling started. I tried to ignore it but had to give up. I reluctantly got up and let Mrs. Moto in. She jumped on my chair, rolled on her back, and meowed insistently until I rubbed her belly.

Finally, I picked her up, sat down, and set her next to me. I logged into my email account and scanned through my messages. My heart skipped a beat when I saw one from Brian Morrison with the subject line, "Watch Out for Lola!"

Watching out for Lola kind of goes without saying. She's someone who would stick a knife in your back, then ask you if you wanted her autograph while she wiped your blood off the blade. Lola fancies herself as something of a celebrity. She's been an extra on a number of science fiction shows, as well as movies that have gone straight to DVD. She usually plays an alien, although she's very picky about which aliens she'll portray. She refuses to wear any prosthetics, wigs, or makeup that conceals her long, red hair, her big, blue eyes, or her curvaceous figure. The casting directors are more than happy to agree to her demands.

I first met Lola five years ago when I attended the FAROUT convention in Texas. She was working at the registration desk, although "working" is a bit of an exaggeration. She was surrounded by a number of nerdy-looking guys, twirling her hair and regaling them with stories of her latest role as Xandra, a sexy alien princess from the outer moon of a planet in a galaxy far, far away. Thankfully, her character didn't have any speaking lines and was killed in the first scene by a large lizard-like creature with two heads. Not that that deterred her fans.

Eventually, I tired of watching her flirt and the guys drool in response. I pushed my way through the nerds, grabbed my badge, and eagerly went to attend my first session on "Signs You've Been Abducted by Aliens." Who knew that session would lead to where I was today—vying with Lola for the investigative reporter job? I sighed and opened Brian's email.

Bad news. Lola submitted her report and it's a doozy. She claims to have evidence of a government cover-up of a UFO landing next to Space Mountain in Disneyland. She states that the government is hiding the evidence inside Sleeping Beauty Castle. She has interviews with some Disneyland employees who've seen the spaceship (their identities are protected, of course) and she has photographs taken with a hidden camera (they're blurry, but you can make out what appears to be aliens in the background). The board of directors is very impressed. I think they're going to recommend that Lola be appointed as the new investigative reporter.

Of course they were going to appoint Lola. Not only did she have the scoop of the century, all four members of the board were also members of Lola's fan club.

I think Mrs. Moto sensed how upset I was. She reached up, batted me on my chin with her paw, and meowed softly. I stroked her back while I tried to figure out what I could do to make sure Lola didn't succeed. Getting a career as a sexy alien extra didn't seem like a viable option in the time I had left before the next board meeting.

Somehow, I had to convince Sandy to speak with me—not only about Jack's illegal sideline, but also about her alien abduction. Maybe I could get her to recall details about the spaceship and what the aliens did to her. It probably couldn't compete with Lola's Disneyland exposé, but it was worth a shot.

Considering the way Sandy had reacted the last time I saw her, I needed to find an opening that would make her want to chat. Mrs. Moto looked at me and meowed. That was it! Sandy had a soft spot for her cat. I'd ask her about taking care of Mrs. Moto when they went out of town, then slowly work the conversation around to Jack and to her abduction.

* * *

Before I tackled Sandy, I stopped by the Sailor's Corner Cafe to pick up some lunch for the guys.

"Hi, there," Alejandra said over her shoulder as she walked past me carrying a tray laden with chocolate shakes. "I'll be right with you."

I picked up a menu from the counter and looked at today's specials. The Captain's Chili sounded good, as did the Boatswain's Burger. But what sounded even better was one of those shakes.

Alejandra set her tray down on the counter. "Are you here on your own today?"

"Just picking up some lunch to take back to the boat."

She whipped out her pad and pen. "What'll it be?"

"I'll take three of the Boatswain's Burgers with fries."

"No problem. Anything else?"

"How about a chocolate shake while I'm waiting?"

The young woman smiled. "Coming right up."

I sat on a stool at the counter and watched as she scooped dark chocolate ice cream into a blender, then added some full-fat milk along with a generous dollop of thick chocolate syrup. A few minutes later she set the milkshake in front of me. "Here you go."

I murmured my thanks between sips. Alejandra sat on a stool next to me, slipped off her sandals, and flexed her feet back and forth. I noticed her toenails were painted with purple-and-silver stripes. "It must be hard to run around on your feet all day," I said, conscious that the only thing my toenails had going for them was a lack of fungus.

"It is, but people tip well, especially the tourists," she said. "Every penny I save means I'm one step closer to opening my own nail salon."

"How did you get into doing nails?"

"During high school, my best friend and I would get together on Sunday nights to do our homework. When we were done, we'd reward ourselves by giving each other manicures." Alejandra looked at her fingernails, which coordinated with her toes. "We had so much fun. When I graduated, I didn't know what I wanted to do with my life, so I found a job waitressing here. I got lots of compliments on my nails, and I thought to myself, here's something I love to do that I could make a living at. I finished nail-technician training, and I'm taking some small-business classes at the community college. Now all I have to do is win the lottery so I can open my nail salon."

A woman at one of the tables waved at Alejandra. "Excuse me for a sec, *chica*," she said, grabbing her tray and bustling over to help. I continued sipping my shake while she refilled ice teas and sodas. After she was done, she came back and perched on one of the stools.

"What about your nails, Mollie? Have you ever thought of having a manicure?"

I looked down at my hands. Although I didn't bite my nails, they weren't much to look at. I kept them short and pretty much ignored them. "I've never really had a manicure."

"Really?" she asked. "Never?"

"Hard to believe, I know. It seems like a lot of work, especially when I see people with full-on nails like Nancy."

"Nancy is very particular about her nails," Alejandra said. "She's actually been one of my biggest supporters, always encouraging me about the nail salon. We get together occasionally for girls' nights. We try out the latest nail products over a few glasses of wine. Lately, she's been into press-on nails. They're really easy to do."

The waitress dashed off to take care of another customer, while I reflected on the state of my cuticles. She pointed out a few of the town's attractions on a souvenir map, then came back to the counter with a smile. "You must have gotten a good tip," I said.

"I'll say," she said, tucking some bills into the pocket of her apron. "Those are the kind of customers I like."

"Did you know I found a press-on fingernail on *Marjorie Jane* the night Captain Dan was murdered?"

"You did?" Alejandra asked while she rolled up silverware into paper napkins. "What did it look like?"

"It was pink with a white starfish on it." I

thought about it for a minute. "You know, I'm surprised that Chief Dalton didn't ask you about it. You must be the local expert on nails."

Alejandra laughed. "Wouldn't that be funny—being an expert witness on nails."

"Well, you'd probably know what kind it was, where it was bought, and who in town had similar nails."

"I don't know about that. But it would be interesting to have a look at it. I wonder whose it was."

I took another sip of my shake. The straw made that disappointing slurping noise that lets you know you're nearing the bottom of the glass. I twirled my straw and said, "The day of the murder, I noticed that Penny's nails were identical to the one I found. At least I think they were. I tried to get a look the next day, but she had destroyed her manicure. She chews her nails by the way." Alejandra made a tsk-tsk sound. "Nancy also had a similar manicure. Maybe the nail belonged to one of them."

"You know, Penny and Nancy did have

identical manicures. Those pink press-on nails were ones that I brought over to Nancy's last week for the girls' nights. Penny's eyes lit up when she saw the pink color. But what would either of them be doing on your boat?"

"That's a very good question," I said.

* * *

After an uncomfortable lunch with Scooter and Ben—I still wasn't convinced that Ben hadn't been responsible for the missing compass—I decided it was time to summon up my courage and go see Sandy. I hoped Jack wasn't on the boat. The last thing I wanted was to run into him again. I rubbed the lump on my head. It was slowly going down, but it still ached a little bit. The bigger issue was that I was having a hard time coordinating its blue-and-purple color to my outfits. Imagine having to coordinate all your outfits to your manicure as well.

I took a deep breath as I walked over to Jack and Sandy's boat. As I got closer, I saw them standing on the dock. "Just stay out of it," Jack said. "It's none of your business!"

"But it is my business," Sandy replied, her voice trembling. "How could it not be my business? You sunk all our money into this venture and look what's happened as a result. We're broke, we have to sell our boat, and—worst of all—we have to give up Mrs. Moto."

"Is that all you're worried about—the cat?" he replied with venom. "You pay more attention to it than to me."

"That's not true."

"No, you're right; it isn't true. You pay more attention to him than to me. Or at least you did. Now that he's gone, all you can think about is the stupid cat and money."

As Sandy started sobbing, I felt something rub against my leg. I looked down and there was Mrs. Moto staring up at me. I scooped her into my arms. "Don't worry, kitty. It'll be okay." She began playing with my earrings, so I guess she was feeling better. Although I don't do my nails, I always wear earrings. We each do girly in our own way, I guess.

As I was cuddling Mrs. Moto, Jack stormed past. He was in such a huff, I don't even think he noticed me. I walked up to Sandy and handed her cat to her.

"Where have you been?" she asked, drying her tears on the soft fur. "I've been searching for you everywhere." She turned to me and sniffled. "Thanks for bringing her back."

"I saw you and Jack arguing," I said. "I thought you could use a cat cuddle."

Sandy smiled. "You're right. Mrs. Moto is the only good thing in my life right now."

"What were you fighting about?"

"I've been trying to help with his business records. I've spent hours entering data into spreadsheets. Next thing you know, he's yelling at me, saying I did it all wrong. But I didn't. I matched everything up with his notes and invoices."

"What does he think you did wrong?" I asked.

"You know how he buys and sells marine equipment? I enter what items he's bought, the quantity, and how much he paid in one spreadsheet. Then in another, I enter what items he's sold, the quantity, and how much he's sold them for. That way I can calculate any profit that's been made." She shook her head. "Who am I kidding? There hasn't been any profit in a long time. It's been all losses."

"I don't know—it sounds like you're pretty organized." I actually didn't have a clue if she was organized or not. Data entry and spreadsheets mystified me. I preferred the written word to crunching numbers. "So what exactly was the problem?"

"I know he ordered twelve bicolor lights, but he says he never bought any at all. But I have a receipt saying that he sold them to some guy. So how could he have sold something he never bought in the first place? I just don't get it."

"What are bicolor lights?" I asked. Mrs. Moto meowed. I guess she was curious too.

"They're navigational lights you have on your boat at night. The port-side lights are red and the starboard lights are green. That way when you encounter another boat in the dark, you can tell by their lights what direction they're going in. Keeps you from crashing into each other."

Red and green lights—not the most fascinating topic, unless it involved decorating a Christmas tree. Mrs. Moto yawned. I was more polite and stifled mine.

Sandy set the calico down on the dock. "I'm so glad you came by, Mollie. Sometimes it's hard not having anyone to talk to."

I looked at Sandy's eyes. Not only were they bloodshot, but she had dark circles underneath them. "You look tired. How have you been sleeping lately?"

"More of the same. Jack tells me he caught me sleepwalking again last night." She shrugged. "I don't remember a thing, but he says he found me trying to climb into one of the dinghies."

"Yikes!" I said. "That could have been dangerous if you'd fallen in the water."

"That's what Jack says. Somehow he managed to guide me back onto the boat and into bed without me being aware of it." She rubbed her eyes. "He's been trying to get me to take sleeping pills at night, hoping they'll knock me out and keep me from sleepwalking."

That sounded dangerous to me. Who knew what was in those things? "Did you talk to your doctor about it?"

"No," she said. "Besides, we can't really afford to go to the doctor these days." I wondered how they could afford the sleeping pills and where Jack got them.

Sandy yawned. "You look like you could use a nap."

"That's probably a good idea." She rubbed her temples. "I feel another one of my headaches coming on again." She picked up Mrs. Moto. "Why don't you come snuggle with me?" The Japanese bobtail didn't look like she would object to a nap. "Was there anything else, Mollie? Or did you just come to drop the cat off?"

I decided to show more sensitivity than I had yesterday and not press her about the abduction. "No, that was it. Dropping Mrs. Moto off." As Sandy was getting on board her boat, I added, "I guess there is one other thing. Why did you and Jack decide not to go out of town? I meant to ask you before, but I completely forgot about it after Captain Dan's murder."

As soon as I mentioned Captain Dan, Sandy turned white and steadied herself by holding onto the side of her boat. "That was Jack. His business plans changed. He said he had to be here at the marina. I didn't ask any questions. Sorry that I didn't let you know about the change of plans."

"That's okay," I said. She was breathing rapidly, and sweat was beading on her brow. "Sandy, you really don't look good. Are you sure you're all right to be here on your own?"

"I'll be fine. It's the headache. I just need to lie down." She squeezed Mrs. Moto tightly. "Come on, time for our nap." The cat squirmed, jumped out of her arms, and tore down the dock. Sandy frowned, then went down below.

I wished I had been able to ask her more questions. There was more going on than simple alien abduction here, but what it was I wasn't sure. What I was sure of was that as soon as I got to the bottom of it, the story would completely wipe Lola's Disneyland scoop off the map.

* * *

As I was walking back to *Marjorie Jane*, I saw Jack come toward me, wearing another gaudy Hawaiian shirt. I tried to duck behind one of the palm trees, but the problem with palm trees is that their trunks are much narrower than my hips. There's really no place to hide.

"Is that you, Mollie?" Jack called out.

I reluctantly came out from behind the tree and glanced around to see if there were any witnesses in case he decided to assault me again. "Did you want to check and see how I'm doing?" I asked sarcastically.

He came closer and looked at my forehead. "That's a nasty lump. There was a tourist who got hit by a coconut last year. He had a bad lump on his head too, but I think yours is larger. It looks pretty painful."

"It wasn't a coconut and you know it,

Jack," I said as I backed up a few steps.

"What do you mean?" he replied. "Sandy found you on the trail with a coconut lying next to your head."

I scouted around to see if there was anything I could use to defend myself if things turned ugly. The only thing I saw were coconuts strewn at the bottom of the palm tree. I picked one up.

"See what I mean, Mollie? Those things are heavy. One of those falling from a tree could easily knock a person out."

"Just stay away, Jack," I said.

"Mollie, what's wrong with you?"

"What's wrong with me? What's wrong with you? You're the one who hit me on the head!"

"What! Are you crazy? I did no such thing." He advanced toward me. I held up my coconut. "Loss of memory can happen when you've had a head injury. I'm sure they explained that at the hospital."

"Just stop lying, Jack. You can't walk all over me like you do to your wife!"

"My wife? Why are you bringing up Sandy?

She doesn't have anything to do with this. She's the one who found you. She probably even saved your life."

"I was just over at your boat speaking with her. She's really upset. Not to mention really sick. I heard you yelling at her. How could you do that to a sick woman?" I shifted the coconut in my hands. They really were heavy. "Can you imagine what it would do to her if she knew what you were up to?"

"What in the world are you talking about?"

"When you realized that I saw you with those two hooligans, Fred Rollins and Wayne Grimm, and heard what it was you were up to, you panicked." Jack looked surprised at the mention of crew-cut guy and his bearded friend's names. "You tried to kill me because I discovered you were involved in something illegal. Isn't that right?"

"You're crazy. Just like Sandy. What are you talking about? I'm not involved in anything illegal."

"Oh yeah, then what were those two guys doing on the beach saying that you owed them money?"

"I don't owe anyone money."

"I don't believe you. I think you're up to your eyeballs in debt. I even heard you talking with someone at Melvin's Marine Emporium trying to sell him some stuff. Probably stuff you're trying to fence."

Jack's eyes turned cold. "Well, aren't you a little eavesdropper? Fine, yes, you caught me. I was trying to sell some stuff to Tony. Some stuff from the boat that we won't need anymore now that we're selling her. You've got quite the overactive imagination, you know. I can't imagine how Scooter puts up with it."

"Well, at least we're happily married."

"So are we." Jack frowned. "Why would you think we weren't?"

"I heard you two arguing, and Sandy says that things haven't been great between you two."

Jack looked down at the ground. "Sandy and I have been married for over thirty years. We've had our ups and downs like any other couple. And I'll admit, our financial difficulties have put a strain on our relationship, but we're working through it. Plus, as you pointed out, Sandy hasn't been physically well for quite some time. Her doctor has tried all sorts of things, but we haven't been able to come up with a treatment plan that works yet."

Things didn't add up. Sandy had said they couldn't afford a doctor, yet Jack said she was seeing one. Maybe all this talk about Sandy's treatment plan was just a ruse to play on my sympathies and make me forget about the assault.

I was about to tell Jack exactly that when Chief Dalton walked up. He looked at the coconut in my hands, raised an eyebrow, and asked, "Is everything okay here?"

"Did you know that this man"—I pointed at Jack with my coconut—"is still claiming that he didn't strike me over the head!"

"But I didn't!"

"Oh yeah, then how did I end up with this?" I said, pointing at my head with one hand and trying to balance the coconut in the other. Both the chief and Jack ignored my bump and stared at the coconut.

I almost threw the coconut at them in exasperation. "Just keep him away from me!"

Chief Dalton turned to Jack. "I was actually looking for you, sir. Would you mind coming down to the police station to answer a few questions."

"Questions? Questions about what?"

"Why don't I explain it to you down at the station?" His tone and manner made it seem like it wasn't an invitation.

"Fine, fine," Jack said. "But I've got a lot going on. I don't have much time for this sort of thing."

"Come along, then," the big man said as he ushered Jack down the path. I saw Mrs. Moto peek around a palm tree and hiss at Jack as he walked past her. Can't say I blamed her.

* * *

Scooter and Ben were determined to install something to do with the navigational lights before they called it quits for the night. They were so focused on the task at hand that they didn't even want dinner. My stomach doesn't let me get away with skipping meals. It lets me know in no uncertain terms that it needs to be fed every few hours.

I pulled Scooter aside, reminded him to keep an eye on Ben, and headed into town to find something to eat.

My earlier encounter with Jack had me on edge, so just to be safe, I took a sturdy flashlight with me. I figured it would come in handy not only to light my way, but also to fight back if needed. I thought about tucking a coconut in my purse too, but it didn't fit.

I walked along the boardwalk and paused at the dinghy dock. There were only two dinghies tied up, one of which belonged to Ben. The skull-and-crossbones sticker on the side made it easy to identify. His dinghy was covered in lots of patches. How long would it hold air before it deflated?

A Styrofoam cooler was floating in the water. Similar ones were used by fishing boat crews to transport fresh fish to the local restaurants. My flashlight kept cutting in and out as I walked to the edge of the dock to get a closer look. I opened it up, pulled out both batteries, and reinserted them, giving it a sharp tap as I closed the lid. I bent down to try to grab the cooler before it floated out to sea.

That's one of the reasons that we don't get more alien visitors. They're appalled by all the litter we have floating in the water and the damage we've done to the environment. I figured it was the least I could do, sparing the ocean from one more unnecessary piece of debris.

Fortunately, there was a nylon handle attached to the cooler, which I was able to reach by lying down on my stomach. I pulled it out of the water and set it on the dock. The cooler was taped shut with duct tape, which of course made me want to see what was inside.

I looked in my purse to see if I could find anything that could cut the cooler open. I didn't find a handy pocketknife, but I did find a bag of M&M'S. I munched on a few while I thought about my options. Then I had a horrifying thought. How was it I didn't know I had M&M'S in my purse? After the whole Ben-compass incident, I'd sworn to Scooter up and down that I knew the contents of my purse inside and out. I wasn't about to admit to him that I'd been wrong, so I decided to destroy the evidence by finishing the rest of them.

As I popped the last candy morsel in my mouth, I saw something out of the corner of my eye floating between the two dinghies. Probably another cooler. I aimed the flashlight toward it. It flashed in and out, then cut out, but not before I caught sight of a Hawaiian shirt. It wasn't a cooler—it was a body.

I grabbed an oar out of one of the dinghies and pulled the body toward me. As I held onto his shirt collar, it didn't take long to realize that the man was dead. And even without my flashlight working, it also didn't take long to figure out that it was Jack.

CHAPTER 12
LITTLE GREEN MEN

I WISHED I HAD MORE M&M'S. Why didn't I save them for a real emergency, like this? I got out my phone and dialed 911. The dispatcher said that Chief Dalton would be out right away and not to interfere with the crime scene, like last time. Yes, she actually said that.

While I waited for the chief and his bushy eyebrows to arrive, I took another look at Jack's body floating in the water. I wondered what had happened. Had he fallen into the water and accidentally drowned? Or had something more sinister occurred?

Then I thought about Sandy. How would she cope when she heard about her husband? Despite their difficulties, they'd been married for many years and it would be a huge shock. It didn't help that Sandy was dealing with so many physical ailments either. And somewhere lingering in her subconscious was the knowledge that she'd been abducted by aliens. Many people didn't remember or want to remember their experiences, but when they had a big enough shock, it all came flooding to the surface. I'd have to look out for her.

"Mrs. McGhie, what a surprise to find you here. You seem to specialize in finding bodies." Chief Dalton raised both of his eyebrows. "That makes two bodies in just four days, doesn't it?" His math was correct. I guess the ability to be able to do simple arithmetic was an important skill for police officers. That's probably why I never joined the force. I struggle with math. I'm also scared of guns.

"It looks like that's Jack Holt from what I can see," I said, ignoring his comment about the number of bodies I'd found to date.

He eyed me suspiciously. "And why would you say that? From his position in the water, you can't see his face. Unless you tampered with the crime scene. Is that what you did? Or perhaps you had something to do with how he got in the water. Is that the case?"

"Me?" I spluttered. "I didn't have anything to do with Jack's death. I just happened to be out for a walk when I saw him floating in the water."

"Then why do you think it's Mr. Holt?"

"From his shirt," I said. "I saw him wearing that same Hawaiian shirt earlier today when I was speaking with him. You were there—you saw it too. You must have had a good look at it when you were questioning him at the police station." I watched Chief Dalton's eyebrows do contortions. "What was that about, anyway? Did you finally get him to confess that he hit me over the head?"

"That's police business, completely unrelated to alien abductions," he said with a smirk. We watched as the EMTs lifted the body out of the water. "In any event, I have to admit you were right. It is Jack Holt."

I noticed a nasty lump on Jack's head. There seemed to be a lot of those going around these days. Maybe he hit his head when he fell into the water, or maybe somebody hit him over the head before throwing him into the water.

As the EMTs removed Jack's body, Scooter and Ben came rushing up.

"What happened?" Scooter asked.

"They found Jack floating in the water."

"They?" Scooter asked dubiously.

"Well, okay, by 'they,' I mean me," I said. "I was walking down to the dinghy dock when I noticed that Styrofoam container floating next to the dinghies. I pulled it out and tried to open it. That's when I saw a body floating nearby."

Scooter clutched his chest and turned pale. "You're not kidding, are you? Jack's really dead?"

"He is," I said, giving him a hug. Ben put his hands over his mouth for a few moments. Then he took a deep breath. "He was a nice guy. Always willing to lend a hand." He knelt down near the container. "I wonder what's inside?" he asked as he tried to pry the lid off. "Maybe it's beer. We could all probably use one about now."

"Hands off that, sir," Chief Dalton said as he came up behind Ben. He shifted his gaze to me. "You weren't going to try to hide this from me like you hid that fingernail the other day?"

"I didn't hide the fingernail. I just forgot about it," I said. "There's a big difference. And I was going to tell you about this. I just haven't had a chance. Besides, you should be grateful I pulled it out of the water, otherwise Jack's body might not have been discovered until the morning. It might have floated out to sea when the tide changed."

I was proud of myself for remembering about the tidal flow in the local waters. Scooter looked at me with pride too. Or maybe that was surprise.

"What might have floated out with the tide?" Nancy asked, sneaking up behind us with Ned in tow.

"Jack," I said.

"Jack? What are you talking about?" Ned asked.

"I found him floating in the water." I looked at their confused faces. "He's dead."

Ned gasped. "Jack...are you sure?" His eyes welled up. "I need to get out of here."

Nancy squeezed his arm. "Do you want me to come with you?"

"No, I just need a few minutes to myself."

Nancy watched him walk away, then looked at me. "That makes two bodies you've found, doesn't it?" Great, another math whiz. I guess simple arithmetic is important if you're a small-business owner too.

"That's not really the point, is it, Nancy? The question is whether or not it was a murder."

Nancy muttered, "That's all we need. Another murder at the marina. This really isn't the kind of publicity that's going to help us attract new customers."

By this point, Scooter had a glazed expression in his eyes and was noticeably unsteady. He pointed at something on the dock. "Is that what I think it is?" he asked.

Chief Dalton reached down and picked it up. "It's just an M&M'S bag, sir."

Scooter stared hopefully at it. "Are there any left?"

Nancy pushed Scooter aside. "Well, Chief, was it murder or not?" she asked impatiently.

"That's not for me to say. That's for the coroner to determine. Hopefully we'll know more tomorrow. In the meantime, I'll need to speak with everyone, just like last time. We'll also need to notify his wife."

"I'll come with you," Nancy said. "She'll probably need someone to support her when she hears the bad news."

"Fine. Why don't you go with Officer Moore? After you're finished there, I'll have a word with you and your husband." He turned to me. "Now, shall we start with you?"

* * *

Scooter had a minor meltdown the next morning when he went to pour some Froot

Loops into his bowl only to find there weren't any left. He looked at me accusingly. I suggested that aliens might have abducted his candy-colored, crunchy nuggets. After agreeing to disagree on the cause of the disappearing cereal, we headed to the Sailor's Corner Cafe for breakfast.

"Did you hear what happened at the marina last night?" Alejandra asked as we walked in the door. "There was another murder!"

"How do you know it was a murder?" Scooter asked.

"I overheard a couple of the police officers talking. They always come in here in the morning before their shift starts. While I was cashing them out I heard one of them say that a man had been struck with a heavy object, and then his body had been dumped in the water." She showed us to our table, handed us our menus, and said, "You know, I can't decide if all these murders are good for business or bad." She pointed to the crowded dining room. "We've been slammed with customers all morning and that's all they're talking about."

"They're probably looking for a side of gossip with their coffee," Scooter said as he pulled my chair out for me.

"Speaking of coffee," I said as I sat down.

"Coming right up." Alejandra grabbed a pot from the counter.

"So, what do you know about what happened?" she asked as she filled our cups up.

"Well, Mollie was the one who found the body," Scooter said as he passed me a couple of sugar packets.

"You were?" Alejandra gasped. "Wait a minute, wasn't it you who found Captain Dan when he was murdered, *chica*?" I nodded. "Wow, that makes, what..."

"Yes, yes, I know. Two bodies in four days," I said. "Can I get a short stack of blueberry pancakes and a couple of strips of bacon?"

"And I'll have a Western omelet with home fries," Scooter said as he handed Alejandra our menus.

"Why do they call them Western omelets?"

I mused as I sipped my coffee. "I know they have ham, green bell pepper, and onion in them, but what makes that Western?"

"Maybe the chefs wear tiny cowboy hats when they make them," Scooter said. "I remember the best Western omelet I ever had was at the little hole-in-the-wall place we ate at in Texas when we were there for your FAROUT convention. Do you remember that place?"

"I do. They had great French toast." I stirred some more sugar into my coffee. It was feeling like a three-pack morning. "Those are the best kinds of places. The ones you just happen to run across. If we hadn't stopped at that drugstore next door, we would have never found it."

"It was right across from that place with the funny name, wasn't it?" Scooter asked.

"Oh yeah, that used-car lot we made fun of. What was it called again?"

Scooter shook his head. "I can't remember. Something corny." He held out his cup for a refill as Alejandra passed by.

"Your order will be right up," she said.

"More coffee for you, Mollie?"

"Sure, why not? It was a long night. I'm struggling to wake up this morning."

As Alejandra filled my cup, she asked, "Who do you think did it?"

"Well, I have my suspicions," I said. The young woman leaned forward. "I saw Jack arguing with two guys on the beach the other night. That's the night I got this." I pointed at my forehead. My lump was going down, but you could still see it.

"Right, that's when the coconut hit you," she said. "I'm always telling the tourists to be careful of falling coconuts."

"It wasn't a—never mind. Anyway, I think Jack was into something dodgy. He was fencing stolen goods and he owed these guys money."

"Now, you don't know that for sure," Scooter said. "Let the police do their investigation."

A bell dinged from the kitchen. Alejandra said, "That's probably your order." As she placed our plates in front of us, Nancy, Katy, and Sam walked through the door.

Katy skipped up to us, followed by her brother. "Hi! Guess what grandma is getting us?" she asked.

"More chocolate?" I ventured.

"No, silly. It's too early in the morning for chocolate!" Katy said.

"Chocolate!" Sam shouted.

I tried again. "A kitten?"

"No, it's not a kitten," Katy said. "Grandma doesn't like kittens."

"Kittens!" Sam cried.

"You're really a terrible guesser," Katy said. "But I'll give you one more chance."

I thought long and hard about it. "Okay, let me see. Your grandma is going to get you an alligator."

Katy and Sam burst into giggles. "No, it's not an alligator," Katy said. "Grandma is going to get us cocoa for breakfast. And since we've been good this morning, we get to have extra marshmallows in it."

"Cocoa!" Sam shouted.

Nancy smiled behind them. "Come on, kids, our table's free. Go sit down, and I'm sure Alejandra will bring you your cocoa straight away." She watched as they ran over to the table. "I let them have cocoa every time we go out for breakfast. I can't figure out why they think it's such a treat. But the promise of extra marshmallows does seem to produce better behavior."

"Hey, whatever works," Scooter said.

"How long were the police there last night?" I asked.

"Thankfully, not as late as last time. Because it happened during the week, there were fewer people around for them to have to question."

"Alejandra was telling us that it was a murder, not an accident." I took a sip of coffee. "Have you heard anything about it?"

"Chief Dalton called this morning and said it could be homicide. It probably happened not too long before you found him, Mollie. Wasn't that around seven-thirty?"

Goose bumps covered my arms. "About then," I said, wrapping my arms around myself.

"Well, someone saw Jack earlier, around six."

"Do you know what happened?" I asked.

"Someone hit him over the head. Then he either fell or was pushed in the water. Who would do such a thing? And why? Sure, Jack had his faults, but he was a nice man. Ned is just devastated. He and Jack have been friends for years." Katy and Sam started to have a pretend sword fight with their knives. "I better go over there and break things up."

Scooter glanced over at the kids and smiled, then asked, "Before you go, Nancy, how's Sandy doing?"

"Not great. She ended up breaking down in hysterics. Pretty understandable. They took her to the hospital for the night and sedated her."

* * *

When I arrived at the hospital, I ran into the doctor who had treated me in the ER. "Hello there, Mrs. McGhie. Is everything okay? Have you been experiencing any side effects from the bump to your head? Those coconuts sure can be nasty."

"It wasn't a coconut," I said under my breath.

The doctor examined my forehead. "It looks like it's healing nicely. You were lucky the coconut didn't hit you harder. So, why are you here?"

"There was another murder at the marina last night, and the victim's wife was taken here. I wanted to check and see how she's doing. I don't think she has any family in the area, and we became close over the past few days. I figured maybe I could help."

"I'm sure she'll appreciate the company. The volunteers at the front desk can let you know where her room is." She smiled. "Be sure to stay clear of palm trees from now on. I don't want to see you back in here for another coconut-related injury."

"It wasn't a coconut," I muttered under my breath as she walked away.

One of the volunteers printed out a visitor badge, circled Sandy's room on a map, and pointed me to the elevators. I pressed the button to the third floor and tried to decide if I should tell Sandy's doctor about her abduction. I knew that most medical professionals scoffed at the idea of alien abduction, but not all of them. Maybe Sandy's doctor was more open-minded.

The door to her room was open. I poked my head in. "Knock, knock."

Sandy looked up from the magazine she was reading and said, "Mollie, is that you? What a nice surprise."

"How are you doing?" I asked as I sat in the chair next to her bed. "I saw Nancy earlier this morning, and she said they admitted you last night."

Sandy put her magazine down and reached out for my hand. "It means the world to me that you came. I can't believe I broke down the way I did last night. They ended up sedating me. It's just so embarrassing."

"Nonsense. It isn't embarrassing at all. I would have reacted the same way if it had been Scooter. Jack was your husband, after all. It's a devastating blow to lose him, especially like that."

"What do you mean, like that?" she asked, looking confused.

"Nothing," I said hurriedly. "I didn't mean anything by it. Have the police been by to see you yet this morning?"

"No, but the nurse said that they'll be coming by soon. Why?"

"Oh, no reason. I'm sure they just want to give you an update on the case."

"What case? Jack's death was an accident. There isn't any case, is there?" I eyed the call button next to Sandy's bed and was debating whether or not to buzz it when she started sobbing. I passed her the box of tissues. "I'm sorry, Mollie, I just need a moment. It's so much to take in."

"Of course. I understand. Can I get you anything?"

"A glass of water would be nice," she said between sniffles. "There's a pitcher over there on that table." She handed me her magazine. "Here, can you put that over there too?"

While I was filling up her water glass, I glanced at the cover. It was one of those tabloid publications that they sell at grocery checkout lines. This one had a ridiculous headline about a UFO crash-landing in a small town in North Dakota. Apparently, the residents had taken a liking to the little green men and were sheltering them inside one of the local churches. Who would believe something like that? Publications like this gave reputable organizations like FAROUT a bad name.

But still, if Sandy was reading this, maybe that meant that she was a believer. Perhaps the memories she had been repressing were beginning to surface.

Sandy interrupted my thoughts. "Mollie, could I get that water from you?"

"Oh, I'm sorry," I said, passing her the cup. "I got distracted looking at your magazine."

"That piece of trash? It was already here, otherwise I wouldn't be caught dead reading something like that. Did you see the headline about aliens in North Dakota? What kind of people believe things like that?"

I sat back in the chair deflated, clutching the magazine in my hand.

"You can have that if you want," Sandy said.

"No, that's all right." I heard a light tapping on the door.

"Mrs. Holt, it's Chief Dalton and Officer Moore. Can we come in?"

"Of course," Sandy said, settling back into her pillows. She looked pale.

"Are you okay, Sandy?" I asked. "Do you want me to get the nurse? You know, you don't need to talk to the police just yet if you aren't up to it."

"Mrs. McGhie, what a surprise to see you here," the chief said, his eyebrows twitching.

"I'm just looking out for Sandy," I said.

He looked at the magazine in my hand. "Do you write for them?" he asked. "I'm sure they've got some great stories about alien abductions in there."

"No, I don't," I said. I tossed the magazine into the garbage can. "Sandy, if you're sure you're okay to talk to the police, I'll get going now."

Sandy reached out and grabbed my hand. "Would you mind staying? I'd feel a lot better if I had a friend here. If that's okay, officers?"

Chief Dalton reluctantly agreed. "Ma'am, I'm sorry to have to tell you this, but your husband was murdered."

Sandy gasped and clutched my hand harder. She had a strong grip. "Murdered? Are you sure?"

"Yes, we're sure. The coroner found—"

Sandy interrupted. "No, please don't tell me the details. I can't bear to think about it." She clenched my hand even tighter. Then she sobbed loudly. My hand was really starting to hurt, and although I hated to see her cry, I was kind of glad, because that meant she needed both of her hands to wipe away her tears and blow her nose.

"Do you want me to call a nurse?" the burly man asked kindly.

"No, I'll be fine. Could I have another glass of water, though?" Officer Moore filled her glass up, while the chief got out his notebook.

"If you're sure you're okay, I just have a few questions. Do you have any idea who might have done this?"

"No, of course not. Why would anyone

want Jack dead?" Sandy asked. "Everyone loved him. He's lived here all his life and has lots of friends."

"I understand he was having some financial difficulties. Is that true?"

Sandy squeezed her crumpled-up tissues in her hand. Better the tissues than my hand. Finally, she replied with a tight voice. "Yes, he was having financial issues. But it wasn't his fault. He got in over his head and then, when Captain Dan swindled him, he didn't know what to do. Ned was nice enough to loan him some money, but it wasn't enough to settle his debts. It was causing him a lot of stress." She took a sip of water. "Do you think it's possible it wasn't murder, but suicide?" she asked with a trembling voice. "Maybe the stress drove him to..." She began sobbing again.

A nurse came rushing in. "Is everything okay here?"

"We were just asking Mrs. Holt a few questions," Chief Dalton said apologetically.

"Well, you're upsetting her," the nurse replied. "I'll have to ask you to leave. You too," he said, nodding to me.

As I was walking out of Sandy's room, she called out. "Mollie, will you look after Mrs. Moto? Nancy has a key to our boat in the office."

* * *

I unlocked Jack and Sandy's boat and made my way down below. After digging through a few lockers, I eventually found where Sandy stored the cat food. Just as I was pulling back the lid of a can of Fisherman's Delight, I felt a set of claws digging into my leg, and a furry face looked up at me expectantly. I scooped out the contents of the can into a dish and set it on the floor. I have to say, Fisherman's Delight certainly didn't smell delightful, but that didn't seem to be stopping Mrs. Moto.

The Japanese bobtail finished her meal, jumped up on the couch, and washed behind her ears. I poked around in the cabinets until I found where Sandy hid the cookies. I made myself some coffee, grabbed a couple of cookies, and sat down next to her. She sniffed at the snacks but decided they weren't nearly as delightful as Fisherman's Delight. She curled up on my lap for a post-lunch nap.

I might have taken a bit of a nap too.

Both of us were woken up by the sound of a couple trying to dock their boat. When we heard a loud thud, Mrs. Moto ran into the aft cabin. I took this as an opportunity to check out the rest of Jack and Sandy's boat. Although I guess it was just Sandy's boat now.

"Here, kitty, kitty," I cried out as I made my way to the rear. It was a similar setup to our boat—a bed against one side with a love seat running along the other side. What they had, which we didn't, was a large closet with a set of drawers next to it. They also had a small sink beside their bed, which seemed strange. I rarely have the desire to get up in the middle of the night to wash my face, but maybe it's a thing for people who live on sailboats.

I couldn't see Mrs. Moto anywhere, so I sat

on the bed and peered out the hatch. I have to admit, the view of palm trees swaying in the breeze overhead was pretty special. I lay down to get a closer look. There was definitely some high thread count going on here. The sheets were soft and silky. I might have had another nap. When I woke up again, I found the calico nestled against me.

I glanced at the clock. How had it gotten so late? Had Scooter noticed how long I had been missing? Or had he been so caught up in boat projects that he hadn't even given my absence a second thought? Both the cat and I had a quick stretch, although hers was far more impressive than mine. If I had attempted what she did, I would have pulled muscles in my body that I didn't even know existed.

After stretching, Mrs. Moto leaped to the floor and stuck her paw into the gap of one of the opened drawers. After a few attempts, she snagged something, dragged it out, and meowed loudly. I picked it up and turned it over. It was a blurry photograph of two people sitting on the hood of a car in what appeared to be a car dealership. I rubbed my eyes and inspected it more closely. The woman had long, blonde hair and was wearing a pink blouse belted over a pair of jeans. The man next to her had a large cowboy hat, cowboy boots, and a three-piece suit that looked like it was made out of some sort of horrible man-made fabric. They had their arms around each other, smiling broadly into the camera.

I looked at Mrs. Moto. "How did a picture of Penny and Captain Dan get into that drawer?" She blinked at me a few times and meowed. I don't think she knew or cared.

CHAPTER 13
BELLY BUTTON LINT

I WASN'T SURE WHAT TO do with the picture. Should I confront Penny? After all, she'd told me that she didn't know Captain Dan prior to moving to Florida, yet according to the date stamp, this picture had been taken a few years before that. But if I did ask her about it, would she tell me the truth?

Amid all these questions, my stomach growled, alerting me to the fact that two cookies and a cup of coffee weren't really going to cut it for lunch. I tucked the picture in my purse, filled up Mrs. Moto's water bowl, gave her a quick cuddle, and headed to the boat to see if the guys were interested in fish-and-chips.

My head was reeling with thoughts of cowboys, cookies, and Penny's poor taste in men when I ran into Ben.

"Weren't you on *Marjorie Jane* with Scooter?" I asked.

"We needed a socket wrench, so I ran back to my boat to grab one," he said, holding up a tool bag. "Scooter doesn't really have a good set of tools, does he?"

"No idea."

"Might be something to think about with the holidays coming up," Ben said. "People always want tools as presents."

"Just like people want sailboats for their anniversary?" I asked.

Ben smiled. "Exactly. Your husband is awesome! I'd love to find a woman who would be thrilled to get a sailboat as a present, like you were," he said wistfully. "But there's so few women out there who are single, let alone who enjoy sailing."

"It must be tough. I think the only single

woman I've met at the marina is Penny."

"Oh, she's amazing. She's smart, she's gorgeous, she's got her own boat, and she's a great sailor. Between you and me, I actually asked her out once. Couldn't believe I got up the nerve, but I'd had a few beers and I thought, what the heck, all she can do is say no."

"So she said yes?" If you had asked me before I'd found that picture, I would have thought there was no way Penny would date an unemployed pirate wannabe. But seeing her with her arm around Captain Dan put a new perspective on things. Maybe she had said yes.

"No, she said no," Ben said, looking down at the dock. "It was kind of embarrassing the next day."

"Why'd she turn you down?"

"She said she had recently broken up with a guy and hadn't gotten over him yet."

"Was he someone you know? Someone from around here?"

"She wouldn't say. She got real evasive. The only thing she did say was that he was an older guy who had swept her off her feet. It might have been a guy back when she lived in Texas. She said that they had been in business together, a business she'd invested heavily in, but when it had started to lose money, he'd dumped her. She thought maybe he had liked her just for her money. She comes from a wealthy family, you know. Talking about it got her really upset, so I dropped it."

"Captain Dan was from Texas, wasn't he?"

"Yeah, he was."

"Do you think they knew each other there? Maybe he was the guy that she was involved with?"

"Captain Dan?" Ben asked incredulously. "I can't see it. That dude was such a jerk. Penny is too nice of a girl to have ever gotten mixed up with someone like him."

I was debating whether or not to show Ben the picture when Scooter walked up. "I was wondering where you got to," he said to Ben with a wink. "Now I know—you've been chatting up my wife."

Ben flushed. "It wasn't like that at all. It

just took longer than I thought. My outboard engine died on me again. Jack helped me last time, and now that he's—you know—no longer with us, I had to try to fix it myself. He knew engines inside and out." Ben shifted his tool bag. "Anyway, I got the socket wrench. Wanna head back to *Marjorie Jane* and see if we can get that bolt out?"

"I'll catch up with you in a few minutes," Scooter said.

Ben mumbled good-bye to me and left without making eye contact. Once he was out of earshot, I punched Scooter in the arm. "Why did you go and tease him? You've totally embarrassed him."

Scooter scoffed. "He knows I was only kidding. It's not like he's one of those creepy guys always flirting with other men's wives."

"Speaking of creepy guys, look what I found on Jack and Sandy's boat."

My husband frowned. "How's she doing?"

"Not great. She's still at the hospital. It was just awful." I smiled. "But there was one bright spot to the visit."

"What's that?"

"Chief Dalton started pestering her with questions and got kicked out by the nurse. You should have seen the look on his smug face."

Scooter pulled me close. "I can't imagine what I'd do if I ever lost you."

"Oh, you'd be fine, provided you had enough chocolate to get you through the mourning period."

He chuckled. "The problem is that you always hide the chocolate. You'll have to leave a note with instructions on where I can find it."

"Enough about chocolate," I said. "You have to see this. It's Captain Dan and Penny."

"Are you sure?" He held the photo at arm's length. "I can't really see all that well without my glasses."

"I'd lay money on it. Or chocolate."

"But why would there be a picture of Captain Dan and Penny on Jack and Sandy's boat? That doesn't make any sense."

"I don't know. There are a lot of things that don't make sense." I put the photo back in my purse and headed off to pick up lunch.

* * *

After a delightfully greasy lunch of fish-and-chips, I decided to bite the bullet and see what I could get out of Penny regarding her relationship with Captain Dan. She was sitting on the deck of her boat with her legs hanging over the edge, polishing a metal railing.

"That looks like hard work," I said.

"Owning a boat isn't for the fainthearted," Penny replied, putting down her cloth. "There's always something that needs to be fixed, installed, or maintained. Like this stainless steel. You have to keep it polished to prevent rust. That's one of the things I like about living on a boat. I've always got a project to work on. It keeps me busy."

"That's probably a good thing, given everything that's been happening at the marina. Jack murdered and Captain Dan before that. I saw Sandy in the hospital this morning, and she's devastated by the loss of her husband. I wonder if Captain Dan had a special lady in his life?" I watched Penny carefully to see what her reaction was.

Penny picked her cloth back up and began polishing furiously. "Not that I know of."

"That's a shame. He seemed like such an outgoing guy. I'm surprised he wasn't dating anyone." Penny didn't respond. I tried again. "You know, I can picture the two of you together. You both like boats and sailing. I thought you guys would have been a good match."

"A love of boats and sailing isn't all it's cracked up to be," Penny said bitterly. "You'd think that would be enough to keep a man interested, but no, it isn't. Trust me. Never date a sailor. They'll cheat on you and lie to you."

"You think Captain Dan was a cheater and a liar?" I asked cautiously.

"I only know what I told you before. Ned and Nancy lost a lot of money when the previous owners of *Marjorie Jane* skipped town, and they blame Captain Dan for it."

"I also heard that Jack wasn't all that fond

of him."

Penny reluctantly agreed. "That's true."

"You know, at first I thought Jack might have been the one who killed Captain Dan, but then he was killed."

"Jack kill Captain Dan? Why did you think that?"

"The two of them were involved in selling stolen marine equipment. Things went sour with the deal. Jack was angry about it, maybe angry enough to kill. Plus, he did this to me." I pointed at my head.

"I thought that was a coconut."

"No, Jack hit me on the head."

"Are you sure?"

"I'm positive. It was Jack. But since Jack's dead, who would have reason to kill both him and Captain Dan?"

"No idea. And to be honest, I have other things to worry about, like my sailing school."

"You moved here from Texas, right?"

"I did."

"Captain Dan moved here from Texas too, didn't he?"

"What are you getting at?"

"I was just curious if you knew him when you lived in Texas. You might be able to give some background information to the police to help them figure out who would have a motive to kill him."

"Sorry, I can't help them. I didn't know him there. You know, Texas is a big state. There are a lot of people who come from Texas," she said wryly.

"That's true. I just thought that maybe the sailing community was relatively small and that you two had met through that somehow."

Penny relaxed a little bit. "It is a small community, but I never ran across him before I came here. Honestly, I'm glad I didn't. He's a sleazeball. Did you notice how he flirts with all the women?"

"I saw him chatting Sandy up at the barbecue. I figured it was harmless, although Jack looked irritated. I thought that might have played into his motive for killing Captain Dan as well."

"I can see that. He had a reputation for

going after married women."

"You don't think he and Sandy ever, you know..."

Penny bit her lip. "I wouldn't put it past him." She stood, picking up her rag and a bottle of polish. "I've got to finish the rest of this. I'll see you tomorrow for the ladies' sailing class. Wear clothes you don't mind getting wet and shoes that won't mark the deck, and bring your PFD." She walked to the other side of the deck and resumed polishing.

I was left not only wondering why Penny continued to lie, but also what a PFD was.

* * *

What did we do before Google? When you want to know the answers to questions you're too embarrassed to ask anyone, like "Why is there lint in my belly button?" or "What's a PFD?" Google is there for you. So I made a plan of action. Step one: stop at the marina office for more chocolate. Step two: go to the marina lounge for Wi-Fi.

Fortunately, Nancy wasn't sitting behind the counter when I entered the office. I'm pretty sure a couple of flies followed me in. I looked at the rack where the chocolate bars were usually kept. Nothing. This was disconcerting. How was I supposed to execute step one of my plan?

Nancy came out of the back room carrying cans of soda. "Where's all the chocolate?" I asked.

"It's all gone," she said. She set the box down and opened it with a pair of scissors.

"What do you mean, gone?"

She paused and held up the scissors in a way that made me regret my question. "A group of boats spent the night at the marina and bought the rest of the chocolate. They also cleaned us out of soda and chips. Big spenders—they're the kind of boaters we like to see here."

"But you have some more in the back, don't you?" I asked, keeping a careful eye on the scissors.

"Nope, that was the last of it."

"But what am I supposed to do now?"

"Live without."

Not the answer I was hoping for. Oh well, if I couldn't get chocolate, maybe I could get Nancy's thoughts on the picture of Captain Dan and Penny. "Here, get a load of this. Don't these folks look familiar to you?"

Nancy took the picture, walked to the counter, and put her reading glasses on. I watched with relief as she placed the scissors down next to the computer. "I don't think so. Like that guy's cowboy hat, though. Ned would look good in a hat. I've been trying to convince him to wear a baseball cap with the marina logo on it."

What was it with women and guys in cowboy hats? "Have a closer look," I said, tapping my finger on the photo.

"No, can't say that they're familiar. Friends of yours?"

"Don't you think they look just like Penny and Captain Dan?" I blurted out.

"Well, the woman does have long, blonde hair like Penny. I guess it could be her. But it's hard to see the man's face underneath that hat. Where did you get this?"

"Oh, I found it lying around," I said, sidestepping the question. "I think this picture was taken in Texas. See the sign in the corner that says 'Lone Star Plaza'? If that's the case, then Penny and Captain Dan knew each other before they moved to Florida."

"But they didn't. They met here."

"Are you sure? How do you know?"

"Penny told me. It's probably just a couple of people who look like them. There are a lot of gals with hair like that." She passed the picture back to me. "Check back in tomorrow. We might have more chocolate then," she said gruffly.

* * *

I sat down in what I was coming to think of as "my chair" in the marina lounge and pulled out my laptop. The car invoice, originally tucked away in Penny's sailing book, fluttered out with it. It was a run-of-the-mill invoice, but something about it niggled away at me. I read the dealership address again—Cowboy Bob's Automotive Ranch, located at the Lone Star Plaza. That was it! I pulled out the photo and squinted at the sign next to Captain Dan and Penny, which read Lone Star Plaza. Penny had referred to Captain Dan as Bob the night of the barbecue. Was it possible they were one and the same?

I decided to add a third step to my plan of action—learn more about Cowboy Bob's Automotive Ranch. But first I was going to find out once and for all the answer to the belly button lint question. I fired up my laptop and did a quick check of my email. Big mistake. There at the top of my inbox was an email from Brian Morrison.

I'm so sorry to have to tell you this, but the board of directors has decided to give the investigative reporter job to Lola. If it had been up to me, I would have selected you, and in fact, I argued strongly for your case at the board meeting, but to no avail. The board is convinced that the publicity generated by Lola's scoop on the Disneyland alien cover-up will advance FAROUT's cause with the general public.

I needed something to distract me from thinking about Lola. Googling about belly button lint wasn't going to cut it. I reached for the TV remote and flicked through the channels. As I was deliberating between a home improvement show and an old black-and-white movie, Ned walked into the lounge carrying his cleaning supplies.

He set his bucket down. "Ooh, *The Thin Man*. That's a great one. I didn't know you liked old films."

"I didn't until I met Scooter. He loves classic movies like this."

Ned perched on the arm of the other chair. "My favorite scene is coming up, where Nick and Nora throw a dinner party for all the suspects. They make investigating a murder look like fun. It's too bad Nancy isn't here. She loves this movie too. Although if she caught me slacking off instead of cleaning, that'd be another story."

While he polished the bookshelves, he kept peeking at the screen, chiming in with trivia about the stars and director. He was telling me about the fox terrier that starred in the film when the door flew open, and Chief Dalton and Officer Moore marched in, followed by Nancy.

Nancy was tugging at the big man's arm. "I'm telling you, he didn't have anything to do with this! You can't do this!"

The chief removed her hand from his arm, raised an eyebrow, and motioned to Officer Moore to escort Nancy outside. "Sir, I'm afraid you'll have to come with us," he said.

"Do you have more questions for me?" Ned asked, while watching Nancy gesticulate wildly at Officer Moore outside. "I thought I answered everything yesterday."

"I'm afraid you're under arrest." I quickly turned off the TV while Ned stared at him in shock. Chief Dalton handcuffed him, read him his rights, and then ushered him out of the lounge.

As I went out onto the patio, I saw the police leading Ned up to the parking lot and the waiting squad car. Nancy was wringing her hands in despair.

"What happened?" I asked.

"I don't know," she said. She sat on one of

the patio chairs and rocked back and forth. "They came into the office and started asking me all these questions about Jack and Ned's business dealings. They mentioned the money Ned had loaned Jack, and then the next thing I know, they're arresting him for Jack's murder. Jack and Ned were friends. There's no way Ned would kill him. He doesn't have a mean bone in his body. He can't even hurt the flies that buzz around the office." She saw Mrs. Moto walking off in the distance. "He even has a soft spot for that mangy cat."

"Was Ned involved in Jack's business?" I asked gently.

"No, of course not. We've got plenty to keep ourselves busy with here at the marina without getting mixed up in other business ventures."

"Then why do the police think he was?"

"That's the thing that doesn't make any sense. When they were going through Jack's computer, they found an inventory of the boat equipment Jack bought and sold, and Ned's name was listed as a seller. They claim

Ned sold Jack used boat equipment on credit, and that when Jack didn't pay him on time he got angry and killed him."

I thought about this for a moment. "There has to be more to it than that. Couldn't that inventory have been falsified?"

"It has to have been. Sure, Ned loaned Jack money, but it was a loan, pure and simple. He never sold Jack any boat parts."

"Do they think this has anything to do with Captain Dan's murder?"

Nancy put her head in her hands. "I don't know. The police didn't say anything about Captain Dan." She raised her head. "But their murders have to be connected. There must be someone who wanted both Jack and Captain Dan dead and it certainly wasn't Ned. I don't know what to do, Mollie."

"Well, the first thing you should do is call a lawyer." She got up wearily. Ned's arrest had sapped all her usual feistiness out of her. While there were times I wished for a kinder, gentler Nancy, this wasn't the way I would have wanted it to happen. I watched Nancy walk slowly toward the office and pondered Ned's arrest. Could he have really killed Jack? Could he have really killed Captain Dan, and if so, why? Were the two murders connected?

CHAPTER 14
DATING SCOUNDRELS

AFTER THE SHOCK OF NED'S arrest, I decided to go back to Melvin's and find out more about Jack's illegal dealings. Maybe I could discover a connection to Ned.

"Welcome to Melvin's Marine Emporium," Chad said with his usual perkiness. "How can I help you today?"

"I'd like to speak with the manager," I said.

"Tiffany, buzz Mr. Dublonski and ask him to come speak with this lady," Chad said. Tiffany rolled her eyes and put down the stack of T-shirts she had been folding. She walked over to the cash register, picked up the phone that was right next to Chad's elbow, and buzzed the manager. Chad pointed at the T-shirts. "Those aren't going to fold themselves, are they?" Tiffany looked like she wanted to strangle him. Can't say I blamed her.

A few minutes later, a man in his midthirties wearing a rumpled blue suit and shiny black shoes approached me. "Welcome to Melvin's Marine Emporium," he said in a high-pitched, squeaky voice as he shook my hand. "How can I help you today?"

"I don't know if you've heard about the recent tragedies at the marina," I said, wrestling my hand back with difficulty. His grip was almost as strong as Sandy's.

"Tragedies?" he asked. "I heard about Captain Dan. Losing him was a real blow to the local sailing community. He also brought a lot of business to our store."

"He did?"

"Sure. Every time he sold a boat, he helped the new owners make up a list of equipment they needed and pointed them our way."

"I suppose he got a commission."

"A little one, sure, but that's normal in our line of work. Plus, we gave the customers a discount if they spent over a certain amount."

"We bought our boat from Captain Dan."

"You did?" he said. "Did he help you put together a list as well? If you have it handy, I can go through it with you and get you all set up. What's the name of your boat?"

"*Marjorie Jane.*"

"*Marjorie Jane.* Isn't that the one that..." his voice trailed off.

"Yes, that's where Captain Dan was killed."

"Oh, that's terrible."

"I found the body."

Mr. Dublonski put his hand over his mouth. "Oh, dear. What a shock that must have been," he squeaked.

"It wasn't pleasant, that's for sure. Did you know he was killed with a winch handle?"

"Yes, the police mentioned it."

"The police? Did they question you? Did the winch handle come from your store?"

"Of course not," he said in shock. "It was just routine questioning. They wanted to know if I could identify the make and model of the handle. It isn't one that we normally keep in stock."

"Ah, so you're a marine equipment expert witness."

Mr. Dublonski looked pleased with that description. "I guess you could say that."

"So you know everything there is to know about boats, right?"

"I know a bit, yes."

"And you know about all the boat equipment being sold in town?"

"Of course. Wait, what do you mean?"

"You knew Jack, didn't you?" He looked at me blankly. "Jack Holt, the other man who was killed at the marina."

"Oh, him. Yes, he was a customer here. Everyone at the marina is a customer, really."

"Did you know he was murdered? I found his body too."

Mr. Dublonski gasped. "Another murder? This won't be good for business." He took a long look at me. "Wait a minute. That means you found..." I gave him some time to do the calculation in his head. "Two bodies. That's got to be some sort of record."

"Jack was more than a customer, wasn't he?" I asked, trying to guide him back to the topic at hand.

"No, just a customer. He came in from time to time."

"Before he died, Jack told me that he was in business with you." Okay, he hadn't exactly told me that, but I wasn't really in the mood to confess to eavesdropping outside Mr. Dublonski's office.

"In business with Jack? I don't know why he would have told you that. I don't even know what kind of business he was in."

"He was a used marine parts dealer. He told me that you were one of the people he sold parts to."

"I think you must have misunderstood. We only buy marine parts from reputable suppliers. We assure our customers that everything they buy from us is high quality. We don't sell anything used here."

"Maybe he told you the items he was selling were brand new."

"I still wouldn't have bought from him. How could I be sure things were brand new unless they came from the manufacturer or a reputable supplier?"

"Well, that's odd. Maybe it wasn't Jack you dealt with directly, but his two colleagues— Fred Rollins and Wayne Grimm."

Mr. Dublonski scratched his head in an unconvincing manner. "Nope, doesn't ring any bells." He pointed to a part of the store devoid of customers. "Oh, I see some folks over there who need my help," he said as he dashed back to his office.

While I was thinking about Mr. Dublonski's evasiveness, I looked at the clothing display. All the women's items were in various shades of pink. Pale pink, salmon pink, bubblegum pink, fluorescent pink—you name it, any kind of pink you could ever want. Penny must love shopping here.

I picked up a rain jacket on display and tried to figure out if it would be best described as ballet-slipper pink or blush pink. Chad tapped me on the shoulder. "That's one of our biggest sellers. All the ladies love it, especially the color."

I held it up against me. "Do you have my size in navy blue or hunter green?"

"No, only our men's jackets come in those colors. We might have a pastel-blue version in the back," he offered.

"I'll think about it," I said. I poked through the racks. "I was just speaking with your manager about Jack Holt."

"Oh yes, Mr. Holt. He comes in here all the time."

"He's a good customer?" I asked.

Chad thought about it. "No, I'm not sure he was a customer so much as a supplier. I often saw him at the loading dock delivering boxes to the store." He picked up a fuchsia T-shirt. "How about this?"

I shook my head. "No thanks, I'm not really in the market for any shirts today."

"Well, I'll leave you to your browsing. Please let me know if I can be of any further help."

"You've no idea how helpful you've been already," I said.

* * *

As I waved good-bye to Chad, I spotted crew-cut guy and his bearded friend driving a blue pickup truck covered with a tarp. They pulled into Melvin's Marine Emporium and drove through the parking lot around to the rear of the store. I hightailed it back there and hid behind a dumpster.

Crew-cut guy hopped out of the truck, stopped to tie one of his sneakers, then adjusted one of the straps holding the tarp down. After exchanging a few words with crew-cut guy through the window, bearded guy got out of the truck and walked to the door next to the loading dock, his flip-flops slapping loudly on the asphalt. He tried to open it, but it appeared to be locked. He dug his cell phone out of his pocket and called someone, gesturing angrily as he spoke. After a few minutes, the door by the loading dock was opened by none other than Mr. Dublonski. All three of them entered the building, leaving me free to check out the back of the pickup truck.

I untied the strap and pulled back the tarp

to see what was underneath. There was a whole bunch of equipment, most of which I couldn't identify. I did see a couple of familiar things, including two winch handles, both of which were smaller than the one that had killed Captain Dan.

I crept around to the passenger side of the truck, opened the door, and poked in the glove compartment. Other than a map of Texas, I didn't find anything interesting. My stomach grumbled when I saw a bag from Alligator Chuck's BBQ Joint on the floor. Ribs were sounding like a real contender for dinner.

"What do you expect us to do with all this?" I heard a man ask. "You're the one who told us to set the whole thing up. You can't back out now."

I quietly closed the passenger door and crouched down next to the truck. I saw three pairs of shoes standing beside the loading dock—Mr. Dublonski's shiny, black shoes, crew-cut guy's sneakers, and his friend's flip-flops. If they walked toward the truck, they would see me. I looked over at the dumpster. It was in direct line of sight of the loading dock. Not an option.

My stomach grumbled again. Something about ribs. I told it to shut up so I could hear what the guys were saying.

"It wasn't my idea." I recognized Mr. Dublonski's high-pitched, squeaky voice. "Captain Dan and Jack organized this. And now that they're gone, I'm wiping my hands of the whole business. I've got enough trouble with the police coming around asking questions."

"You can handle the police," either crew-cut guy or his friend said. It was hard to tell just by looking at their shoes.

"It's more trouble than it's worth. Plus, I had some nosy lady in here just now asking questions about what Jack was up to."

"Nosy lady?"

"Yeah, some broad Captain Dan sold a boat to," Mr. Dublonski said. "I didn't catch her name, but her boat is called *Marjorie Jane*."

"Maybe that's her name."

"No, that's the boat name. I remember him telling me about her. That's the one they brought the stuff over from Texas on."

"Oh, I remember now. We helped the owners of the boat unload it last week and put the stuff in the warehouse. That boat was a mess. It's in such bad condition that I'm surprised it made it over here in one piece. If I ever own a boat, it'll be a brand-new fishing boat. I'd call it *Reel Nauti*."

"Well, you're never going to get the chance, are you, if you end up in jail?" Mr. Dublonski said, rocking back and forth on his shiny, black shoes. "And that's what's going to happen if you don't get yourselves and your truck out of here."

"Sure, we'll do that. You just have to take the stuff we've got back there and pay us what you owe us."

"I'll do no such thing! Listen, you guys do what I say. You don't want to end up like Captain Dan and Jack, do you?"

"Hah, like you had anything to do with that. You don't have the guts to off anyone."

"Oh yeah, are you saying you guys knocked them off?"

"It wasn't us. Besides, we have an alibi for

both murders. And they sure were good alibis too. Curves in all the right places, if you know what I mean. We met them at the Tipsy Pirate."

"Well, if you guys didn't do it and I didn't do it, who murdered Captain Dan and Jack?"

"Who cares? I know I don't. They ended up eating into our profits and your profit too. Come on, admit it. You liked the money."

"Fine, but we can't do this now. Why don't you guys lay low for a while, and I'll give you a call once things get quieter here?"

One pair of shoes walked back to the building while the other two pairs headed my way. I took my chances and ran for it.

"Hey, who's that?"

"Get her! It's probably that nosy lady from *Marjorie Jane.*"

My heart pounded as I ran around to the front of the building. Just as I was about to collapse, someone grabbed my arm. "Are you all right?" I looked up and saw Tiffany staring at me with concern.

"I'm fine," I said as I gasped for breath. I glanced behind me. The two men glared at me. I guess they figured they couldn't make a scene in front of a witness. "What are you doing out here?" I asked.

"I just quit my job. I've had enough of Chad acting all superior. Can you believe he still had the nerve to ask me out?"

Actually, I could believe it. I could also believe I hadn't seen the last of crew-cut guy and his bearded friend.

* * *

After hearing more about Tiffany's teenage dramas, I walked a few blocks to the police station. Even though it had only been a few hours since they arrested Ned, it felt like ages since I had last seen Chief Dalton's bushy eyebrows in action.

The receptionist did a double take when I told her my name. "Oh, the chief's told me about you."

"That must be because the first murder took place on our boat," I said.

She hesitated for a moment. "Yes, that must be it."

"Any chance he can squeeze me in for a few minutes?"

"Can't promise anything, but I'll see what I can do."

While I waited, I looked at the bulletin board. Next to some Most Wanted posters was a takeout menu for Alligator Chuck's BBQ Joint. It had a five-dollar-off coupon on the bottom. I took it off the bulletin board and stuffed it in my purse. We were definitely having ribs for dinner.

I heard a distinctive voice in the hallway behind the reception area. "You didn't tell her I was here, did you?" Even though I couldn't see him, I could picture him raising his eyebrows.

I took that as my cue that he was free to see me now. I poked my head into the hallway. "There you are," I said as I steered him toward his office. As he walked by the receptionist, he said, "See what I mean?"

He sat at his desk and shuffled a few file folders back and forth. "Mrs. McGhie, I've got a lot to do."

"Then I'll make it quick. How's the

investigation into Captain Dan's and Jack's murders going? Why did you arrest Ned?"

The chief stared at me quietly for a few moments, then shuffled his folders again. I took this to mean that he didn't have an update.

"Okay, then, why don't I start? Remember those two guys who were talking with Jack at the beach that night when he hit me over the head?"

He raised an eyebrow. "I thought we had established that a coconut hit you over the head."

"No, we didn't. It was Jack! Why doesn't anyone believe me? Listening to what everyone says, you would think all the coconuts in this town were intent on harming humans at an alarming rate. You should probably put up flashing neon warning signs."

He raised his other eyebrow.

"I was just at Melvin's Marine Emporium and I saw them talking to the manager, Mr. Dublonski. Well, I didn't exactly see them talking, but I saw their shoes talking." He raised both his eyebrows this time. No wonder he had so many wrinkles on his forehead. "Remember how I told you they were all mixed up in something? Well, now I have proof."

"Proof?" There went those caterpillars again.

"Yes, proof. I heard the three of them talking about how they worked it. Captain Dan loaded up stolen marine equipment on *Marjorie Jane* in Texas. The previous owners sailed her to Florida. Then they took off and left *Marjorie Jane* behind. Crew-cut guy and his bearded friend—"

"Who?" Chief Dalton asked.

"You know. Fred Rollins and Wayne Grimm. One of them has a crew-cut and one of them has a beard. I have no idea which one is Fred and which one is Wayne."

"How much longer is this going to take?"

"Let me finish. Once they got to Florida, they helped the previous owners of *Marjorie Jane* unload the stuff and hide it in a warehouse. Jack was going to sell it all to Mr. Dublonski, who would then turn around, pass it off as brand-new equipment, and sell it to unsuspecting customers. Jack was supposed to get the money from Mr. Dublonski and give crew-cut guy and his friend their cut. When Mr. Dublonski refused to buy it, Jack was in a pickle. Those two guys were expecting to be paid for their share, but he didn't have it. They threatened him and then you know what happened next."

The chief sat back in his chair and stared at the ceiling. "Both Fred and Wayne have alibis for the night Mr. Holt was killed."

"I know. They were at the Tipsy Pirate chatting up some girls." Chief Dalton nodded ever so slightly. "And they were at the Tipsy Pirate the night Captain Dan was murdered too." He looked at me and nodded again. "And I think Mr. Dublonski has an alibi too." More nodding. "But even if they didn't kill Jack and Captain Dan, they sure were happy about it. It meant they didn't have to deal with any middlemen anymore. They got the rest of the stuff out of the warehouse, took it over to Melvin's, and tried to get Mr.

Dublonski to take it. He said he couldn't do anything until the murder investigation cooled down."

"And how do you know all this?"

"I overheard them at the loading dock behind Melvin's."

"Overheard them?"

"It really doesn't matter, does it? The important thing is that you need to investigate this."

He sighed. "I'm just going to cut to the chase because it's probably the fastest way to get you out of here. We've known about this little operation for some time. It's not the first time these guys have done this. We're investigating, and we should be able to make some arrests soon."

"That's good to hear. Now, since we can rule crew-cut guy, his bearded friend, and Mr. Dublonski out of the picture, the question is, who did murder Captain Dan and Jack? It sure wasn't Ned."

Chief Dalton was lifting that eyebrow when the receptionist poked her head in the door. "Sir, we need you urgently in the conference room."

Just my luck. I was sure the chief had just been about to open up to me about the case.

* * *

There were two things I couldn't forget to pick up on my way home: Scooter from our boat and ribs from Alligator Chuck's. I was so hungry I almost collected my husband second, but he was the one with the cash. The smell of the barbecue was intoxicating on the ride back, but I managed to restrain myself from ripping open the container until we were inside the house.

After washing the last of the sticky barbecue sauce off my hands, I turned on my laptop, sat on one of the kitchen stools, and got back to my action plan. First up, I found out more than I'd ever wanted to know about belly button lint. Then I did a search for Cowboy Bob's Automotive Ranch. I came up with several hits. One was for the car dealership, one was for a consumer affairs site, and the last one was for a dating site.

I clicked on the dealership site first. The top of the page had a banner that read, "Cowboy Bob's Automotive Ranch—You Won't Wrangle a Better Deal Anywhere Else." Underneath was a picture of a large car lot. When I tried to click on the section labeled "Find Out More," I got a message that said, "Sorry, but we're out of business."

After hitting that dead end, I debated whether to check out the consumer affairs site or the dating site. Curiosity made me click on the link for Dating Scoundrels. Turns out it wasn't a dating site. It was a site warning women about scoundrels who'd tried to con women they'd met on matchmaking sites. There were pages and pages of pictures of men, each with a caption underneath detailing his name, occupation, and dating scoundrel crime, such as "married," "gold digger," or "cheater." I scrolled through a few pages until I saw Captain Dan's face staring at me. Or should I say, Bob Kincaid, owner of Cowboy Bob's Automotive Ranch and gold digger? And guess who reported him? None other than

Penny Chadwick. Bingo.

Next, I clicked on the consumer affairs site. As I was reading about consumer fraud and protection, Scooter entered the kitchen. He opened the freezer and got out a tub of double-chocolate ice cream. As he walked over to the cupboard where we keep the bowls, he glanced at my laptop. "Consumer affairs? What's that all about? Are you filing a complaint?"

"Not exactly. It's more like I'm investigating a complaint. I found proof that Captain Dan did own a used-car dealership in Texas." I clicked over to Cowboy Bob's website and showed it to Scooter. "They went out of business, but the name of the dealership and logo match the car invoice I found in that sailing book Penny loaned me." I grabbed my purse and pulled out the sales invoice. "See, it's an exact match."

"Okay, they're the same." He put two bowls on the counter. "But what does that have to do with Captain Dan?"

I clicked over to the Dating Scoundrels site and showed him the picture. "See, that's

Captain Dan right there, listed as the owner of Cowboy Bob's Automotive Ranch."

"But that doesn't say Captain Dan. It says Bob Kincaid."

"It's him. Look closely. You can't deny they're exactly alike."

"Lots of people look like other people. Maybe it's just a coincidence."

"Or maybe he changed his name because he got into trouble. That's where the consumer affairs site comes in. There's gotta be something on here that implicates Captain Dan."

Scooter scooped ice cream into the bowls. "Here it is. A report on Cowboy Bob's Automotive Ranch, owned by Daniel Robert Smith, who goes by the alias of Bob Kincaid." I tapped my fingers on the counter. "Aha! That's it. I knew I had seen Captain Dan before. Remember that place we had lunch at in Texas? You know, the one with the Western omelets that was across the street from a used-car lot? It was Cowboy Bob's Automotive Ranch. There was a huge billboard next to it with his face plastered on it. That's why he looked so familiar!"

Scooter handed me a bowl and smiled. "You're quite the investigative reporter."

"No, I'm not," I said glumly. "I heard from Brian. Lola got the job."

Scooter gave me a kiss, and then handed me his bowl of ice cream. "Looks like you might need this one too." And that's the secret to a successful relationship—knowing when your partner needs extra chocolate.

CHAPTER 15
MR. AND MRS. DIAMOND

THE NEXT MORNING, SANDY WAS discharged from the hospital. I popped by her boat to check on her, bringing a box of assorted pastries fresh out of the oven from Penelope's Sugar Shack. I had my eye on the one *pain au chocolat* in the box. I knew it was selfish on my part, but I really hoped that Sandy was the kind of hostess who offered a cup of freshly brewed coffee and allowed her guest to have first dibs on the pastries. If she wasn't, I'd have to create a distraction and snatch it before she did.

When I got to Sandy's boat, I realized that

in the state she was in, she probably wouldn't have noticed or cared if I took the pain au chocolat. She was sitting in the cockpit staring into space. I waved the pastries in front of her. No response. Even the smell of chocolate wafting from the box wasn't enough to get her attention.

She finally noticed me and motioned for me to join her. She looked at the box. "Is that for me?" I nodded. "That's sweet of you, but I just don't have an appetite. I couldn't eat a thing."

"How about a cup of coffee, then? I could make you one," I offered.

"Sure, that'd be nice," she said with a vacant stare. I placed the box next to her and went down below to put the kettle on. After the water came to a boil, I poured it over the grounds in the French press and set it aside to brew for a few minutes.

"Sandy, do you want cream or sugar in your coffee?" She mumbled some sort of reply. I couldn't make out what she said. I stuck my head up into the cockpit and repeated the question. That's when I noticed that she was covered in little flaky pieces of pastry.

She wiped away some chocolate from the side of her mouth and said, "Just cream, please. I think I already ate enough sugar in this pain au chocolat. It was delicious!"

Lesson learned—never leave a box of pastries unattended, even if the other person claims they don't have an appetite. I passed Sandy a cup of coffee and then quickly plucked out a blueberry muffin before Sandy laid waste to that too. "What did the doctor say?" I asked in between bites of muffin.

"She said I was fine to go home," Sandy said. "When I explained that I lived on a sailboat, she was surprised, but it's my home, you know. I love living on the water and being able to take my floating house with me wherever I go. I really hated being in the hospital. It's good to be back in familiar surroundings."

"Are you still going to sell the boat and move into the condo?" I asked.

"I don't know," Sandy said. Her eyes welled up with tears. "I'll have to talk to our lawyer and accountant first and get a handle on exactly how much money Jack wasted away. When we first got married, he seemed like such a go-getter. I thought for sure he'd be a successful businessman, but everything he touched turned sour." She reached into the box and grabbed a blackberry Danish.

"Look at me," she said, tearing bits off the Danish angrily. "I've got nothing to show for our life together. I should have divorced Jack when I had the chance. If I had, then things would have been different. I could have started over with someone else." She dried her eyes with one of the napkins that Penelope had provided. "Would you mind making me another cup of coffee, dear?" she asked as she held out her empty mug.

I nabbed a glazed donut on my way to the galley. It was tasty, just not as tasty as a pain au chocolat.

"While you're down there, can you get the bottle of pills out of my purse for me?" Sandy asked as she burst into tears. "The doctor gave me some antidepressant tablets. I should probably take one."

I was surprised by her comments about Jack. I knew they'd had troubles, but I didn't realize how bitter Sandy had been about her marriage. It made me realize how lucky I was to have Scooter.

While the coffee brewed, I spotted Sandy's purse on the table and opened it. It was amazing how much stuff she managed to cram in there. I pulled out an eyeglass case, her wallet, a packet of tissues, a hairbrush, a makeup bag, a romance novel, and chewing gum. Finally, at the very bottom, I found a bottle of pills from the hospital pharmacy.

After plunging the coffee, I poured a glass of water and handed Sandy the bottle along with it. "Thanks. I don't think I'm supposed to take these on an empty stomach. Good thing you brought those pastries," she said. "It was really thoughtful of you."

"So what did you think about Ned's arrest?" I asked. "Do you really think he could have killed both Captain Dan and Jack?"

"It's hard to believe, isn't it?" Sandy said. "We've known them for years. Jack and Ned used to race sailboats together. But I guess you never really know someone, do you?"

"But if Jack and Ned were such good friends, why would Ned have killed him?"

Sandy hesitated and then said, "Well, now that he's dead, I guess there's no harm in telling you. Besides, the police are already aware. You know Jack's business selling marine goods? Well, turns out that he was selling stolen goods. He knew some guys who would break into boats that were unoccupied, steal things, and then give them to Jack to fence. Jack would then sell them to unsuspecting people and get a cut of the profit."

"How long had this been going on?" I asked, keeping to myself what I already knew about Jack's illegal activities.

"I can't be sure. Jack started his marine equipment business four years ago after he lost his job. He pretended he hadn't been fired and told everyone he had taken early retirement. At first, he had high hopes for his new business, and I did too. I thought it was going to be the answer to our financial problems. We both were so excited about it initially. But after the first year, it was apparent that he wasn't making much money. We squeaked by for another year, then things picked up and he began bringing home more money. Not enough to let us keep both the boat and our condo, but enough that we could get by. I think that was when he'd started fencing stolen goods."

"Did you realize that right away?" I asked.

"No, it took me a while to even be suspicious, but I finally found proof. You know how I do the bookkeeping for Jack?" I nodded while I listened to my stomach make very unladylike noises. Perhaps two pastries on top of the big rib dinner I had had the night before was a bad combo.

"Well, at first the bookkeeping was straightforward." She took a sip of coffee. "He'd give me receipts from people who he'd bought equipment from. I think I told you before how I'd enter them into a spreadsheet, then enter sales invoices when he sold something. All was good and well but then things changed. He'd just tell me what amounts to enter. He said that he had misplaced the receipts and invoices, but he knew what all the transactions were."

"But wouldn't that get him in trouble with the IRS if he were ever audited?"

"That's exactly what I said, but he told me to mind my own business. That's when things got really bad between us. It was really hard because, to be honest, I didn't have anyone to talk about it with. I still wasn't sure what was going on, but I knew something wasn't right."

"That must have been so hard not to have anyone to confide in."

"Well, there was one person I could talk to, for a while at least." She twisted her wedding ring nervously. "Then I found out..."

"What did you find out?" I prompted.

"Nothing important," Sandy said. "Anyway, it turns out he couldn't be trusted either."

"When did you know something was wrong?"

"A couple of days ago. Jack's cell phone

rang and I picked it up. A guy was on the line, but he didn't even wait to see if it was Jack who had answered the phone. He started screaming that if Jack didn't come up with the money he owed, he was going to make sure the police got wind of what he was up to and that he'd take the fall for everything. I ended up confronting Jack about it that night, and he didn't deny it. I kept quiet about it, but once he was killed, I told the police what I knew."

"I still don't understand how Ned was involved."

"I'm not sure. All I can think of is that it had to do with the previous owners of *Marjorie Jane*. They blamed Captain Dan for what had happened with them."

"Okay, maybe Ned might have had a motive to kill Captain Dan, but Jack?"

"Ned's always been a straight shooter. He probably threatened to turn Jack in, there was a struggle, and Ned accidentally killed Jack."

I thought about this while I finished my coffee. "So you don't think it was murder, just accidental homicide?"

"I hope that's the case, for Nancy's sake," she said. "Oh, no, look who's coming." Sandy pointed at Penny, who waved while making her way down the dock. She was closely followed by Mrs. Moto, who meowed loudly when she reached the boat. "She's got some nerve, showing her face," Sandy whispered.

"Hi there," Penny said as she scooped the Japanese bobtail up and put her on the deck. "I thought I'd check in and see how you're doing, Sandy."

Sandy gave her a brittle smile. "I'm just fine, Penny. I see you found my cat. I was looking for her everywhere this morning. She must have sneaked off the boat when I wasn't watching."

Penny scratched behind her ears. "She's such a lovely cat. I bet she missed you while you were in the hospital."

Sandy reached out her hand. "Here, Mrs. Moto, come say hello to mama." The cat stared at her, then jumped in my lap and purred. Sandy looked crestfallen.

"Penny, we were just talking about Ned's

arrest," I said. "It seems hard to believe he could have been responsible for Jack's death. What do you think?"

Sandy turned and scowled at me. She grabbed the coffee cups. "I better go wash these out."

After Sandy was down below, Penny whispered to me, "How's she actually holding up?"

"Okay, I think."

"She doesn't really think Ned killed Jack, does she?"

"Well, she thinks it could have been an accident," I said. I decided not to share what Sandy had told me about Jack's shady business.

"Well, if that's the case, why would they have arrested Ned?" Penny asked.

"That's a good question. Unless the police got it wrong. In a small town like this, they probably don't have to deal with murders very often. Maybe they made a mistake."

"I can't imagine Chief Dalton admitting the police made a mistake, can you?" Penny asked. "Although, going up against Nancy—

that took guts on his part. She's a pretty tough lady."

"I don't know. This may be too much, even for her. I should go check on her later," I said.

"I'm sure she'd appreciate that. I've gotta skedaddle. I'm helping a young couple check out a couple of boats for sale. Say good-bye to Sandy for me."

Sandy popped her head out of the companionway. "Is she gone?"

"She just left. I should probably get going too," I said.

"Oh, no, you don't have to leave. It's nice having the company. It's just Penny I don't want to talk to."

"Why's that?" I debated whether or not to mention the picture I'd found of Penny and Captain Dan the night before. "I thought everyone got along with Penny."

"I used to think she was all right, but then I found out something about her that changed my mind." When I gave her a questioning look, she shook her head and said, "Never mind. I don't want to spread gossip. Just suffice to say that she isn't somebody you should trust."

I was starting to get a bad feeling about my sailing lesson. But then again, Sandy might be overreacting. After all, her husband had just been killed, and that had to have been a shock, no matter what difficulties they were having. Plus, the alien abduction experience wouldn't be helping matters either.

"What do you mean, you wouldn't trust her? Is she dangerous?"

"She's definitely the backstabbing type." Sandy thought about this for a few minutes. "Backstabbers can become dangerous when they don't get what they want."

"But is she the type to bash your head in with a winch handle?" I asked.

"Poor Dan," Sandy said, evading the question. "What a horrible way to go." She put her hand on the side of her head. "I think I'm getting another one of my headaches."

"Why don't you go lie down? I need to get going anyway and find a PFD, whatever that is."

"I think I will. Come on, Mrs. Moto, want to go take a nap with mama?" The calico stared at Sandy, then jumped off the boat and ran down the dock.

* * *

Although I'm sure I earned plenty of good-calorie karma from sharing the box of pastries with Sandy, I figured it couldn't hurt to go for a walk on the beach to burn off any residual calories that hadn't gotten the message about my good deeds. I kicked off my flip-flops and scrunched my toes in the sand. As I walked along the water, I saw Mr. and Mrs. Diamond wading. I sat on a piece of driftwood and watched them splash each other playfully. Mrs. Diamond's pendant glistened as the sun's rays bounced off it. They walked toward me hand in hand, giggling at some private joke.

"Sorry, were you sitting here?" I asked when I noticed a straw bag with water bottles, sunglasses, and towels propped up against the driftwood.

Mrs. Diamond picked up the towels, handed one to Mr. Diamond, and wrapped the other around her waist. "Not at all, there's plenty of room for everyone," she said, sitting next to me. "I've seen you around before, haven't I?"

"Yep, at the marina office." I decided not to mention that I had originally seen them at Chez Poisson. I really wasn't in the mood to hear about their romantic dinner or tell them about my less-than-romantic dinner that night.

"That's right," she said. "Isn't the water great? So refreshing on a hot day like today."

"I've had so much going on that I haven't really had a chance to go swimming lately." I watched the waves crashing on the beach. "Although I do get a little nervous swimming in the ocean. I'm not a very strong swimmer."

Mrs. Diamond pulled out her sunglasses and put them on. "I'm a real water baby. If I could, I'd swim in the ocean every day. We were just away for a couple of days at a marine biology conference." She pointed at

Mr. Diamond. "He's a marine biologist, specializes in sea turtles. Sometimes I think I'm a sea turtle too, I'm in the water so much."

"So you weren't here for all the drama, then," I said.

Mr. Diamond pulled a water bottle out of the bag. "What drama?" he asked as he twisted the cap off.

"Jack Holt was killed on Monday night. I found him floating by the dinghy dock."

Mrs. Diamond gasped. "We know him. We were talking to him about buying a used outboard motor for our dinghy, weren't we, sweetie?" Mr. Diamond nodded. "I can't believe you found the body. How horrible," she said, patting my arm.

Mr. Diamond looked at me curiously. "Weren't you the lady who found Captain Dan as well?"

"Yes, that was me. I found him on our boat."

"So that means you found two bodies." He shook his head in amazement. "That must be some kind of record."

"Not exactly the kind of record I'd like to have," I said. I decided to change the subject. "You know Ned Schneider, the owner of the marina? They arrested him for Jack's murder. They might also be charging him with Captain Dan's murder."

"Ned? I don't know anything about the night that Captain Dan was murdered, but we saw Ned on Monday night, didn't we, sweetie?" Mrs. Diamond said. "We went for a swim and then had a picnic on the beach. He was sitting right here on this driftwood the entire time we were here."

"What time was that at?" I asked.

"We were here from about seven to ten. It was all his idea," Mrs. Diamond said as she squeezed Mr. Diamond's hand. "It was so romantic. A full moon, warm night, no rain. My sweetie had a picnic basket, wine, candles—the works."

Mr. Diamond really was setting high standards in the romance department for the rest of the guys at the marina. A diamond necklace and a romantic picnic dinner. I was going to have to introduce him to Scooter.

"Nancy told me that Ned doesn't have an alibi for the night of Jack's murder. She was at her daughter's house that night. While she was gone, he went for a walk on the beach. He said he didn't see anyone and no one's come forward to say they saw him."

"Well, we did wave at him when we walked by that night, but he was just staring out into space, oblivious. Wasn't he?" Mrs. Diamond asked her husband. Mr. Diamond agreed.

"We need to sort this out," Mrs. Diamond said. "He's such a sweet guy." She pulled out her cell phone. After a quick conversation, she said, "Chief Dalton is going to come talk to us."

* * *

The next morning, I sat on the patio with the sailing book Penny had loaned me, doing some last-minute studying. My first lesson began in a couple of hours, and I still didn't know what a PFD was. Mrs. Moto helpfully jumped on the table and lay on the book. She stretched out on her back, obscuring the section on man-overboard drills.

While I scratched the calico's belly, Ned came out of the office carrying a broom and dustpan. He started sweeping the patio, slowly making his way over to where I was sitting. He put the broom down and smiled at Mrs. Moto. "You better not let Nancy catch that cat out here."

I returned Ned's smile. "It's so nice to see you back here!"

"It's good to be back," Ned said, sitting in one of the chairs and scratching behind Mrs. Moto's ears.

"What exactly is it that Nancy has against her? She's as sweet as can be."

"It isn't this one specifically as much as it's all cats and dogs. She doesn't like how they roll around on the beach and then deposit sand everywhere. She's a bit of a stickler for everything being neat and tidy." He pointed at his broom. "Whenever I say I'm all caught up on things, she manages to find something for me that needs to be cleaned. To be honest, it's actually kind of nice taking a break from time to time and getting out of the office."

The feline jumped onto Ned's lap. "She likes you," I said. "But you better not let Nancy catch you with cat hair all over you."

"I've got one of those hair-remover rollers in the storage shed. I make sure to clean up all her hair before she catches me. Isn't that right, Mrs. Moto?" he asked.

"I meant to ask Sandy why she named her that. It's a rather unusual name."

"Oh, she didn't name her. I did."

"You did? But I thought she was Sandy's cat."

"She is. But I'm the one who found her late one night yowling on the patio. I think her owners abandoned her, or she jumped off a boat and they left without her. I knew Sandy was feeling down about things, and I thought a cat would cheer her up."

"But why that name?"

"You know how I like old movies?" I nodded, remembering our discussion in the lounge right before the police had arrested him. "Well, some of my favorite movies are the 'Mr. Moto' ones, starring Peter Lorre as a Japanese secret agent. He wears these glasses that kind of remind me of the black circles around Mrs. Moto's eyes." He saw the look of confusion on my face. "I realized after I picked the name that was a she, not a he, hence the Mrs."

"What do you think happened to her tail?" I asked. "Was she in an accident?"

"No, she was born that way. I think I told you she's a Japanese bobtail? Their tail, or lack of tail, is characteristic of the breed. They're also known for being very talkative. Isn't that right, Mrs. Moto?" he asked. She enthusiastically agreed with a loud meow.

"I have to say, it was strange to see a cat without a tail, but I think it suits her," I said.

Ned smiled. "It sure does." Then his face sobered. "You know, Mollie, I wanted to thank you for what you did for me, finding that young couple who could back up my alibi. I can't imagine what I would have done if the police didn't release me. The thought of being locked up and apart from Nancy, our kids, and the grandkids—well, I don't even want to think about it." There was a loud meow. Ned chuckled. "And of course, you too, Mrs. Moto."

"I'm just so glad I was able to help."

The calico yowled, jumped off Ned's lap, and ran toward the beach. I heard the marina office screen door bang shut. "Ned, what are you doing sitting there?" Nancy asked. "That patio isn't going to sweep itself."

"Just having a little chat with Mollie, thanking her for her help. Maybe we should give her one of those chocolate bars to show our appreciation."

"Humph," Nancy said. She narrowed her eyes, then turned and went back into the marina office.

As soon as the screen door closed, Ned stood and rushed toward the storage shed. He quickly used a roller to remove Mrs. Moto's telltale hairs from his clothes.

A few minutes later, Nancy came out and put a chocolate bar in front of me. "Here," she said. "It's a new kind. Dark chocolate mint swirl." She took a deep breath, put her hands on her hips, and said, "Thank you."

* * *

"Scooter, can you take this? I've got to get going," I said, holding up a paper bag.

"Just a minute," he said. He walked up to the bow of the boat and handed Ben a toolbox. Ben rummaged through it, plucked out a wrench, opened the anchor locker, and started doing whatever it is you do with a wrench. Scooter leaned over the lifelines and grabbed the bag from me. "What's this?" he asked.

"Some sandwiches I picked up from the Sailor's Corner Cafe for you guys to have for your lunch."

Ben stopped what he was doing and set the wrench down beside him. "Thanks, Mollie! You didn't happen to get any brownies as well while you were at it?" he asked with a sly grin.

"Nope, sorry. Maybe next time," I replied, neglecting to mention that I had a dark chocolate mint swirl bar in my purse. Mrs.

Moto had followed me down the dock, and now she jumped up and sat next to Ben. "Make sure you don't feed her any human food. Sandy said it isn't good for her tummy."

"Aren't you going to be joining us for lunch?" Scooter asked.

"No, we're having lunch as part of my sailing class. Unless you think I should stay here instead," I said, half hoping he thought I should cancel the lesson. The section on man-overboard drills in the sailing book had made me slightly nervous.

"That's right," Scooter said. "I forgot about that. No, you should definitely go. You're going to love sailing."

"Hey guys, look what I found," Ben said. He reached into the anchor locker and pulled out a compass. "It's the one we found on *Marjorie Jane* the other day, the one that Scooter said went missing." He sat back on the deck and smiled. "Looks like I've got a streak of good luck going lately. First, I win eight hundred dollars from a scratch-off lottery ticket the other day, then I find this compass that you lost."

"Eight hundred dollars? Wow, that's a lot of money," I said.

"Well, it *was* a lot of money," Ben said sheepishly. "I repaid some money I owed, and I'm afraid I spent the rest at the Tipsy Pirate. Oh well, easy come, easy go."

Scooter set the paper bag down and inspected the compass. "I wonder how that got in there?" Mrs. Moto stuck her paw into the sandwich bag and tried to fish one of the sandwiches out. Scooter seized the bag from her. He looked at the cat, then back at me. "Remember how you left your purse by the anchor locker when we had sundowners? Well, I think I know how the compass might have found its way out of your purse and into the anchor locker." He pointed at the calico. She meowed and twined herself around Scooter's legs. I'd like to say she looked guilty, but we all know she didn't.

* * *

When I got to Penny's boat, I saw Sandy

sitting in the cockpit giggling and chatting away with Penny. It appeared that she had gotten over her concerns about the sailing instructor.

"There she is," Sandy said. "We were beginning to wonder if you were going to make it, Mollie."

"Sorry about that. I was speaking with Scooter and Ben about..." I hesitated, not wanting to mention the compass until I'd found out more about it.

Sandy leaned forward. "Speaking with them about what?"

"About Mrs. Moto and how cute she is."

Sandy beamed. She patted the seat next to her. "Come sit beside me, and Penny will show us where we're going on the chart."

"Oh, are you coming with us?" I asked. "I thought this was the ladies' sailing lesson. Don't you know how to sail already?"

"I do, but when I heard Louise and Wanda couldn't make it today—food poisoning, you know—I offered my services to Penny. It'll be easier for her to have a third person aboard." Sandy's eyes sparkled. "You'll be glad I came. Not only did I bring lemonade and shortbread cookies, but I also brought you a PFD to use. I remember you saying you weren't sure if you had one." Sandy held up something that looked like a harness.

"Is that what a PFD is? A life jacket?" I asked. "I always thought they were bright orange and bulky."

Sandy handed it to me. "PFD stands for personal flotation device. If you should fall overboard—not that that would happen," she said with a wink to Penny—"then this will automatically inflate."

I sat next to Sandy and put the PFD on while she explained to me how it operated. While I was buckling it up, Mrs. Moto jumped on the boat, darted over to me, and played with the straps. "Did you follow me?" I asked, pulling the straps out of her way and cinching them tightly.

Sandy went down below to stow the lemonade and cookies. Penny whispered to me, "You don't mind if she comes, do you, sugar? I figured it would do her good to get off her boat and get some fresh air."

"No, that's fine." We listened to Sandy cheerfully singing to herself. "She does seem to be in a better mood than yesterday. I guess those antidepressants are working."

* * *

Turns out sailing is actually quite a rush. The feel of the salt air on my face and the wind whipping through my hair as we tacked the boat back and forth was exhilarating. Watching dolphins frolic alongside the bow of the boat as we slipped through the water was so mind-blowing that when I reached up and felt how tangled and frizzy my hair had become, I didn't even mind. Of course, I didn't plan on telling Scooter that I liked sailing right away. He can be a nightmare to live with when he thinks he's right. He would feel that he deserved two bowls of Froot Loops for breakfast instead of one.

After a couple of hours, we dropped anchor in a small cove on the north side of the bay for lunch. Penny let me operate the controls for the windlass to lower the anchor. I could see why this might be a useful gadget to have on board *Marjorie Jane*.

"Why don't I go down and get us some lemonade?" Sandy offered.

"Thanks," Penny said. "Can you grab the sandwiches as well?"

"Of course I can, honey," Sandy said. "Anything for you."

Penny and I exchanged glances while Sandy went down below. A few minutes later, she put a plate of sandwiches on the cockpit table and handed us each a glass of lemonade. "You've got really darling glasses, Penny," she said. "I like how each one has a different pattern. I chose the one with the dolphin for you, Mollie, because you enjoyed watching the dolphins so much. And I chose the one with the octopus for you, Penny, because you have your tentacles in everything."

"My tentacles?" Penny asked, taking a sip of her lemonade.

"You know, having your fingers in so many pies. I just don't know how you do it, balancing running your sailing school with your love life."

"I can't say I have much of a love life these days." She took a sip of her lemonade. "Mmm. That's tart, just the way I like it." She drained the glass quickly.

I snagged a ham-and-cheese sandwich and sipped on my lemonade thoughtfully. What had gotten into Sandy? Just yesterday, she had hinted that Penny had some dark secret, but today she was acting as if they were best friends.

"Let me refill that glass for you, Penny," Sandy said. "Better yet, why don't you come down with me, and I'll give you the recipe so you can make some for yourself."

I finished off my sandwich and counted how many were left on the plate. Darn, there weren't enough for everyone to have a second one. Hopefully, Sandy would break out the shortbread cookies soon.

"Penny is going to take care of a few things down below," Sandy said as she came up into the cockpit without any cookies. "The wind has really kicked up. See those waves rolling in? Penny wants you and me to check to make sure the anchor is set properly."

I followed Sandy to the front of the boat, feeling *Pretty in Pink* swing back and forth on the anchor. "Watch out for that boat hook," she said, picking the long metal pole up off the deck. "We don't want you to trip."

Sandy spent a few minutes explaining how to check and make sure the anchor was set properly and why it was so important. "I remember one time, Jack and I were anchored in this very same cove. We had problems setting our anchor, and the next thing we knew, we had dragged and were drifting across the bay toward that rocky shore. Thankfully, we managed to get the engine started in time before we crashed."

After that story, I was reconsidering my newfound love of sailing, but then I saw two dolphins swimming nearby. "Look!" I said, tugging on Sandy's arm. "I wonder if they're the same ones as before."

"Wouldn't it be fun to go swimming with them?" Sandy asked. "Why don't you stand over here and watch them for a while? I'll go check on Penny."

I watched the dolphins leap in and out of the water, wishing I could swim as well as they could. As I leaned against the lifelines to get a closer look, I heard someone come up behind me. I saw the boat hook out of the corner of my eye. It crashed into the side of my head. I tried to steady myself by grabbing onto a lifeline, but the boat hook came down hard on my hand, and I pulled back in pain. Two hands seized me by my shoulders. I lurched forward. The lifelines snapped. I fell into the water, screaming for help.

When I surfaced, I tried to tread water. Waves crashed into me, making it hard to keep my head above the surface. Why hadn't my PFD automatically inflated? I pulled on the cord to manually inflate it. Nothing happened. I tried to swim back to the boat, but the current was pulling me in the opposite direction. I watched helplessly as someone in the cockpit turned on the engine. The windlass creaked and groaned as it lifted the anchor. I waved my hands frantically over my head so they could see where I was, coughing as I swallowed sea water. Then the boat turned toward Coconut Cove, leaving me drifting out to sea.

CHAPTER 16
KILLER COCONUTS

"MOLLIE, MOLLIE, ARE YOU OKAY?" A dinghy pulled up beside me. I struggled to reply, barely able to keep my head above water. "Here, give me your hand." I reached up and saw Ben looking at me with concern. He pulled me into the dinghy, setting me next to a case of beer, a fishing pole, and a tattered orange life jacket.

"What were you doing in the water?" he asked as he tossed an anchor over the side. He examined my PFD. "What happened here? This isn't inflated. Did you fall off a boat?"

I sat up carefully, wincing as I bumped my shoulder on the fishing pole. "I didn't fall. Someone..." I tried to catch my breath. "Someone tried to kill me."

"Kill you?" Ben asked. He moved the fishing pole out from underneath me.

"Yes, kill me. See this lump on the side of my head? That's from a boat hook."

"That does look pretty nasty," he said. "You sure it wasn't from a coconut?"

"A coconut?" I asked incredulously. "How would I get hit by a coconut here in the middle of the water?"

Ben shrugged. "I don't know. Sometimes I see them floating in the bay."

"But they'd have to fall down from something in order to hit me. Do you see any palm trees floating out here?" I gestured out across the water.

Ben put his hands over his mouth and scanned the horizon. "You're right. I don't know what I was thinking. It's just that... well, it's hard to believe." I started coughing. Ben handed me a water bottle. "Here, have a drink. You look terrible. Let's get you back to the marina."

"Okay, but first we need to alert the authorities. There's a killer on the loose. Do you have one of those walkie-talkie things?"

"You mean a VHF?"

I shrugged. "I'm not sure what they're called."

"I used to, but it doesn't work anymore, and I can't afford to replace it."

"Well, what about your cell phone?"

"Sorry, I don't have it with me. I forgot it on your boat. Scooter had to go back to Melvin's to pick up some supplies, so I decided to take off and do some fishing."

"Okay, no phone and no VHF. Let's turn on the motor and hightail it back to the marina so we can catch this killer."

Ben got the outboard engine started after a few attempts. "Luckily, I managed to get this fixed, Mollie."

"Just hurry, as fast as you can," I said. "We need to make sure they catch the killer before she escapes."

"Are you really sure someone tried to kill you?"

"I am. Someone hit me from behind and shoved me off Penny's boat."

"Are you saying Penny did this?" he asked.

"It was either her or Sandy. They were the only two people on the boat."

I curled up in the bow of the dinghy, listening to the engine sputtering. At the rate we were going, the killer would be long gone by the time we got back. As I struggled to keep my hands from shaking, I wondered what had happened to my PFD.

* * *

The sound of the dinghy hitting the dock alerted me to the fact that we were back at the marina. "Wait here, Mollie," Ben said as he tied it to a cleat. "I'm going to get help."

I struggled to hoist myself out of the dinghy, flopping ungracefully on the dock. I shuddered when I looked over at the small boat, remembering that I'd found Jack's body floating nearby. I tried to sit up but couldn't find the energy to move. I lay on the dock, staring at the seagulls circling overhead.

After a few minutes, Ned came running toward me.

"Are you all right?" he asked, bending down and pushing my wet hair out of my eyes. "Ben said he found you in the water off Pirate's Cove."

"Can you help me up?" As Ned pulled me to my feet, I groaned in pain.

He put his arm around my waist to hold me steady. "That's a nasty lump, Mollie. How did that happen?"

"Someone whacked me with a boat hook and then pushed me overboard," I said. I bit my lip. "Did Ben call the police?"

"He didn't mention anything about the police. He just told me you were hurt and went to find Scooter."

"I don't need a doctor—I need you to call the police!" I screamed, my voice cracking with hysteria. Ned stared at me in shock. "I need you to trust me. Please, just call them," I pleaded.

"Okay, I will. Let's just get you settled first." Ned helped me over to the patio. He got out his cell phone and placed the call. As

I sank down on a chair, Mrs. Moto ran across the patio, catapulted herself onto my lap, stretched up, and nuzzled my face.

"Hello, you beautiful girl," I said, snuggling her against my neck. She meowed loudly. "Wait a minute—if you're back at the marina, that means *Pretty in Pink* is back." I set the calico on my lap. "Ned, have you seen Penny and Sandy?"

"They docked a little while ago." He looked at me quizzically. "Weren't you on *Pretty in Pink* today for your sailing lesson?" I nodded. "But if that's the case, why did Ben fish you out of the water?"

"The boat hook and being pushed overboard. Ring a bell?"

Ned stroked his chin. "You were serious about that? I just figured you—"

"Imagined it?" I asked. Ned looked chastened. "Never mind. The important thing is to track down Penny and Sandy. Did you see both of them when they docked?"

"Now that you mention it, I just saw Sandy. She said Penny was down below doing something with the engine."

"I have a feeling that something may have happened to Penny, just like it did to Captain Dan and Jack." I shooed Mrs. Moto off my lap and pushed myself up. "Hurry, we've got to get to the boat and make sure Penny is okay."

I stumbled, and Ned held my elbow. "You're in no shape to go anywhere. I see Chief Dalton coming this way. You sit back down, and we'll let him take care of this."

Ned walked over to the chief. I watched as he tried to explain the situation, pointing toward me, then pointing to where *Pretty in Pink* was docked. The burly man seemed unimpressed. Even from a distance, I could see his raised eyebrows. I was about to go over and try to get him to see reason when I saw Sandy dashing across the patio in the direction of the parking lot.

"Hey!" I shouted as she ran past me. Sandy stopped in her tracks and looked at me in shock. "You! What are you doing here? You should be at the bottom of the sea by now." She grabbed my arm and yanked me out of my chair. "Now I'm going to have to find another way to deal with you." Mrs. Motc arched her back and hissed at Sandy. Sandy tried to push her out of the way with her foot, but the cat jumped back too quickly.

I fought to break free of Sandy's grasp, but she dug her fingers into my arm, adding new bruises to the ones she'd given me a short while ago on Penny's boat. I stepped down hard on her foot, pushing her off-balance and causing her to let go of me. I lifted my arm to wave at the chief, but she yanked me back. She wrapped her powerful hands around my neck with a vise-like grip. With a crazed look in her eyes, she squeezed her fingers. I tried to yell for help, but no words came out. As I struggled to breathe, I could feel the world fading away.

Then I felt an abrupt jerk and Sandy's hands were no longer around my neck. I collapsed on the patio, gasping for air. Hearing a gruff voice say, "You're under arrest," I looked up and saw Chief Dalton pulling Sandy back. While the big man handcuffed her, Ned rushed over and helped me to my feet.

After reading the handcuffed woman her rights, the chief turned to me. "I'm going to need you to come down to the station and tell me what happened. But we'll get you to the hospital first." For a second, I thought I saw a hint of a smile as he raised one of his eyebrows. "Looks like you got hit by a whole bunch of coconuts this time."

I gingerly rubbed my neck. "Feels like it too."

"I'll make sure she gets medical attention," Ned said.

The chief nodded and escorted Sandy toward the parking lot.

"Oh, no! I forgot about Penny," I said frantically. "You have to go check on her."

Ned hesitated. "Are you sure you'll be okay?" I assured him I was fine for the time being. The Japanese bobtail and I watched him hurry down the dock.

Nancy poked her head out of the marina office and peppered me with questions. "What's all the commotion out here? Where's Ned going? He should be cleaning the shower room. What's that mangy cat doing here?"

I smiled, picked up Mrs. Moto, and said sweetly, "Better close that door before you get flies in there."

CHAPTER 17
THE MYSTERIOUS TOTE BAG

THE NEXT DAY, I STOPPED by Penelope's Sugar Shack to pick up a tray of brownies. No, they weren't for me, they were for the barbecue—although one of the brownies did accidentally fall off the tray and into my hand on the way back to the marina, so I had to eat it. It would have been wasteful not to, right?

I have to confess, I did feel guilty about it—not about eating the brownie, but about not baking my own award-winning, gooey, quadruple-chocolate brownies. But really, when you've been investigating not one but two murders and an alien abduction, someone bashes you in the head when you're out for a walk, someone else throws you overboard, you're up for a promotion at work (which gets snatched away from you by that evil, red-headed Lola), and your husband surprises you with a sailboat for your anniversary, there's really not a lot of time left for home baking.

By the time I got to the patio—I needed a few moments to wipe the brownie crumbs off my clothes—the barbecue was in full swing. I watched everyone chatting, laughing, and having a good time, then pulled out my cell phone. My mom had left a number of text messages over the past couple of days, which I hadn't had a chance to read properly. Rather than continue to exchange endless texts trying to correct misunderstandings, I decided to phone her instead. We had a nice talk, once she got over the shock of what had happened to me. I think I even convinced her to come visit and see *Marjorie Jane* for herself.

After promising to call more often, I wandered over to join the crowd. I put the

:ray of brownies on one of the tables. The
;mell of the barbecue was heavenly. I
:ouldn't help but check out what Ned was
;rilling.

"It's one of my specialties—chicken legs
narinated in lemon, garlic, Dijon mustard,
and olive oil. The secret is to let them
marinate for at least twenty-four hours,"
Ned said as he checked the chicken, turning
over pieces to make sure the skin got evenly
crisped. "Of course, the other secret is
expert grilling, and that's where I come in."
He smiled.

"They look delicious," I said. "How long
until they're ready?"

"About another five minutes or so."

"I don't know if I'll be able to hold out that
long."

"Who put these over here?" Nancy asked,
pointing at the tray I had set down.

"Might as well get it over with, and confess
to your crime," Ned said. "It'll be easier that
way. Trust me."

I held my hand up meekly. "It was me."

Nancy summoned me over. "This table is

for side dishes," she said as she pointed to an impressive array of salads. All of them seemed to feature plenty of vegetables prepared in a variety of low-fat dressings. Fortunately, I spotted a dish of potato salad oozing with mayonnaise. "These brownies do not belong on this table. They belong over there, on the dessert table." I muttered my apologies and placed the tray of brownies next to a lonely bowl of fruit salad.

"Come and get it!" Ned yelled out. He placed a big platter of chicken on the table and set aside a few legs for Nancy and himself before the crowd rushed over. While they were fighting over the chicken and salads, I put a brownie on my plate. Then I found a gap in the crowd, made my way to the table with the side dishes, and scooped up some potato salad.

"There you are, my little sweet potato," Scooter said. He held out his plate. "Can you put some of that on mine too? No, not the quinoa salad, the potato salad." He took some napkins and pointed to the far side of the patio, where Penny, Ned, and Nancy were sitting. "The gang's all over at that table. Come on, let's go join them."

As we sat down, Penny looked at my plate and smiled. "I see you got some of my potato salad."

"Did you make this?" I asked as I sampled it. "It's delicious! You make it with plenty of mayonnaise, just the way I like it."

"Oh, that's not mayonnaise. That's tofu that I whipped up in a blender. Tastes like the real thing, doesn't it?"

I put my fork down slowly and grabbed one of my chicken legs. At least this was real chicken and not something made out of tofu. Maybe I was going to have to start bringing coleslaw with extra mayo, plus dessert, to these barbecues.

Ben sat in the chair next to me. Today's T-shirt advised me to keep calm and say "Arr." He appeared relatively neat and tidy. His hair looked like it had been recently shampooed, and his shorts didn't have any holes or stains. "You shaved your beard off," I said as I toyed with the misleading potato salad on my plate.

"What do you think?" he asked. "I thought I'd go with a clean-cut look for my new job."

"Your new job?"

"Didn't you hear? Ned and Nancy hired me to work in the boatyard," he said with a huge grin. "Beer's on me tonight at the Tipsy Pirate."

Nancy leaned over and poked Ben in the ribs with one of her long fingernails. "Don't forget, Ben, it's for a trial period. If you do a good job, then maybe we'll talk about hiring you on a permanent basis."

"I'm going to do a great job, just you wait and see," he said, digging into his baked beans. He set his fork down. "You know, these baked beans are good, but not as good as the ones Sandy made. I still can't believe she tried to kill you, Mollie."

Ned polished off the potato salad on his plate. Clearly, he wasn't averse to tofu being disguised as mayonnaise. "I can't believe Sandy killed Captain Dan and Jack," he said. "I would have never thought she had it in her."

"I still don't get why she did it," Penny

said. I noticed she was eating some of the quinoa salad. It probably had tofu in it too.

"Well, it was because of you," I said.

"Me?" Penny put her fork down. "What did she have against me?"

"It all had to do with you and Captain Dan."

"Captain Dan? I don't know what you're talking about," she said. Her eyes began to water. I got a tissue out of my purse and passed it to her.

"It's okay, Penny. It happens to the best of us, falling for the wrong guy," I said. "It wasn't your fault that he conned you. He conned lots of people." Ned, Nancy, and Ben all nodded in agreement.

"But how do you know about Bob—I mean, Dan?" she asked, dabbing at her eyes.

"Who's Bob?" Nancy asked.

"Bob was an alias for Captain Dan. Before he moved to Florida, he had a used-car dealership in Texas called Cowboy Bob's Automotive Ranch. Penny knew Captain Dan back when he was Cowboy Bob. He sold her that pink convertible she has. I'm not sure when or how it happened, but at some point, they became romantically involved."

Penny put down her tissue. "I met him at a bar one night. He was a smooth talker. I fell head over heels in love. My family warned me about him, but I didn't believe them. He asked me to invest money in his car dealership, and I did. I ended up losing every last cent." Nancy patted Penny's arm sympathetically. "Turns out he was conning other women out of money as well. He got in some trouble with the law, so that's when he moved here."

"But why did you follow him up here to Florida if you knew he was no good?" Nancy asked.

"I was curious about that too," Scooter said. "You reported him on that Dating Scoundrels site, didn't you?"

"That's the part that's so embarrassing," Penny said. "He convinced me that everything that happened in Texas was a misunderstanding, and that he wanted me to come to Florida and be his partner in the boat brokerage business. What was I thinking? He was a used-car salesman, for goodness' sake. And I was stupid enough to believe he could make a success of being a boat broker, something he knew nothing about, and that things would work out between us." She put her head in her hands and groaned.

"You weren't the only one who believed him," I said. "Sandy fell for his charms too. That's what started this all. He flirted with her, and she fell for him, hook, line, and sinker. Then she found out about you and him."

"How did she find out about us?" Penny asked.

"I'm not sure, but Mrs. Moto found a picture on Sandy's boat of you and Captain Dan, or Cowboy Bob, in Texas with your arms around each other. Sandy wanted to leave Jack and marry Captain Dan. She was convinced that you were the reason why Captain Dan was hesitating. She didn't like being part of a love triangle."

Scooter looked at me quizzically. "How do you know about Sandy wanting to marry

Captain Dan?"

"Oh, I ran into Officer Moore when I was at Penelope's Sugar Shack. She's so much nicer than Chief Dalton. She was at the police station yesterday when I went in to give my statement about what happened on *Pretty in Pink*. We had such a nice chat. Then when I saw her today, I gave her one of the brownies, and she told me all about the case and Sandy's confession."

"What else did you find out?" Scooter asked.

"Yeah, tell us about the murders," Ben said. "Let's hear all the details about how she whacked Captain Dan over the head with that winch handle."

Scooter sat back in his chair and shuddered. I don't think he really wanted to hear all the details. I passed him my brownie. He ate the whole thing in two bites.

"After the barbecue last week, Captain Dan told Sandy in no uncertain terms that he didn't want her leaving Jack, and that they should continue to have an affair behind his back. He needed Jack to help him fence stolen marine equipment, and he certainly didn't want to be tied down to one woman."

I looked over at Penny's hand. "Remember how you were chewing on your nails when you had a fight with Captain Dan at the barbecue?"

"Yeah, but how did you know about that?"

"Never mind," I said. "It's not important. Sandy found one of your press-on fingernails on the patio and picked it up."

"See, I told you it wasn't my fingernail," Nancy said. "What happened after that?"

"She followed him to *Marjorie Jane* when he supposedly went there to leave a boat-warming present for us. They got into a fight, she picked up the winch handle, and... well...you know what happened next. She must have decided to leave the fingernail to implicate Penny."

Everyone thought about this for a few minutes while Nancy cleared the table. When she sat back down, she asked, "What do you mean by Captain Dan *supposedly* going to *Marjorie Jane* to leave a boat-warming present?"

"Oh, that." I nodded at Ben and Scooter "The guys found an antique compass hidden on *Marjorie Jane*. Turns out Captain Dan had stolen it from some people in Texas and tucked it in a secret compartment before the previous owners of *Marjorie Jane* sailed her over to Florida. He was planning on retrieving it when no one else was around. That's why he said he wanted to leave a boat-warming present for us. But before he could get it, Sandy surprised him, they argued, and then she murdered him."

Scooter blanched at the reference to murder and pointed at my purse. "Do you have any more chocolate in there?"

"No, sorry," I said. "At the rate things have been going, I'll have to start stocking up on a lot more emergency chocolate."

"You sure are." He dumped the contents of my purse on the table. "Maybe there's some in here you forgot about." Scooter sighed. "Nope, nothing." He fiddled with my keys. "So was it high school kids who broke into *Marjorie Jane* originally, or was that Captain Dan?"

"No, Captain Dan had a key. He didn't need to break in. That was Jack. Jack overheard Captain Dan talking on the phone with a prospective buyer for the compass. Jack told Sandy he was going to get to the compass before Captain Dan did, as payback. So he cut the padlock and searched the boat. That's how that large winch handle ended up on the floor. He found it when he was tearing the boat apart. Crew-cut guy and his bearded friend must have left it behind when they unloaded the stolen goods."

"Crew-cut guy and his bearded friend? Who are they?" Ben asked.

"A couple of local bad guys—Fred Rollins and Wayne Grimm. They helped Captain Dan and Jack fence the stolen marine equipment."

"Oh, Fred and Wayne," Ben said. "I know those guys. They hang out at the Tipsy Pirate."

Penny folded her hands together. "Okay, so I understand now why Sandy killed Bob," she said, sniffing slightly. "But why did she kill Jack?"

"Jack and Sandy had been having problems for years," I said. Ned and Nancy nodded. "She couldn't bear to be around him anymore. She blamed him for their money problems. And in her mind, Jack was the reason that things didn't work out with Captain Dan. She snapped that night. When he got back from the police station, they had an argument on the dinghy dock. She hit him over the head with an oar, and he fell into the water. I'm not sure if she meant to kill him or not, but either way, he ended up dead."

Nancy pursed her lips. "She tried to frame Ned for that," she said angrily. She squeezed Ned's hand. "Thankfully, you found that young couple who could vouch for his alibi."

"That's when Sandy really got desperate. She thought I was asking too many questions, so she decided I was going to be her next victim."

Penny shivered. She zipped up her pink jacket. "I'm so sorry about that, Mollie. I should have known what she was up to. I should have checked that PFD she brought

'or you to use. I had no idea she had taken
:he cartridges out so it wouldn't inflate."

"It wasn't your fault," I said.

"But it happened on my boat," Penny said.
'She even undid the clasps on the lifelines so
:hey'd be loose and you'd fall overboard."

"You can't blame yourself. She put
;leeping pills in your lemonade."

Nancy shook her head. "No one is to
3lame, especially not you. You just put that
idea right out of your head. You hear me,
Penny?"

Penny nodded, but I had a feeling it would
:ake some time before she could forget the
impact Captain Dan and Sandy had had on
her life.

"What I want to know is what was in that
Styrofoam cooler you found the night Jack
was killed," Ben said. "Was it beer?"

"No, Officer Moore told me it was full of
illegally caught fish," I said.

Ben reached for another beer. "I've heard
rumors that there's been some poaching
happening lately."

Ned frowned. "Where did you hear that?"

"At the Tipsy Pirate. Who knows if it's true or not?" After cracking open his bottle of beer, Ben looked at me with a big grin. "Hey, maybe that's what you should investigate next, Mollie—the case of the mysterious fish poachers."

Scooter put his arm around my shoulders. "No way is Mollie getting involved in that. We have enough to keep ourselves busy with all of the boat projects we need to do on *Marjorie Jane*. She won't have time for any more investigations. Isn't that right?"

"Well, there still is the matter of the mysterious green and red lights I saw on the water last week. It could be a—"

Scooter interrupted. "That didn't have anything to do with aliens. I'm sure those were navigation lights on a boat. They use them at night so you know which way other boats are going, and you don't crash into each other."

"Or were they?" I asked. "You'll have to wait until I complete my report for FAROUT."

"Another report?" Scooter asked.

"Yep, turns out Lola faked those pictures at Disneyland. Those weren't aliens hiding in Sleeping Beauty Castle. Those pictures were from the annual staff Halloween party. Some of the guys dressed up as little green men, thinking it would impress Lola. That means the investigative reporter job is all mine now!"

* * *

After the barbecue, Scooter and I went back to *Marjorie Jane* for sundowners. "You wait here in the cockpit. I'll go down and fix us some drinks," I said. I listened to Scooter humming away happily to himself while I cut up a lime for the gin and tonics.

It was nice to see my husband so happy. He had received a call earlier in the day about a potential new business opportunity that had him excited about the future. Hopefully, that meant *Marjorie Jane* wouldn't be occupying all his time anymore. With Scooter busy, I would be able to put my investigative skills to good use unraveling the case of the poached fish, or look for another story to pursue for FAROUT, or just enjoy a well-deserved rest. It would be a nice change from finding dead bodies. But tonight was for celebrating, not thinking about work.

"Here, take these," I said, passing him the glasses and a bowl of potato chips. After he set everything down on the table, I told him to close his eyes. "I've got a surprise for you," I said as I set his present in his lap. "Okay, you can open your eyes."

"But this is a cat," he said.

"Not just any cat. This is your cat—Mrs. Moto. She's my belated anniversary present to you. Remember how you surprised me with *Marjorie Jane*? You told me that I'd love having a sailboat?" Scooter reluctantly nodded while the calico nudged his hand. "Well, now I'm surprising you with your very own cat. See, I even put a ribbon around her neck. You're going to love her."

Scooter sighed. I think he knew that I had beaten him at his own game. "Welcome aboard, Mrs. Moto," he said, scratching under her chin.

"Speaking of surprises, what was in that navy-blue tote bag you had the day you first showed me *Marjorie Jane*? You said it was something for me."

Scooter handed Mrs. Moto to me. "I can't believe I forgot all about that. The bag is somewhere here on the boat." He went down below and searched for a few minutes before coming back up and triumphantly presenting me with the tote bag. "Have a look in there."

I pulled out a couple of sailing magazines, a water bottle, and a sweatshirt. At the very bottom of the bag was a small velvet jewelry box. "Is this what I think it is?" I asked.

"Go on, open it." And there it was, my very own diamond necklace. I took it out of the box and looked at the pendant. "I meant to give this to you on the day we bought *Marjorie Jane*. See the diamond at the top of the lighthouse? It's meant to represent the light that they shine to guide mariners safely into port. Lighthouses are a symbol of the way forward. I can't imagine going forward in life without you by my side," Scooter said as he put the necklace around my neck.

Yeah, he really did say that. Kind of mushy, but sometimes you need a little mushiness. As we sat in the cockpit with Mrs. Moto by our side, watching the sun go down, I realized that I just might be able to get used to this sailing life.

AUTHOR'S NOTE AND ACKNOWLEDGMENTS

Thank you so much for reading my book! If you enjoyed it, I'd be grateful if you would consider leaving a short review on the site where you purchased it. Reviews help other readers find my books and encourage me to keep writing.

My experiences buying our first sailboat with my husband in New Zealand (followed by our second sailboat in the States), learning how to sail, and living aboard our boats inspired me to write the *Mollie McGhie Sailing Mysteries*. There's a little bit of Mollie in me.

I want to thank my wonderful beta readers who were so generous with their time, graciously reading earlier drafts and providing insightful and thoughtful feedback: Alexandra Palcic, Angela Wooldridge, Duwan Dunn, Elizabeth Seckman, Greg Sifford, Liesbet Collaert, Rebecca Douglass, and Tyrean Martinson.

I have been amazed at how supportive the

online writing community has been to me during my journey to becoming a published author. I'm especially grateful to the Insecure Writer's Support Group and the Women Who Sail Who Write Facebook group.

The followers of my blog, *The Cynical Sailor* have been a huge source of inspiration. Their kind words and encouragement motivated me to publish my first book. I've been fortunate to have made good friends (both virtual and in-person) through the blogging community.

Many thanks to Chris Brogden at EnglishGeek Editing (englishgeekediting.com) for his keen eye, thoughtful edits, and support.

Most of all, I want to thank my family for their support and encouragement. My mother enjoys cozy mysteries and first gave me the idea of writing one of my own. My sister's love of books and her work at her local library inspires my writing. I have two wonderful nieces whose enjoyment of reading reminds me that imagination is something we should nourish in young people. My husband, in particular, played a huge role in turning *Murder at the*

Marina from an idea bubbling away in my imagination into a published book, reviewing endless drafts and providing feedback at every stage of the writing process.

Any many, many thanks to all of my readers. Your support and encouragement means everything.

ABOUT THE AUTHOR

Ellen Jacobson is a chocolate obsessed cat lover who writes cozy mysteries and romantic comedies. After working in Scotland and New Zealand for several years, she returned to the States, lived aboard a sailboat, traveled around in a tiny camper, and is now settled in a small town in northern Oregon with her husband and an imaginary cat named Simon.

Find out more at ellenjacobsonauthor.com

ALSO BY ELLEN JACOBSON

Mollie McGhie Cozy Sailing Mysteries

Robbery at the Roller Derby
Murder at the Marina
Bodies in the Boatyard
Poisoned by the Pier
Buried by the Beach
Dead in the Dinghy
Shooting by the Sea
Overboard on the Ocean
Murder aboard the Mistletoe

Smitten with Travel Romantic Comedies

Smitten with Ravioli
Smitten with Croissants
Smitten with Strudel
Smitten with Candy Canes

North Dakota Library Mysteries

Planning for Murder